The Queen of Minor Disasters

a novel with recipes

Antonietta Mariottini

This is a work of fiction. The characters, places, and events portrayed in this book are fictitious. Any similarity to real persons, living or dead, is coincidental and not intended by the author.

Recipes by Antonietta Mariottini and Graziella Iacovino

Cover art by Tom Delaney

Chapter 1

I can imagine it already.

Drew will walk through the front doors holding a big bouquet of roses (not that he's ever brought me flowers, but you never know, people can change. And anyway, tonight's a *special* night). I'll be at the hostess stand, juggling a million things like I always do, but as soon as I see him wearing one of his Brooks Brothers suits, the world will stop. Slowly, he'll walk towards me and hand me the bouquet. Before I can even say "thank you" he'll cup my face in his hands and give me kiss. At this point, the entire restaurant will be watching; service will stop for a minute, as everybody awaits what's coming next. Then, without saying a word, Drew will drop down to one knee and take my hand. He'll look up at me with those gorgeous blue eyes and say…

"Um, Stella," I hear a female voice snapping me out of my thoughts. Oh, right. I rest my hands on the hostess stand which I've been leaning on for the past couple hours. I must start taking this job more seriously. But honestly, it does get a little boring. Not that I *mind*. I really do enjoy managing my brother's restaurant, but the truth is, the place pretty much runs itself.

Ask anyone what the best restaurant down the shore is and they'll say "Lorenzo's." Not to brag or anything, but it's true. And from the way this night is going, it looks like our fifth season is off to a great start. If it stays like this, the summer will be smooth sailing.

"Stella?"

Oh, right.

I turn to look at Michelle, one of the waitresses here. She's been with us for two summers and is usually fully capable of handling her own section. "What's up?"

"Disaster at table twelve."

I scan the restaurant trying not to look too obvious, and then focus my eyes on the single lady on table twelve. She looks normal enough. Her black hair is pulled into a tight bun and her skin is a little too bronzed for the second week of June, but besides that, I don't see any red flags. "What's the problem?"

"Her husband left," Michelle says with a hint of tension in her voice. She scans the restaurant, looking at the rest of her tables.

"He's probably just in the bathroom." I look at the table again, and see the lady slumped in a chair. Maybe her husband did leave. Or maybe this is a ploy to run out on the bill. Well, not on my watch.

I keep my cool, but the thing is, I'm a little nervous. It's times like these that I really wish my brother Mario was here. He's the General Manager of my family's other restaurant, La Cucina, and he'd know *exactly* what to do.

I hear a sob and my eyes dart directly to table twelve.

Michelle looks at me. "I think you need to go over there. She's pretty drunk."

I sigh. Sometimes being a restaurant manager requires more than putting on a nice dress and smiling at the customers. Those are the times I dread, because honestly, I never wanted this job in the first place. It was sort of handed to me with my college diploma (which was in English, *not* Restaurant Management, by the way). "Let's go," I say and move towards the table.

The sobbing continues and a few other people have turned to look at the woman. I can't help feeling bad for her, I mean, what if her husband really did *leave* her? Right here in our restaurant? That can't be good karma.

"Hello," I say when I get to the table.

She looks up at me and gives me a weak smile. Her cheeks are stained with mascara streaks, and she looks a bit severe. I pick up a napkin and hand it to her.

"You okay?" I ask gently.

"Yes, I'm fine. Just a little lonely." She slurs the word "little."

And a little drunk.

"Maybe I can help," I offer.

"Oh, it's really not a big deal," she sniffles. "My husband just had to go. He's on call."

I give her a strange look.

"He's a *doctor*," she snaps.

Oh, right. I knew he wouldn't just leave her. Not at Lorenzo's, our food is too good.

"What kind of doctor?" I ask to keep the conversation going. Her tears have dried up and she's sort of smiling at me. See, it just goes to show you that a little kindness goes a long way. That's the trick to being a manager, of course. I mean, all you need to do is recognize what people need and serve it up to them. No biggie.

"He's a…" she pauses and her face wrinkles into a scowl, "surgeon." She sobs again. "He said he got an emergency call but I know better. I'm not stupid." I nod my head because it seems like the right response.

"His girlfriend called and he just up and left," she continues. "My therapist said I should just ignore it, but how is that possible?" She looks at me as though I have the answers. The only thing I know for sure is that she needs a new therapist.

I shrug my shoulders.

"And the worst part is she's only *thirty*," she nearly screams. Slowly, she gives me an accusatory look, as if my being nearly thirty is a mortal sin.

I look around to see other customers staring at us. Just as I'm about to walk away, it hits me. Of course! This woman doesn't need a crap ass therapist to tell her how to react. She needs Food Therapy!

I'm a strong believer in Food Therapy, which is the theory that all of life's problems can be solved by eating the right foods. I'm not talking about nutrition here, people. I mean *comfort foods*. And I personally know Food Therapy works because just last night I was feeling frazzled, so I ate some hazelnut gelato and poof, I was one hundred percent better!

The major players in my personal Food Therapy repertoire are Bindi hazelnut gelato, a slice of Chuck's chocolate orange cake, or my mom's famous meatballs. I think of which option would be best for this situation.

"I have just the thing to make you feel better," I say putting my arm on the woman's shoulder.

She looks up at me in interest. "Vodka?" She turns to see if we have a bar, which unfortunately we don't. Like most restaurants down the shore we're BYOB.

"Even *better*," I answer quickly. "Just wait here."

I rush up to the dessert display case and reach in for a piece of decadent chocolate cake. Our sous-chef, Chuck, does an amazing job with all the pastries, but his specialty is this cake, with its dark chocolate and hint of orange.

I cut a thick slice and lay it on a plate, then drizzle some vanilla crème over it and add candied orange peels as a garnish. If *this* doesn't cure a heartache, I don't know what will.

I grab a fork and rush back to the table, just in time. The woman is standing and scanning the restaurant, looking for God knows what.

"Have a seat." I gently push her down into her chair and place the cake in front of her.

She looks at it as if she's mentally calculating all the calories, and then looks back up at me in frustration. Perhaps vodka would have been a better choice.

"Take a bite," I urge.

Skeptically, she forks a tiny piece and pops it in her mouth. I see the corners of her lips curl up into a smile. I *knew* it would work.

"Just eat this and I'll call you a cab," I say. "Where do you live?"

"29th Street."

Our restaurant is located on one of the most prestigious islands on the Jersey Shore. About forty miles south of Atlantic City, our island is the smallest of the cluster off Jersey's coast and is only seven miles top to bottom. There are two towns here but little distinction between them, and most people just call this place "the Island."

Lorenzo's is on 96th Street, the southern part of the Island, and this lady's house is on the northern part. Still, a ride will only cost about five bucks, and she looks so sad and depressed even though she's eating the cake that I'll just spring for the cab.

And the cake.

Oh, what the hell. I'll spring for the whole bill, after all her husband stuck her with it. She might not even have a credit card with her. I think about this for a second then confirm my decision even though Lorenzo is constantly yelling at me over giving things away for free. Sometimes it really is the best option though. Plus, what does he know about service? He's cooped up in a closed kitchen pumping out entrées—not in the circus ring with angry lions like me.

The cab arrives about ten minutes later, and by then, the heartbroken lady has cleaned her plate. I walk over to the table and give her my arm. She stands, though a bit wobbly.

"Dinner is on me tonight," I say as I lead her through the restaurant.

"Thanks!" she gives me a strange look, and then asks, "What's your name?"

"Stella."

"That means star!" she squeals. She's right, it does. I smile at her.

"The cab will take you home. Don't worry about paying him, I got it covered."

She throws her arms around me. "Thanks, Star," she slurs and stumbles out the door.

I take a deep breath and walk back towards the hostess stand.

I must say, I'm pretty proud of the way I handled the situation. I'm quite good at this management stuff. Too bad I don't plan on making a career out of it though. Basically, this is my last summer here. I haven't told anyone yet; I realized it's best not to spring this kind of stuff on the family until you've got a solid plan—and my plan depends on Drew and a little (ok, maybe medium sized) diamond.

I take my place behind the podium and look around the restaurant. Though I hate to admit it, I'll miss this a little. I still remember the exact day, four years ago, when I stepped foot in the place for the first time. It was a total nightmare. The previous owners were gothic/animal print enthusiasts (I have no idea how that combination came about), and the place was clad in dark velvet drapery and a leopard print carpet. Honestly, it looked more like a seedy lounge than a restaurant. Lorenzo and my parents had already bought the place, and I remember thinking that it needed a special touch. That's where I came in and suggested the Tuscan theme, which we have now. I basically hand selected these burnt ochre walls and stone archways. My mom chose the terracotta tiles that line the floors and hired a painter for the mural of the Tuscan hillside covering the back wall. Yes, it's a tad stereotypical, but people seem to love it.

And for the most part we're lucky because in the four years we've been in business we've acquired so many regular customers. On any given night I'll know about ninety percent of the people who walk in the door, which can be a good and a bad thing.

For example, tonight I've already been asked *three* times about Drew. Two older women glared at my bare left hand asking me about marriage. I mean, honestly, why are people so nosey? We've only been dating for three years and we're taking our time. Besides, we're both so busy that we hardly have time to *think* of marriage, let alone get engaged.

Drew is on his way down from New York right now, and who knows what might happen tonight.

I've got a good feeling about tonight.

Actually, I've had a good feeling all day. And just in case something *does* happen tonight, I've dressed accordingly. I'm wearing a very classic canary yellow dress with a full skirt and modest neckline. Generally I don't wear such pale colors to work because I'll inevitably spill something on myself in the midst of the rush, but this is a Marc Jacobs dress and I've always imagined that I'd be wearing Marc when Drew…

Oh never mind. I don't want to jinx anything.

Anyway, tonight, Frankie the bus boy has been on his A game, so I haven't had to clear one plate off a table, which means I look as fresh as when I walked in here at three this afternoon.

The phone rings, bringing me back to reality.

"Lorenzo's how may I help you?"

"Stell, it's me," says my best friend Lucy. Lucy is a teacher at St. Ignatius with my oldest brother Dante. She's been working with us since day one and has become like the sister I never had. My mother wants her in the family and has been trying to set her up with Dante for the past four years. She's not biting though, which is fine by me.

"Hey Luce, what's going on?"

"There's a major accident on the expressway," she sounds frazzled. "I've been in stopped traffic for three hours now."

My heart begins to race. Drew could be in that accident. Images of Drew crunched up in his black BMW fill my head. "Lucy, Drew isn't here yet, I gotta go." I hang up without waiting for a reply.

Oh God. Oh God. Oh God.

I patter through the kitchen and into the office where I've left my cell phone plugged into the wall. I grab it. Two missed calls from Drew. My mind reels. He could be in a hospital somewhere.

The phone rings two times before he picks it up. "Drew," I yell. "Are you okay?"

"Hey," he whispers. "Did you get my message?"

"Where are you?"

"In the office, there's a big project at work and I need to be here. I left you a message."

"Oh," I say a bit relieved. Then it hits me. He's not coming down. Tonight's not *the night*. "I left my phone in the office."

"Sorry. Listen I have to run," Drew says in a hushed tone. I imagine that he's in the middle of an important meeting and his boss is standing over him so I resist the urge to make him feel worse. When he took the job at Connective Global Marketing, I knew it would be hard for us, especially in the summers. Still, sometimes I can't help but wish he'd make more time for me. But that's Drew; he's dedicated, hardworking, and honest. How can I be mad?

"It's fine. I'll be up on Monday. I have to go too; we have 9:00 reservations coming in."

"Ok," he says.

"I love you," I add, just to let him know that he's not in the dog house.

Silence.

He must not have heard me. "I love you," I repeat.

"Ditto," he replies and hangs up.

I shoot Luce a text asking her to pick up a bottle of wine, then exit the office, and walk through the kitchen to the front of the restaurant. As I approach the door to the dining room it swings open at full force. Frankie runs through carrying an armful of dirty dishes. I try to get out of his way but we collide and some melted ice cream lands directly on my chest. Lorenzo and Chuck laugh as my face gets red.

"Watch where the hell you're going," Lorenzo yells.

"Sorry," Frankie says, setting the plates on a work station and pulling a napkin out of his back pocket. I grab it out of his hand and rush through the kitchen into the bathroom to wash off my dress.

I do my best to scrub the stain out of my yellow dress but in the process it becomes completely see through. Cream-colored-lace-bra see through, and there's *no way* I can walk around the restaurant like this.

I quickly tie a clean napkin around my neck like a bib and twist it to the side. It doesn't look *that* bad. It's sort of fashionable, in a very Parisian way. Not that I've been to Paris. But you know what I'm talking about.

Just to add to the effect, I undo my loose bun and let my long brown hair fall over my shoulders. I just got layers cut into it, so it cascades nicely down my back. I can pull this off. No problem. After all, confidence is the key to success.

At least, that's what it said in *Restaurant Management for Dummies*.

I mean, I *think* that's what it said. I didn't actually read the *entire* book (as I mentioned earlier, this is not my life's ambition, so why waste the energy). But I did sit in the bookstore and flip through it one day.

Regardless, it seems like good advice.

Back at the hostess stand there's a line at the door. I look at the clock on the phone. 8:51 p.m. People are so punctual when it comes to eating, like they're afraid if they show up at 9:01, all the food will be gone.

Luckily, we keep a stocked fridge.

"Hello," I greet the first couple in line with a smile. I grab two menus and seat them at a table in the back corner.

As I walk back towards the hostess stand I touch my hand to my dress. Still damp. I adjust the napkin.

I look towards the next group and notice Trisha Motley standing with her friends. I'd roll my eyes but she'd see me. Trisha and I used to run in the same circle down the shore, but to be honest, we never *really* liked each other. Of course, we pretend to.

"Trisha!" I squeal. "It's *so* good to see you. You look *amazing*," and really, she does. God, she must have grown since last summer. I don't remember her being so tall. Or so thin. She probably doesn't use Food Therapy, or *eat* for that matter.

Already bronzed for the summer, Trisha is wearing a light green off the shoulder mini-dress and four inch heels. She towers over my petite frame and bends to give me a hug while her equally tall Amazonian supermodel friends watch.

"Stella how was your winter?" she asks. I can only imagine her winter jet-setting to exotic places while I was stuck working lunches at my parents' restaurant. I need to think of something good.

I can tell her I traveled to India and worked with impoverished children.

Only that's not as glamorous as say, spending the winter in Buenos Aires. That's it. Perfect.

She's looking at me strangely, as if waiting for an answer.

"Oh, it was great, I spent so much time in New York," I mutter. Shit. I meant Buenos Aires.

"I *love* the city." She pauses to look at her friends. "I just moved up there for my job."

"Nice," I say politely, though I could care less what fabulous job her daddy got her.

"Are you still dating Drew?" she asks suddenly and I feel my face get hot. I know that at twenty-seven I should be more secure and not let petty things like that bother me but I can't help it. Trisha and Drew went to this uber-exclusive private school in Philadelphia, and were prom king and queen or something. Apparently, they were the "it" couple in high school, and even though that was ages ago, it still makes me uncomfortable. The fact that Trisha is the one who introduced me to Drew makes it all the worse.

"Of course," I snap.

"I guess you're just waiting for a ring then?" she asks in the bitchy-but-friendly tone that she's mastered. One of her friends snickers a little. I give her a tight smile. Just wait until I get that ring, then I'll flash it in her face. I grab the menus and begin walking them to their table.

As I walk back, I look around to see what people are eating. People love specials and tonight, Lorenzo made two terrific ones: Chicken alla Patria, a chicken breast topped with fresh tomatoes, spinach and melted mozzarella cheese, and Filet Mignon topped with a wild blueberry sauce.

God, the boy is talented.

Sometimes he makes me feel inadequate. I mean, we *are* twins and all. Actually, all four of my brothers are talented. Dante is an awesome teacher, Pietro is a big lawyer in New York City, Mario is the general manager of the restaurants, and Lorenzo is an amazing chef. Then there's me.

Two hours later, as I'm counting the money in the office, Lucy arrives, flustered.

"Five hours in traffic," she whines in the doorway of the office. "You almost done? I need a drink."

"Yeah." I divide twenties into swift piles. "How are the waiters doing out there?"

"It looks like they finished all their side-work. They're all folding napkins."

"Good. Can you tell them I'll be out in a minute?"

"Sure," she says, leaving the office.

I gather up each waiter's pile of tips and write it all in my book. I look at my phone as I walk out into the dining room. No calls from Drew. He must *still* be working. Or maybe he's on his way down. He probably changed his mind and decided to blow off work and surprise me. Not that he's ever done that, but you never know.

The waiters are all sitting in chairs, folding napkins to restock the side stations. They look like a strange bunch of businessmen, ties loosened or removed and crumpled into balls on the table, shirts unbuttoned and untucked. Lucy is right in there with them, folding napkins with precision and chatting with Dante about some school stuff.

"Great job tonight guys," I say. They all look up and shuffle around for their things. I hand them each their tips and say goodbye.

"Where's Drew?" Lucy asks when all the servers are gone.

"He's not coming. Did you bring the wine?"

"That sucks," she says and stands. She moves over to her purse and lifts out a brown paper bag. "I did better than wine," she removes the bag dramatically. "I brought Andre."

I laugh. Andre is the cheapest of all champagnes, good for nothing except maybe cooking, yet the two of us love it. It's our little secret. I stand and take the bottle from her hands, hugging it. "The only man who never lets me down."

"It'll go perfect with some chocolate."

"I like the way you think," I say and move towards the dessert case. Since Drew is not coming, I may as well scarf down an extra-large piece of Chuck's chocolate cake. Not that I'm heartbroken or anything.

By the time I return, Lucy's already put the bottle on ice and cleared away the place settings from the table. She looks so at home in the restaurant that it's hard to believe that we've only been friends for four years. She just fits into my family, which is not an easy feat. Plus, she's a natural beauty, with long lean legs and wavy chestnut hair. No wonder my mom has been trying to get her and Dante together. I sit down next to her and place the cake in the middle of the table.

"Why isn't Drew coming down?" she asks taking a fork.

"Work" I wave it off and take a sip. The champagne instantly makes me feel better.

She smiles sympathetically. "It's just temporary. Drew's a great guy and he loves you."

I take a bite of cake. She's right. I really did luck out with Drew but sometimes I get impatient about the whole marriage thing. "Luce, I thought tonight was the night," I confess.

"Don't worry Stell. It's coming. I can feel it."

I smile but a small part of me can't help but wonder if it is true. I stab another forkful of cake and shove it in my mouth.

Recipe: Chocolate Cake for a Heartbreak

Yields 8 servings*

If you're following Food Therapy, this is the Tylenol of Cakes. It can fix just about any ailment you might have, from a hangover to a heartbreak (which, by the way, usually go hand in hand).

*If, by chance you see that you've eaten the entire cake, don't worry. Just don some elastic pants and nurse yourself back to health. You can always diet tomorrow.

8 oz semi-sweet chocolate
1 oz unsweetened chocolate
1 3/4 sticks of butter
2 oranges (zests and juice)
1 teaspoon vanilla
5 large eggs
1 tablespoon flour
1 tablespoon dark cocoa powder

1) Preheat oven to 375. Butter an 8" cake pan and line with parchment paper. Butter the paper and set prepared pan aside.
2) Using a double boiler, melt together chocolate, butter, orange zests, orange juice, and vanilla. Stir to incorporate.
3) Remove chocolate from the double boiler and allow to cool for 5 minutes.
4) Add eggs, one at a time, stirring well to incorporate. Add the flour and cocoa powder and stir until dissolved.

5) Pour batter into prepared pan. Place pan in middle rack of the oven and bake for 20-25 minutes, until set.
6) Removed pan from oven and allow to cool for 15-20 minutes. Gently invert the cake onto a serving platter. Remove parchment paper and dust with powdered sugar.

This cake will keep in an airtight container at room temp for 5 days. It also freezes nicely.

Chapter 2

When I board the bus in Atlantic City on Monday morning I'm full of nerves. Only a few hours until I see Drew.

The Casino busses to and from New York are about as high class as the Andre Lucy and I like, but it's yet another strange thing that relaxes me. I've always loved bus rides, and the trek from the Jersey Shore to New York City gives me three prime hours to relax and read.

As much as I normally love my bus rides, I do not like getting stuck sitting next to people, and if I time things correctly, I can usually get my own seat. The trick is to sit relatively close to the driver, so as people board the bus, they see the empty seats in the back rows and move towards them. The other trick is to sit in the aisle seat, making it difficult for people to get to the free window seat. As selfish as it sounds, it's the *one* area when I think of myself before others. A relaxing three-hour bus ride can be hellish if seated next to someone who is

a) Weird
Or
b) Talkative.

The Atlantic City to New York busses are usually full of all the aforementioned folks, so I stick to my guns. If all else fails and someone is still trying to snag the seat next to me, I usually breakout in an uncontrollable fit of coughing. Even the freaks and degenerate gamblers are scared of germs nowadays.

But today I hardly care at all. My stomach is in knots and my mind is racing. Luckily, the bus is pretty empty, so I'm able to get a good seat. Before boarding, I bought a bunch of gossip magazines at Quick Mart, but not even Brad and Angie's new baby can hold my interest for very long. Still, I open a magazine to distract myself.

Things have been so awkward since Friday night that I'm a little nervous to see Drew today. He's been sort of weird. I don't know how to explain it, but something is off. I can tell. He's been pretty short on the phone the past couple of days and he didn't really sound too excited when I said I was coming up to visit.

Of course, this could all be a plan to distract me.

Maybe he wants me to think he's working all day, but really he'll be waiting for me in his apartment.

I can imagine it already.

I'll unlock the door and make my way into the apartment only to see flower petals strewn all over the floor. Then I'll look up and see him, kneeling on the floor, ring in hand…

I must have fallen asleep in the midst of my fantasy because before I know it, we are pulling into Port Authority Bus Terminal. I look at my watch. It's 2:45, which gives me plenty of time to go grocery shopping and get a head start on dinner before Drew gets home.

I step off the bus and take a deep breath of the city I love. New York feels like an entirely different world from the Island, though I suppose Manhattan is actually an island too. Anyway, it's a different kind of island, and the rushed pace of people around me is a nice change.

Yes, this is where I *need* to be. This is our city. It was made for Drew and me.

And the other eight million people here.

I make my way through the labyrinth under Port Authority without getting lost and walk towards the subway. I only have to wait two minutes before the 1 train arrives.

I ride the train up to 72nd Street and Broadway. I get out there, forty blocks away from Drew's Harlem apartment, but only two blocks away from Fairway Market, where I can find the best olives and cheese in the neighborhood.

I don't want to waste too much time in Fairway, so I walk right over to the cheeses and pick up some fresh Parmigiano Reggiano and ricotta salata. There's nothing better than being able to make my boyfriend's favorite pasta dish to surprise him.

He'll probably think I want to go out for dinner, but tonight I feel like staying in, because if tonight is the night, I want him all to myself.

I walk back towards the produce and pick out seven Roma tomatoes, an onion, and an eggplant. Before walking to the check-out I grab a box of penne and some sparkling water.

Don't worry; I haven't forgotten dessert.

I walk a few blocks and pick up some crisp Riesling on 79th Street. Then I trek up to Café Vola, my favorite spot in the entire city. It's pretty much the happiest place on earth. Always brightly lit, the café sticks out like a Christmas tree in a street full of dimly lit trendy bars. The brick walls are covered with vintage posters filling the ambiance with bright orange, bursting red, and sunny yellow hues. This place exudes happiness.

Tiny bells jingle when I walk in. See what I mean? Who in New York still has bells on their doors? In June?

Two cute girls in black Café Vola t-shirts greet me.

"Can I help you?" one of them asks as I eye up the pastries in the big glass case.

Finally, I decide on two chocolate Napoleons and four mini apricot tarts. Perfect Food Therapy treats.

I make my way underground at 86th Street. The subway platform is surprisingly empty for a summer afternoon. Sometimes I forget most people are at work at this hour. When the 9 train arrives, I take a seat on the cold plastic chairs and search around in my bag. Even though I live with my parents in the suburbs of South Jersey (pathetic, I know, but I'm saving up to buy one day), I'm proud to say that I carry the keys to two very posh New York City apartments. Ok, one posh one (my friend Julie's in the Village) and one not so posh one (Drew's in Harlem).

When Drew got the job at Connective, I thought he'd move to a better neighborhood, but instead, he bought himself a

BMW convertible and pays to keep it in a garage. It's a little frivolous to have a car in New York City, but Drew says it's a sign that he's "arrived." I'd rather arrive in a nice apartment, but I keep that thought to myself. Besides, once we're married we'll have to move.

I get off the subway at 116th Street, right near Columbia University and walk three blocks up Broadway. Drew lives on the third floor of a five story walk up, and by the time I make it up the steps I'm drenched with sweat.

God, I need to start working out or something. I wipe my brow, thankful that he's not home to see me like this. And if he is, he'll be too wrapped up in the moment to care about a little sweat.

My heart pounds as I put the key in the lock. This could be it. This could be the moment…

I open the door to an empty apartment, which honestly looks more like a college dorm room than the apartment of a successful businessman.

His studio apartment is organized with small messes here and there. The Ikea coffee table/dining room table is littered with papers and old copies of *The Wall Street Journal;* there's a small pile of socks at the foot of the bed, and an almost empty water glass rests on a pile of mail on the nightstand.

Even though I know I shouldn't, I let my eyes scan his mail. Looks like some boring bills and…

Wait a minute. It can't be.

I rush towards the nightstand and pick up the glass of water. Under all the bills is a lovely light blue catalogue. I knew it. I can recognize Tiffany Blue anywhere.

My heart starts racing as I flip it open. The entire booklet is devoted to engagement rings, which can only mean one thing.

Oh my God. He bought a ring. HE BOUGHT A RING!

I knew it. I knew it was coming!

Quickly, I shove the catalogue back under the pile of mail and do a little happy dance right there near his bed.

How did he know to go to Tiffany's? I bet his mom helped him. She's a bit stuck up at times but at least she has good taste.

Or maybe he called Luce?

Who cares, really, the point is HE BOUGHT A RING!

Suddenly, the entire apartment looks different. Each little quirk will be an element in our story, and when I retell it to our kids in a few years, I won't forget to mention how Daddy left his gym socks under the bed to make it look sloppy so Mommy wouldn't suspect a thing.

As I walk towards the micro-kitchen I try to calm myself down.

I shake my head as I unload the groceries and get to work. Cooking for someone is an intimate experience; it's a chance to share your innermost thoughts and feelings, without words. My cooking most always reflects my mood and tonight I'm feeling saucy and spicy, anxious to see my beautiful boyfriend for the first time all week. Plus tonight is THE NIGHT!

Ok Stella, you need to act surprised. Just calm down and don't think of the ring.

Got it.

Only, how can I *not* think of a Tiffany's ring? That's like asking the Pope not to pray, or Joan Rivers not to get any more plastic surgery.

I concentrate on cooking and start by dicing the onion into small pieces, which will eventually crisp up in the hot oil until they caramelize to a golden brown. I move on to the eggplant, which I cube in small pieces with the skin on and then throw into the pan with the onions. Once that cooks for a bit, I add slices of Roma tomatoes and fresh basil, reducing the heat to low and allowing the vegetables to simmer together. I take a taste.

As the sauce thickens, I jump in the shower to rinse off the bus ride film I've collected in my travels. I change into a flowing green circle skirt and white tank top. Not exactly what I always pictured I'd be wearing when I get proposed to (this is so not Marc Jacobs), but it's all I've got. Plus, I'm not supposed to know anything anyway. If I got too dressed up, I'd blow the whole thing.

I pull my hair into a low bun, dot on some concealer and swipe mascara on my lashes. I wear heels even though we are staying in. I'm sorry, I just can't get proposed to wearing flats for God's sake. I'm not that kind of girl.

I take a look at myself in the mirror. I'm the future Mrs. Dzinski. Stella Dzinski.

DiLucio sounds *so* much better.

Maybe I can keep my last name.

Lots of women do it. It's very chic. Very New York.

At a quarter to six I place a pot of water to boil, knowing that Drew will be home in twenty minutes. I ask him not to call before he comes home, because I love the surprise of him opening the door and seeing me in the kitchen. I imagine what our life will be like after we're married, when I cook for him every night. In my mind's eye, I'm living the comfortable life with Drew. Sure I'd have to compromise on a few things, like always coming in second to his career. But lots of women compromise for the comfort of a husband. And at twenty-seven I'm not getting any younger. Plus, there's nothing wrong with wanting a comfortable life, is there?

I start setting the table but something about it doesn't look, right. We can't be sitting on the couch when Drew pops the question, can we?

Then, I get a brilliant idea. I move the table to the center of the floor and remove the seat cushions from the couch, placing one on each side of the table. It'll be romantic to sit on the floor and I know that despite his height, Drew will find it charming.

I look around the apartment for the candles that I bought a few months back. I open cabinets in the kitchen, look on top of his dresser, fumble through the closet, and finally find them on top of the toilet in the bathroom. Gross.

I give them a quick wipe with a wet rag before placing them on the table.

Back in the kitchen, I drop the pasta in the boiling water and give it a stir. That's when I hear the key in the door.

"Hello." Drew calls from the doorway, and I waltz over into his arms and stand on my tiptoes to kiss him since he's a foot taller than me.

Ok, so maybe I don't *waltz*, but anyway, you get the point.

"I'm so happy to see you," I squeal and look into his eyes. All my nerves melt away as I realize this man loves me. And I love him.

Drew looks good in a Brooks Brothers' black suit. He's wearing a blue oxford shirt, which enhances his light eyes, and he's loosened the striped silk tie around his neck. Despite his crisp appearance, his face looks flustered, which totally makes sense. He's probably nervous.

"What did you cook?" he asks and walks towards his bed, not noticing the effort I put into decorating the table. I watch as he slips off his tie and plops onto the bed.

"Get changed. I'll set everything up," I tell him, though *obviously* he won't get changed. He probably has the ring in his jacket!

"Alright," he says and ducks into the bathroom.

I feel my face get flushed. This is probably all part of the plan to make me think that it's a normal night. I look over at the table in a panic. Maybe I overdid it just a tad. I walk over and blow out the candles just as Drew emerges from the bathroom wearing old gym shorts and a ratty white t-shirt.

He's really playing up this casual thing.

"Go sit." I move towards the kitchen. By now, the pasta is cooked and needs to be drained. I save a bit of the pasta water and add it to the sauce, stirring it a few times to incorporate everything, then I add the cooked pasta to the pan and toss it all together. I spoon a large portion of penne in his bowl, a smaller serving for myself. As a final step, I grate both the Parmigiano and the ricotta salata on top, and then drizzle a tiny swirl of olive oil over each bowl.

"Nice," Drew says as I place a bowl in front of him. He's moved the table back in front of the couch and is sitting there, flipping through the channels.

I take a seat on the floor in front of him, blocking his view to the TV. "Can we listen to some music instead?" I say.

Drew sighs and gets up from the couch. He walks over to his iPod, which is docked in the sound station I bought him for Christmas. "What do you want to hear?" he asks.

"Surprise me," I answer and close my eyes. This is his chance to up the romance and turn this night around. Maybe he'll put on some Nora Jones, or Frank Sinatra.

"How about U2?" he asks.

U2. Hum. U2 is good. They've got a few romantic tunes.

Suddenly the sound of snare drums hits my ears. "Sunday Bloody Sunday" wouldn't have been my first choice, but I can roll with this.

Drew sits back down and starts eating his pasta. I let my eyes linger on him for an extra second then start to pick at my pasta as well. Out of the corner of my eye, I watch him take the first bites. If there's one thing that annoys me about Drew it's that he never gives me any compliments on my cooking. I know he likes it because he always finishes his plate, sometimes even goes for seconds. But he never says "wow" or "delicious" like you'd expect. I mean, what's the point of cooking for someone, if not to hear his satisfaction? That's why I could never cook in the restaurant. You basically slave away in a hot kitchen all night long and only get to hear praises from your customers when you make your obligatory round around the restaurant. No, instead, I like to see people enjoying themselves. That's where the magic of food (and Food Therapy) really come into play.

Once we're married I'll tell Drew how I feel. I'm sure he'll be really embarrassed that all these years he's never said anything about my food.

"How's the pasta?" I ask, not that I'm fishing for compliments or anything.

"Ok."

Ok? Just ok? This pasta is delicious, and I'm not just saying that because I made it. Then it hits me. He's nervous. Of course the pasta's just ok. He's not thinking of taste or textures. He's focusing on the proposal. He's probably fixated on getting the words just right. How adorable.

An awkward silence passes between us.

Here it comes. I can feel it.

"Stella, there's something we need to talk about," he says and takes my hand. I can feel him shaking ever so slightly.

Oh my God. Oh my God. Oh my God.

"I know you want to get married." He looks away. "But I've been doing a lot of thinking and I just don't think I'm ready to marry you."

Suddenly the room gets hot and I realize I've been holding my breath. I exhale and wait for him to say "just kidding, I'd be honored to spend the rest of my life with you." Only, he doesn't say anything.

"Ok," I say, still wondering if this is part of the surprise.

"Look, I'm sorry. I've just been thinking this through and I realized you're not the one for me."

His words hit me like a slap in the face. This can't be part of his proposal speech. I feel numb.

"Stella, say something."

"What about the Tiffany's catalogue. I saw it on your nightstand." I confess.

Drew sighs. "That's sort of what started me thinking about all of this. I went to buy you a ring and I couldn't do it."

Ok this all makes sense now. It's not as bad as I thought. I reach for his hand. "Drew, I don't need a Tiffany's ring." I look at him, but his face is blank. "I don't need a ring at all," I lie. "Just as long as I've got you in my life, I'm happy."

He looks like he might get sick. "Stella, you don't get it. I don't want to marry you. Ever. We're not a good pair. I live in New York and you live in your parents' house."

"I'm saving up for a place!" I yell as if I need to defend myself. I stand up quickly and feel the blood drain from my face.

"Look, Stella, you manage your family's restaurant in the summers and waitress during the year, that's what makes you happy and it's all good. But I'm more career-minded than that. I'm working my way up the corporate ladder and I need a wife who can keep up."

I'm about to yell "I can keep up," but I stop myself. What's the point?

I grab my bag off the floor and fling it over my shoulder then turn towards the door.

"Do you want me to drive you to Pietro's?" he asks.

I look at him incredulously. "No!" I snap and head for the door. This is his last chance to stop me.

I take a pause in the open doorway, but he doesn't follow, so I ceremoniously cross over into the hallway and slam the door shut.

Recipe: Penne alla Norma (or The Last Supper)

Yields 2 servings

Ok, I don't really know who the hell Norma is, but apparently, this is *her* pasta, (or my version of it anyway). I've taken the liberty of naming this the Last Supper. You can figure out why.

1/2 pound penne
1/4 cup extra virgin olive oil
1 medium onion, finely chopped
7 Roma tomatoes, diced.
2 cups eggplant, diced
salt and pepper to taste
1/4 cup grated Parmigiano Reggiano cheese
1/4 cup grated ricotta salata
4 fresh basil leaves, chopped.

1) Bring ten cups of water to boil. Add salt to flavor the pasta.
2) Heat olive oil in a medium saucepan. Add the onions, salt and pepper and cook until translucent.
3) Add the tomatoes and eggplant. Reduce the heat to low and allow the sauce to simmer for 15-20 minutes, adding a few spoonfuls of the pasta water if necessary. (While the sauce is simmering, you can cook the pasta).
4) Once the pasta is cooked, add it to the saucepan, and toss to coat it.
5) Top the pasta with grated Parmigiano Reggiano, ricotta salata, and fresh basil.

Chapter 3

It's only about 7:00 when I exit Drew's apartment building. It's early enough that I could take the train to my brother Pietro's place on Long Island. In fact, I'm pretty sure he's still in the city; he usually leaves work around this time. But something in me can't bring myself to call him. I just stand on the corner of 117th and Broadway and watch the people go by. There are so many faces in Manhattan, and with each one a different story. Who knows how many other people right on this street corner are heartbroken like me. I could really use some chocolate cake right now.

Before I can stop myself, I feel a fat tear fall down my cheek. Seconds later, another one drops and I realize I need to get out of this neighborhood before Drew leaves his apartment and finds me. The last thing I need is his pity.

I start walking towards the subway, when it hits me. I have Julie's keys. I'm sure she wouldn't mind if I crashed at her place for the night. Plus, given the situation, I need a little Julie time, though she'll probably go off about what an asshole Drew is. At the moment, I sort of agree.

Julie just doesn't get it though. She thinks the whole idea of marriage is a farce. But that's only because her parents' dysfunctional relationship screwed her up at a young age. Her mother rivals Elizabeth Taylor in marriages and divorces, and her father, a plastic surgeon in LA, changes Botox Bunnies like some men change their ties.

Julie's on the same path, unfortunately. I can't even count the number of guys she's been through since I met her freshman year of college and she seems to only get worse with age. Plus, now that she's a staff member at *GQ* she's all into the models that roam the place in their boxer-briefs.

But the thing is, Julie's never been in love—not like Drew and me at least. She's never had that lasting, withstanding love that bonds people together for life.

As I walk I try to call her, but I get her voicemail. I don't bother leaving a message.

I board the 1 train going downtown to West 4th Street, and snag myself a seat next to an old man. The train is filling up with college students (Columbia kids) who are making their way downtown, probably to get liquored up at some dive bar. I try to ignore their idiotic chatter as I fumble through my bag. When I finally find my compact, I almost wish I hadn't.

My reflection shows a tired girl with mascara streaked cheeks and rumbled up hair. If I were a little skinnier, I'd almost have the whole heroin-chic look down, but instead, I just look like a hot mess.

No wonder Drew broke up with me.

I furiously dig for a tissue and find a crumbled up Starbucks napkin in the bottom of my bag. I lick it and wipe it over my cheeks repeatedly, like a stray cat trying her best to groom herself.

By the time we hit 59th Street, I almost look presentable.

For the rest of the ride, I just stare out the window and replay the events in my head. On one hand, I hate Drew for being so shallow, but on the other hand, I can't help but feel a small spring of hope. I mean, he was close to buying a ring. We dated for three years. He's not just going to throw all of that away on the spur of the moment.

And neither am I.

I reach Julie's by 8:15 and unlock the front door of her building. Even though Julie is a trust-funder, her apartment building is pretty average and doesn't even have an elevator. Thankfully, she lives on the second floor.

I try to call her as I walk up the stairs but her phone goes to voicemail again.

Honestly, I don't even remember when I talked to her last. For all I know she could be on a business trip.

Once the thought enters my head, I can't help but hope it's true. I'd really love to just be alone tonight, take a hot shower, and roll up in bed.

But as soon as I get to her door, I know she's home. I can hear her fake laugh, which can only mean one thing.

I almost don't want to knock on her door, but I'm desperate.

I ring the bell.

She doesn't answer.

I ring it again and wait a few minutes.

I can still hear her laughing so I ring the bell again and bang my fist on the door. "Jules, it's me," I yell.

The door opens a crack and Julie peeks her head out. Her hair is pulled back and her neck and shoulders are bare. I almost think she's naked, but then I see her hot pink tube top. Thank God.

"Hey Stella," she whispers. "Why didn't you call?"

"I did, your phone is off."

She wrinkles her nose and looks back into her apartment. "Oh, sorry. I'm kind of busy. Do you want to hang tomorrow for lunch or something?"

I sigh. "I sort of need a place to crash."

"Just stay at Drew's. Tell Momma DiLucio you're staying here. I'll cover for you." She's about to close the door when I stop her.

"He dumped me, Jules."

Her face softens. "Oh shit. Give me a minute."

I nod and she closes the door. Two minutes later she opens it and a short, pudgy, balding man walks out. "I'll call you," she says and waves him good-bye. So much for the *GQ* models.

I give her a strange look as I enter her apartment. "Who was that?"

"That's George. He's a photographer," she says and plops onto an oversized pillow in the center of her living room floor.

Every time I visit Julie's apartment she's got some new theme going. From the orange and purple sheers billowing from the ceiling, I'm guessing she's doing Moroccan now. Even Winston, her enormous Chow Chow, has a purple doggie bed, which he's snuggled into. He's supposed to be a great watchdog, but the thing is so friendly that if a burglar ever did get through her fifteen locks, Winston would just sniff him a few times and lick his feet.

"He doesn't seem like your usual type," I say trying to be nice, in case this is the one time she's actually in love.

"Ew, Stella!" she squeals and flings her long blonde hair to one side. "I can't believe you thought that."

I give her a look.

"George is a photographer that freelances with us. He's helping me with a project." She pauses to light a cigarette and the offers me one. I decline. "I'm starting a fashion blog. George's doing the photography and I'm doing the styling." Her blue eyes flash with excitement.

It's just like Julie to take on a new project and give it her all. She's motivated, driven, and successful. The exact opposite of me. Drew should be with her. "Do you have any wine?"

"Oh my God, of course," she says jumping up from her pillow. I take a seat on an embroidered foot stool and wait for my drink.

"So, tell me everything." She hands me an oversized goblet of white wine, pours one for herself, and sits back on the floor.

As painful as it is to recount, I give her all the details.

"What an asshole," she says when I finish. "You're better off without him." She blows a puff of smoke, and stands to get another bottle of wine.

"Maybe," I say half convinced. As I was retelling the story though, things started falling into place. In my heart of hearts I know I can get Drew back. Now I just need to figure out how.

When my phone rings at seven the next morning, my first thought is that it's Drew, calling to tell me that he's made a big mistake.

Instead, it's my future sister-in-law Gina, calling to tell me that I'd better high-tail my ass up to the Bronx because we have an appointment with her caterer at the Botanical Gardens at ten.

As I listen to her talk, I contemplate canceling, but then I realize that if anyone can help me get Drew back, it's Gina. After all, she changed my brother Pietro from an uncommitted playboy to a whipped, love struck puppy in just under two years. Honestly, the girl has talent. She'll know just what to do.

Gina has hundreds of close girlfriends, but no sisters, so she chose me as her Maid of Honor, which really surprised me. She and I were never such close friends, but that gesture made it clear; she thinks of me as a sister. Since then, I've looked at her the same way, and though the whole wedding process can be a bit much at times, I've *tried* to be excited and supportive through it all.

Of course, no one's perfect.

There was that one time when Gina was interviewing photographers and made me look through *thousands* of slides. It would have tried anyone's patience. Trust me.

But anyway, besides that, I've been really keen on wedding plans, even when I really don't feel like looking at another color swatch.

Today is going to be a big effort for me, given the circumstances. But as I walk towards the D train I know I'm doing the right thing. I just need to build my strength with a little Food Therapy. A good breakfast will give me the stamina to make it through this day, so before getting on the train, I stop at Café Reggio for a chocolate cornetto and overpriced cappuccino.

My phone starts vibrating the minute I get my cappuccino.

"Stella, how are you?" my mom asks, and for a split second I'm tempted to break down and tell her everything, but I stop myself because she already can't stand Drew.

"I'm ok," I lie. "I just left Julie's apartment."

"I wanted to tell you some good news," she says in a voice that is a little too chipper for this hour.

"What's up?"

"Roberto is back from Italy." She pauses and waits for my reaction. Thankfully she can't see me roll my eyes.

She's talking about Roberto Lancetti, the only son of our bread providers, who also happen to be our close family friends.

Roberto spent the last eight years in Rome doing a PhD in Latin or something, and apparently just got home.

Since I've been about five, my mother and Mrs. Lancetti have been planning an arranged marriage between Roberto and me, even though the kid made my childhood a living hell. One time, he threw gum in my hair and laughed while his mom had to cut it out. I had to get my hair cut all short to even it out, and my brothers called me "shaggy dog" for an entire year. The whole thing was pretty traumatic. Granted, I was eight, but still, these are the things that stick with you. I could have been permanently damaged. Come to think of it, I haven't had short hair since.

The wedding talk went on hiatus when Roberto left for Rome, but apparently it's still fresh in my mother's mind. "That's nice," I reply.

"Maybe the two of you can see each other. I think he's living on the Island this summer."

"I'm sure we'll bump into each other then," I start walking down the steps of the subway. "I gotta go, Mom. I'm meeting Gina in the Bronx."

When I get to Fordham Road in the Bronx, Gina is waiting in her car at the subway stop. She's dressed like a bride in a light pink strapless sundress with a white mini cardigan on top. Her long chestnut hair is freshly highlighted and pulled into a low ponytail and she's even taken the time to curl it so that the ends unravel like a ribbon on a gift box. She wears the large diamond studs my brother gave her last Christmas. Her makeup is fresh, as would be expected on a Bobbi Brown makeup artist, enhancing her naturally thin nose, bright eyes, and pursed lips.

I'm dressed exactly how I feel, dark and depressed.

Honestly, I have no idea why I packed black wide leg trousers and a black tank top. It's like *I knew* I'd be getting dumped or something.

But that's in the past. Today is a new day and I have a fresh take on life.

"What's wrong?" Gina asks in her nasal New York voice as soon as I take a seat. "You look like death." She fishes through her purse and pulls out a concealer stick and some light pink cream blush. "Dab this under your eyes, and dot this on your cheeks."

I do as I'm told. Gina has been working the Bobbi Brown counter at Saks for three years now and knows how to make a girl look good in a pinch. Instantly, my eyes look bigger and brighter. I hand them back to her.

"Keep them," she says. "What happened to you?"

"Drew dumped me," I reply, still in a sort of shock. "He thinks we're not right for each other."

"What?" She rolls her eyes and then says exactly what I hoped she'd say. "It's just cold feet. You'll get him back."

The New York Botanical Gardens are vivid with luscious pinks, golden yellows, deep purples, and fields of green. As we walk through the flagstone paths, Gina describes every detail of the reception, pointing out the outdoor cocktail hour area before we get to the restaurant. "Pray for good weather," she says as we pass it.

We're meeting the caterer in the private ballroom to go over a few options for the cocktail hour. Pietro and Gina already selected the menu choices, but the caterer called last week, about new options for the hors d'oeuvres.

The room was designed specifically for weddings and other special events, so I should have expected it to be beautiful, but as we enter the opulent room, I'm stunned. The walls scream elegance, with their hand painted murals, soaring windows, and Palladian Architecture.

Ok, I'm not really sure what Palladian Architecture is, but the brochure says that it adds elegance to the room.

And, believe me, it does.

"Do you love it?" Gina asks.

"It's amazing!" I squeal and for a minute, I actually try to imagine Drew and me sitting at a sweetheart table, on our wedding day. I did go to Fordham, and that's right across the street. We could get married in the church there and take pictures next to Keating Hall.

My head starts to spin remembering our break-up. But as Gina pointed out, it's just a minor glitch in the plans. No big deal.

I arrive on the Island on Thursday evening just before sunset. After New York, I spent a few days at home near Philadelphia, and then came down the shore a day early. This is the last time I'll have the house to myself all summer and I want to savor every bit of it. Plus with Operation-Get-Drew-Back in the works, I needed to get out of my parents' house.

Of course, they found out about the breakup even before I got home. That's the problem with my family—no one can mind their own business. As soon as Gina dropped me off at Port Authority she called Pietro and told him the news, who in turn called Mario, who just happened to be at Lorenzo's apartment. Dante was the last of my brothers to know, as usual. Of all of us, he's the only one who sort of steers clear of family drama. I'm not sure who exactly told my parents, but as soon as I walked through the door my mother came running up to tell me how I'm better off. My father added that, even though he liked Drew, I'd be better suited with an Italian. I ran up the stairs before my mother could start matchmaking. So you can see why I needed to get to the Island as fast as possible. Plus, just being there has a calming effect on me.

Our house on 99th Street, which overlooks the bay, is prime real estate. My grandparents bought the house in 1952 back when this town was nothing more than a bunch of shacks on the beach. Land down here was cheap because, unless they were going to Cape May, no one ventured this far down south, especially no one from Philadelphia. In those days Atlantic City was *the* place to be, but my grandparents couldn't afford a piece of land on those beaches.

Over the years, my grandparents, and eventually my parents, put a lot of their money into the original little shack, which has now morphed into a four-bedroom home, with bay views in three of the bedrooms. Not that it's even big enough for everyone though.

My room is the smallest in the house but has the best view, and when I wake up the first thing I see is water. It's lovely, it truly is.

I open the door and step inside. The floor boards creek to welcome me. I switch on the lights and see that the house has remained exactly as I left it on Monday morning. A flannel blanket is draped over the plush plaid sofa, the coffee table is centered perfectly in front of it, and the woven rug sits firmly in place. The TV cabinet doors are shut. To the right, a big wooden staircase leads to the upstairs bedrooms.

To the left of the living room is the dining area, which is home to our old kitchen table and eight chairs. When we were young the dining set was in our kitchen, but since all of my brothers have moved out of my parents' house, they downsized to a smaller table. The big table looks out of place in this small dining room, yet also surprisingly comforting. The kitchen is modest to say the least, but since we've opened the restaurant, we never make anything more than a bowl of cereal, some toast, or a sandwich in here.

I open the fridge to see what we've got. I really hope there are some meatballs in there. Whenever I'm stressed, I need a meatball.

It's empty besides a large tank of water, some mayo, and a jar of Dijon mustard. I make a mental note to hit the grocery offshore later on.

I pour myself a glass of water and flip through the mail. We never really get anything important at the house. Most people know to send stuff directly to the restaurant. But still, there's something calming about looking through the mail.

I flip through grocery store flyers, a Val-U-Pack addressed to Dear Residents, and the postcard invitation to the Lancetti's Fourth of July barbeque.

Honestly, I don't know why they even bother sending out the invites, they know we go every year and have been for the past fifteen years. It's a staple of the summer. I guess Roberto will be there this year. I have to admit, I'm curious as to what he looks like nowadays. In my head he has an overgrown beard and long hair pulled into one of those man ponytails that people with PhD's in Latin have. Gross.

I hang the postcard on the fridge and throw the rest of the mail out, then decide to call Lorenzo to see if he wants to come off shore with me.

Out of everyone in my family, Lorenzo is the only one who doesn't love the shore house. Well, I shouldn't say he doesn't *love* it, he probably does. But what he doesn't love is the fact that my family eats together, works together, and sleeps all in the same place.

I don't blame him. It's a bit much at times.

Anyway, last year, he nearly gave my mother a heart attack when he announced that he found his own apartment to rent for the summer. She thought it was ludicrous to spend money on a tiny apartment when we have a big house. "No one's even there during the week!" she shrieked and looked at my dad for support. My dad listened to Lorenzo's side of the story and finally agreed with his son. My mother still hasn't gotten over it.

The phone rings three times before he answers. "What's up?"

"Nothing. Do you want to go grocery shopping?" I ask.

"I'm still in Philly," he replies.

That's strange. Lorenzo never comes down the shore on Fridays. "Really?"

"Yeah, I wanted one last night out in the city before the season starts."

"Where are you going?"

"I don't know yet. I gotta see what Biv and Jason want to do. Thursday nights are good in Old City."

Lorenzo and I used to have the same group of friends, but when I started dating Drew I sort of lost touch with everyone. Besides, Lorenzo's friends are hit or miss; they're great, loyal guys, but sometimes they're really immature. Then again, so are Drew's. "All right. Have fun."

When we hang up I walk through the den, and outside to the bay, where I take a seat in our chaise lounge and watch the colors of the sky turn to night. The sun is a big rosy ball, ready to make its descent into the horizon.

There are beach people and there are bay people and really, the difference comes down to whether you enjoy a sunrise or a sunset. My grandmom Stella was alone in her beach preference, because we DiLucio's are definitely bay people, though since we've opened the restaurant, we've hardly caught a sunset.

But still, we love them.

It's the third week in June but the air still has a slight chill to it so I pull my knees to my chest and hug them for warmth. I think about the week, and try not to replay the events of the breakup.

Then, for some reason, I start thinking of my grandmother. It's times like these, times of high crisis, that I wish she were still around. She'd know exactly what to say and do to get Drew back.

Even though everyone says I take after her, there's one important element that I'm missing. My grandmother was the spunkiest woman I'd ever met, and I unfortunately lack that spark.

Recipe: Meatballs

Yields 4 dozen medium sized meatballs

Perfect for when you're stressed. Just try them, you'll see.

1 pound ground beef
1 pound ground veal
1 pound ground pork
3 eggs, beaten
1 cup breadcrumbs
1/2 cup milk
2 gloves of garlic, finely chopped
1/2 cup Italian parsley, finely chopped
1 cup pecorino romano cheese, grated.

1) Preheat oven to 400 degrees F.
2) In a large bowl mix all the ingredients together until thoroughly incorporated.
3) Roll meat into a small, tight ball using the palms of your hands (some people use a small ice cream scoop to get meatballs that are all the same size).
4) Place on a baking sheet.
5) Bake for one hour, or until fully browned and cooked through. Allow to cool before eating (I know it's hard).

Chapter 4

Ok, it's been exactly 3 days, 16 hours, 36 minutes, and 57 seconds since Drew broke up with me.

The bad news: he still hasn't called.

The good news: Food Therapy works. Last night after sitting on the bay for a few hours, I got tired of thinking, so I walked over to the restaurant and cut myself a slice (or three) of Chuck's chocolate cake. It really did make me feel better, and it helped to formulate a plan of action for Operation Get-Drew-Back.

Ok, here's the thing. Drew thinks we're not compatible because I am just a lowly waitress/restaurant manager working for my parents, while he is a big bad marketing executive (aka, slave to the cubicle in some shitty office).

Obviously, he doesn't understand just how much effort and expertise it takes to deal with people all night long. Honestly, if he could only *see* what I do on a daily basis, he'd realize that I'm not some slacker, mooching off of her parents, but a highly motivated, well rounded woman, capable of multi-tasking and, eventually, achieving global domination. All of that, and I can stand on concrete flooring in six inch heels for eight hours straight, seven nights a week.

Not that restaurant management is my life's dream or anything, but I am working with what I've got.

So, my plan is simple. I'm going to show Drew exactly what I do.

And since tonight officially kicks off our full time season, I'll have plenty of opportunities to show him my talents.

The only glitch in the plan is that Drew is in New York City and I'm on the Island, so how could he possibly see what I'm doing?

Other girls would end right there. They'd throw in the towel and accept defeat. But not this girl. No way.

In a sheer stroke of brilliance I've decided to film myself in action, doing what I do.

When I called Lucy at six this morning to tell her the plan, she brought up the point that customers might not want to be caught on film when they enter a restaurant. But I figure I can get around that by blurring out faces, just like they do on reality TV. And once I've gotten enough footage, I'll post the videos on YouTube and email Drew the link. Once he sees me in action he'll be begging for me back.

I can imagine it already.

He'll be at his desk at work and open the YouTube link, thinking it's a stupid video of a cat dancing or some other nonsense, and he'll be mesmerized by me, in a Kelly green BCBG dress (tonight's outfit), answering phones, greeting customers, flirting like a champ (hopefully a cute guy will come in—that'll make Drew jealous on top of proud), and handling the unexpected situations that will surely arise. All while looking fabulous (thanks to Gina's crash course in make-up the other day).

He'll be so awe-struck, in fact, that he won't even hear his boss standing over his shoulder. And once he does turn around, his boss will say "who's that girl" to which Drew will respond "my ex." His boss will shake his head, confirming what Drew already knows; that he lost a gem. Then his boss will say "she's a star," and send the link to all of his bazillion contacts. The video will go viral in a matter of minutes and I'll have agents phoning me about TV shows and movies. I'm sure of it.

So sure of it, in fact, that I went off shore to buy a larger memory card for my camera. Right now the thing can hold thirty minutes of video. That's a lot, considering the average YouTube video is fifty-seven seconds. But I figure I'll have to scrap *some* footage.

I've set the camera up right next to the hostess stand on my left (my better side) to optimize the light and angle from which I'm shot.

The only thing is, tonight we have another packed house, and with my family coming in, I'm busier than usual. Both Dante and Lucy are late getting down. School ended and their grades were due by 3:00 p.m. They jumped in the car together and made it here thirty minutes after the other waiters. That set us back a bit. I tried to help Michelle and Ryan get the side work done but the phone just kept ringing.

My main job as manager of Lorenzo's is to control the reservation book. I've got it down pretty well; I assign each table a two-hour time slot so in theory we can seat the same table at 5:00 p.m., 7:00 p.m., and 9:00 p.m. With seventeen tables we have the potential of seating 180 diners a night. Now, of course, there are tables (like two tops), which are in and out in less than an hour, and others (like parties of twelve) who will sit for forty minutes before even ordering a thing, but for the most part, my method works. When it doesn't and people have to wait for their reservation, I find that the only thing to do is flirt.

I'm a master flirt. I don't discriminate between men and women, though the tactics differ greatly from person to person. I mean, you have to be *smart* about it. You can't just bat your eyelashes like they do in the movies. Flirting is an art form.

Take, for example, these two scenarios.

Scenario one: a middle-aged woman comes in to check on her table, which is nowhere near ready. No need to panic. Just quickly find something you like about her outfit and divert the conversation that way. You must be sincere though, you can't say you love her Lily Pulitzer pants if the only color you ever wear is black. No, no, no. On the Island, you must dress the part if you want to be a successful restaurant manager, even if that means sporting the occasional Capri pants with embroidered umbrellas on them, straight out of page twenty-six in last year's J. Crew catalogue.

Scenario two: an elderly gentleman comes in after waiting fifteen minutes for his 7:00 reservation. He's *not* accustomed to waiting like younger people so he's pretty angry. Just gently touch his hand and explain how sorry you are. Then, with a big smile tell him the people who are currently sitting at his table have their check and should be paying the bill soon. Even if this *is* a little white lie, it generally calms down the customer. It's really pretty easy.

When all else fails and the customer is *really* mad there's nothing left to do but start giving stuff away for free. As you know, this infuriates Lorenzo (so don't tell him). Not that this happens often or anything. Usually flirting works just fine. I'm an expert; remember?

The phone rings again at 5:00, just as we are opening for the night. "Thank you for calling Lorenzo's how may I help you?" I say looking directly into the camera. I've restarted recording because I figure the opening footage was mostly boring stuff.

"I need to make a reservation," the man on the other end says.

"Ok, when would you like to come in?" I flip through the reservation book busily, as if the man on the other end is very important. Then I hold a pencil between my fingers as if it were a cigarette, and do my best to channel Audrey Hepburn à la *Breakfast at Tiffany's*.

"How about 7:00? There are six of us."

"Tonight?" I ask wide eyed. I drop the pencil to look like I'm in shock.

"Yeah, tonight."

I look down at the reservations and see that our tables are all booked up.

"I'm sorry sir, I don't have 7:00 available. My only available times are 5:00, 5:30, or 9:15."

"What about 7:30?" he asks.

Obviously he's not paying attention.

"I'm sorry sir, I don't have that either," I try to be peppy for the camera.

"Listen," he says frankly. "It's my wife's birthday and I forgot to make a reservation. Is there any way you can squeeze us in?"

Now I just feel bad. His wife's birthday. How could he have forgotten? Drew would never forget. For a minute I'm flustered, remembering the three birthdays I spent with Drew.

"Hello?" the man on the phone says.

Oh right.

"I'm really sorry." I sigh. "If you want, I can take your name for the waiting list. If we get any cancellations, I'll give you a call."

He quickly gives his name and cell number then hangs up without saying goodbye.

It's not *my* fault he forgot to make a reservation.

"I hate people," I mumble to myself as the front door opens. Oh crap. I'll have to edit that out.

My parents arrive with boxes of food from La Cucina. They've decided to close on weekends for the summer. The restaurant is in my hometown, which is just a little speck on the map outside Philadelphia and the town pretty much dies from June to September so it makes sense for them to close.

I look at the boxes my mom and dad are carrying and assume Lorenzo doesn't know about the food they're bringing in. He's *not* going to be happy about it. I turn off the camera and stash it in the hostess stand before they start asking questions.

"Stella!" my dad beams when he sees me, even though I was just home two days ago. I walk over to hug them and take a box out of my mom's hands.

"What'd you bring?"

"Don't even ask," my dad whispers rolling his eyes. My mom shoots him a look.

"I made baked rigatoni," she says. "We can use it for a special or eat it ourselves, if Lorenzo doesn't want to serve it."

They move past me and into the kitchen. I see that they've also brought two bags of spring mix, seven zucchini, two oranges, and a gallon of milk.

I follow them into the kitchen.

"What the hell, Mom?" Lorenzo shrieks when he sees the food. "I told you not to bring anything down."

"I had these things left over," she says, her voice getting loud. "What was I supposed to do? Let it spoil?"

We all know the baked rigatoni was *not* leftover. My mom is always making things purposely to bring down. It drives Lorenzo crazy.

Lorenzo takes the box out of my hands and looks through it. This could get ugly.

"Mom, I don't even *use* zucchini," he says, hovering over the boxes. "And I have three bags of my own spring mix. What am I supposed to do with all this salad?"

"You'll figure it out," she says, detonating the bomb. "You're the chef."

I leave the kitchen and move towards the waiters' station where they have all convened. "Go a little heavy on the salads tonight guys," I say, trying to solve the produce issue before walking back to my podium. Damn I wish that was on film.

My parents emerge from the other kitchen door. "We're not staying to eat here tonight," my mom says. My dad is holding the baked rigatoni pan in his hands. "I'll be cooking dinner at home." She's flustered and red in the face.

My dad shrugs.

Lorenzo must have won.

"Cancel our spot, and if Pietro and Gina come here, just send them home," my mom says.

They leave before I can protest. I erase their reservation from the book, and notice that a 7:00 spot is now open. I look at the man's name on my waiting list but decide not to call him back.

Rudeness gets you nowhere. Besides, I know I'll fill the spot with walk-ins.

The rest of the night goes off without a hitch, and to be honest, it was pretty boring. I mean, there was nothing to film. Not an angry customer, or a waiter flub. The only slightly eventful thing was Mr. Beister, a once a week regular, telling me how beautiful I look. Luckily I caught it on film, but it's hardly worthwhile. I mean, the man is in his seventies, so I doubt if Drew would get jealous about that.

When I get home at night, my mom has already divided up the bedrooms. Mario and Dante are sharing one room. Pietro gets the other. Gina gets my room (no rooming with Pietro), and Lucy and I are on the couch.

"Hello," my mom yells as I open the door. Somehow it's impossible for her to keep her voice down, even though it's after midnight.

My parents, Gina, and Pietro are sitting in the living room, pawning over wedding invitations, which is pretty much the last thing I want to do after work. But Gina was so nice to me the other day, and has been texting me strategies for getting Drew back, that the least I can do is look at an invitation or two.

But knowing Gina, she'll have brought the entire book.

"How was it tonight?" my dad asks, looking thankful that he can take a break from the wedding talk. Honestly, I don't blame him.

"Busy." I place my purse down on the table. The pan of baked rigatoni is still in the kitchen. I make my way towards it. Only the smallest bit of baked rigatoni remains and I scoop it out and pop it in the microwave.

It's past midnight and I'm just eating dinner. That's the funny thing about the restaurant business. The owners and workers rarely eat during service hours. Lorenzo serves family meal to the staff every night after his last order, but I was talking to a few tables and missed it. Lucy offered me half of hers but I said no, so now I'm starving. I pick at the pieces of pasta stuck to the pan while my dinner heats in the microwave.

"You want some wine?" Pietro asks. Even *he* looks thankful for a small break.

I survey the situation and decide that yes, I do.

If we are going to talk wedding talk at midnight after a long night of work, I'm going to need alcohol to get me through it.

He pours me a glass and brings it into the den. I take my dinner out of the microwave and follow him.

“What are those?” I ask placing my plate on the coffee table and taking a seat on the couch next to Gina.

“They’re our top two choices for invitations. We’ve narrowed it down to these. We *need* your input,” Gina explains.

I take a bite of pasta. “Ok, let me have a look.”

The wedding colors are pumpkin, oak, and cream, an unconventional combination, which somehow works. The first invitation reflects the colors nicely. It’s brown cardstock with cream- colored embossed writing. The typeset is casual, and gives the invite a playful tone. A large orange chiffon bow sits on top. The invitation screams modern and sophisticated, which is exactly what Gina wants the reception to be. She does work at Sak’s for God’s sake.

The second is totally traditional. It’s a textured cream cardstock that unfolds to reveal a different textured cardstock with brown embossed cursive script. The pumpkin is decidedly absent from the invite. This is more for the Bergdorf Goodman crowd, and honestly, I like it better.

I take another bite and survey the situation. Since I am the Maid of Honor, I should think of what the bride wants, and the first invite has Gina’s imprint all over it. I know my mother probably likes the second one, and for that reason I put my finger on the first. “This is the one.”

Gina beams. “I told you,” she says to Pietro and he shrugs his shoulders. My mom looks at me strangely.

“I’m glad that’s settled,” my dad says standing up. “Now I can go to sleep.”

“Antonio!” my mom shrieks as if my dad is being rude. Or maybe she just doesn’t want to be left alone with the wedding brigade.

“Teresa it’s *midnight*, I’m going to bed.”

He waves his hand at all of us and embarks up the wooden staircase. My dad is so cute. Gina holds her invitation and admires it a bit more as I polish off the rest of the pasta.

Lucy and Dante come in together. I’m usually the last person to leave the restaurant, but Lorenzo offered to close up. Everyone in my family has been so nice since Drew dumped me, it's like they think I'm suicidal or something. Regardless, I was happy to get a chance to leave early.

"Lucy, I hope you don't mind, we're sharing the pull out couch tonight," I say as she enters the living room.

She smiles at everyone as she walks into the den. "I'm actually going to stay at my aunt's tonight. My dad's coming down for the weekend."

Lucy rarely stays at her aunt's house because it's usually more packed than ours. Her family goes to bed early so by the time we finish work, they're all asleep. I look at her.

"My dad's awake," she says. "I just called his cell."

"That's nice Lucia," my mom says. She has the habit of turning everyone's name Italian. Though, now that I think of it, she never did that with Drew's.

"I'm just going to get my stuff," Lucy says and moves towards the stairs. She comes back a few minutes later, still wearing her waiter uniform. She's carrying a small duffle bag and her hair is hanging loose around her shoulders. She smiles at us. "Goodnight guys," she says and waves.

I don't remember Lucy telling me about her dad being in town, but I've been so preoccupied that maybe I just forgot. Still, I'm disappointed. We haven't had much of a chance to talk this week with her students taking finals and all and I'd really like her advice on the whole Drew situation.

I watch her leave and turn towards Gina who is still admiring the invitations. She catches my eye and winks.

"Babe, why don't you go to bed?" she says to my brother. "I want some girl time with Stell."

Pietro gets up a little too quickly, like he's been waiting for her permission to go to bed for hours. I told you the girl was good.

"Goodnight guys," he says, and follows Dante up the steps.

We both wait to hear his bedroom door close.

"Ok, has he called yet?"

I slump a little lower on the couch. "No. It's been five days!"

"Stop it!" she replies. "You're sounding desperate. Trust me, you do not want to sound desperate in this situation. Remember you *always* want to have the upper hand."

I give her a look.

"You called him didn't you?" she asks.

"No," I lie. I mean, technically I did call, but I blocked my number from caller ID so there's no way he knew it was me. Plus it went right to voicemail anyway.

"Stella, I know it's hard not talking to him now. In fact, this is the hardest part of the whole plan. But if you can make it one month without calling him, I'm positive he'll come running back." She looks so confident that I almost believe her.

"But what if he doesn't?" I say in a small voice.

"Then we pull out all the stops with my no-fail back-up plan." She smiles, proud of herself.

Recipe: Baked Rigatoni

Yields 4-6 servings

Though this can certainly be eaten any time of the day, somehow, it tastes even better at midnight, when you're ravenous.

This pasta really relies on the sauce, so you'll need that recipe first.

Meat Sauce*:
2 28oz cans of tomato puree
1 small onion
1 carrot
1 stalk of celery
1/4 cup of olive oil
1 teaspoon salt
1/2 teaspoon black pepper
2 tablespoons fresh basil leaves (chopped)

1) Finely chop the onion, carrot and celery (this can be done in a food processor).
2) Heat olive oil in a large stockpot and add the onion, carrot and celery. Cook until golden, stirring occasionally. (This should take 3-4 minutes.)
3) Add the tomato puree plus one can of water per can of tomato (just fill the can after adding the puree to the stockpot and add the water).
4) Add salt, pepper, and basil. Simmer on medium heat for one hour, stirring occasionally.

Any leftover sauce can be frozen in an air-tight container for up to 1 month.

For the pasta:
1 pound of rigatoni
1 pound of fresh ricotta cheese
1 cup of Parmigiano Reggiano cheese (grated)

1) Bring 10 cups of salted water to boil. Cook the rigatoni for 10-12 minutes, until al dente.
2) Preheat oven to 400 degrees.
3) Pour one ladle of sauce onto the bottom of a large baking dish.
4) In a large bowl, toss pasta, ricotta cheese, and 1/2 cup Parmigiano Reggiano cheese together. Add enough sauce to coat the pasta. Toss again.
5) Pour pasta into prepared baking sheet. Top with the rest of the cheese.
6) Cover loosely with aluminum foil and bake in oven for 20-25 minutes.
7) Uncover the baking dish and cook for an additional 5 minutes (or until pasta gets golden brown).

*Technically there is no meat in the meat sauce. We call it meat sauce because you can add meatballs to it, which gives it an amazing flavor.

Chapter 5

The next morning I awake to the smell of bacon frying. My mother's already dressed, her short dark hair freshly washed and neatly combed. She is making her fantastic bacon and eggs, and the smell radiates through the kitchen and tickles my nose in the den.

I follow it into the kitchen. "Good morning," I grumble and look at the clock; it's 8:30. I don't know why my mother is up so early. It's Saturday for God's sake.

"Good morning," she says. "Your father and I are having breakfast on the deck, do you want to come out?"

"Sure," I say fixing myself a cup of steamed milk from the stove. I pour a shot of espresso into it and swirl it around on the counter top. Then I look at the spread that my mom has made. There's crispy bacon, fluffy scrambled eggs, and rosemary grissini. "How long have you been awake?"

"Since five."

I look at my mother to make sure she's okay. Usually she's a really late sleeper, and, like me, my mom uses a sort of food therapy when she's stressed. Only instead of eating the food, she just cooks it. "Are you ok?"

"Yes, why?" she asks, as if it's normal to get up at five on a Saturday morning. She turns back to the stove and fixes a plate for my dad. Then she takes a mug and fills it with hot milk and espresso for herself and moves through the kitchen. I follow her. We're almost in the den when she turns, looks at my empty hands, and says, "You're not eating."

To my mother, not eating can only mean two things: snobbery or sickness. Once, Drew's parents came over for dinner and his mother didn't clean her plate (she's one of those women who is perpetually pushing food around on the plate to make it look like she's eating). This was the greatest offense to my mother, who, from then on, referred to Drew's mother as "la strega," roughly translated as "the bitch." I tried to lie and say that she was sick, but my mom saw through the entire thing.

Obviously, I'm no snob, so according to her theory, I must be sick. Forget the fact that I might just not be hungry. Before she can check my pulse and diagnose me with depression, I walk back into the kitchen, grab a breadstick, and take a hearty bite.

"I'm just tired," I say and with my mouth full.

She seems content with my answer because she turns and walks through the den, and out the sliding doors.

"Good morning Stella," my dad says when he sees me. He's reading the newspaper and already sipping on a mug of hot coffee. My mom places the plate down in front of him. "How did you sleep?"

"Ok." I take a seat facing the water

"Did you hear Roberto Lancetti is back from Italy?" my mom says looking at me.

"Yes, you told me." I take a sip of coffee and stare out at the bay.

"Maybe you should give him a call," my dad begins. "You can go to the beach together or something."

I try my hardest not to roll my eyes. Honestly, my dad still acts as if I'm twelve and all I care about is body surfing until the sun goes down. Doesn't he know that I'm a mature, hardworking, career-driven woman?

"That's a great idea," my mom nods.

"I don't *want* to go to the beach with Roberto Lancetti!" I whine. "I just want to be left alone."

I can already imagine what would happen if I did call Roberto. He'd greet me in Latin and then look at me from behind his dorky glasses, waiting for a response, to which I would say "Mihi licet ire ad latrinum," which translates to "may I use the bathroom," which is the only phrase I retained from three monotonous years of high school Latin. Of course, he'd then go off (in Latin) about the bathrooms in ancient Rome—or something equally as enticing—and I'd literally die of boredom. I'd rather not.

"Stella, we just want you to have a friend. We know this is a hard time for you." My dad looks at me with sincerity. Obviously they have no idea about my master plan to win Drew back.

"I'm totally fine," I snap. "In fact, I'm pretty sure that in a few weeks everything will blow over and Drew and I will get back together." I replay the details of Gina's master plan in my head. Like I said, that girl is good.

My parents look at each other.

"Stella, why don't you try to forget him? Move on with your life," my dad suggests.

Honestly, they are taking this a little far. I mean, we broke up a week ago. They're acting as if it's been months.

"Dad, there's really no need to lecture me. If Mom dumped you, would you just try to move on?"

My parents look at each other again.

"Stella, he's not right for you. It's for the best," my dad says.

"Look at his family," my mother chimes in. "They're a bunch of stuck up snobs."

"Oh, and I suppose someone like Roberto Lancetti *is* good for me?" I stand up from the table. "Get this straight," I say with conviction. "I will never date Roberto. Never."

I walk back into the house, wishing that I had someplace to go besides the den. It's not as dramatic of an exit when you're only walking a few feet away, and there's not even a door you can slam.

After the fight with my parents, I spent the rest of the morning on Craigslist, looking at New York City apartments. Honestly, Drew was right, I need to move out of my parents' house, even if it means spending 1,500 dollars a month to live in an East Harlem two bedroom with three other girls and seven cats, which, by the way, was my best option. I'm waiting for them to email me back. Apparently by the time I left for work, seventeen other people were interested and we may get into a bidding war. I'm remaining hopeful.

Now it's 9:30 and service is almost over. Even though it's a Saturday night, nothing, and I mean nothing noteworthy happened. What a waste of a perfectly good dress. I'll have to trash all of tonight's video and at this rate, I'll never get this YouTube clip up and running. Maybe it's for the best.

When I told Gina about the whole idea, she was totally against it, saying that it was borderline creepy and how would I feel if Drew sent me a link of himself at work. I didn't tell her, but actually, I'd kind of like it. I've always wondered what they do at those board meetings.

The phone rings as I'm saying good-bye to Mrs. Junip and her friends. You'd think that a table of five cougars would have made some sort of scene, but not even Frankie could capture their attention. I think one of them is going through a divorce because they were all somber looking and kept saying things like "you're better without him" and "milk him for all he's worth." The saddest part was that the woman in question looked totally out of touch with her friends. You could just sense that she wasn't listening to them, but since she didn't confide in me, I wasn't about to just send over the chocolate cake.

"Thank you for calling Lorenzo's, how may I help you?"

"Hi, is this Stella?" a male voice asks me.

"Yes."

"Hey Stella. It's Rob."

I frantically start thinking of all the regulars who come in, yet I can't think of anyone named Rob. I'm about to pretend like I know who it is, when the voice stops me.

"Lancetti," he says and I can tell he's smirking on the other end.

I'm so going to kill my mother.

"Oh, hi! How was Italy?"

"It was great. Listen, I need to make a reservation for tomorrow night. Do you have 7:00 available for two?"

"Are you bringing your dad in for Father's Day? I ask as I scan the reservation book. We don't have room, but I'll have to squeeze them in somehow. My parents take personal offense if I ever deny one of their friends a seat.

"Oh shit, tomorrow is Father's Day, isn't it?" he pauses as though he's thinking. "Um, okay forget it. I'll see if she's free next weekend."

"Okay."

"I'll let you know. Thanks," he says and hangs up without waiting for a reply. Weird.

I walk through the dining room looking for Lucy and finally find her in the kitchen laughing with Lorenzo.

"What's going on?" I ask and they both seem to jump a bit.

"Nothing, we're just laughing at something dumb this lady at my table said," Lucy replies. I wait a second for her to tell me what the lady said but she stays silent.

Ok.

"Do you want to grab a drink after work?" I ask. "We can keep it chill and just go to Bob's."

Bob's is the biggest dive bar on the planet and only exists on the Island because it's been there for like fifty years or something. Basically it is a small, windowless room with a huge center bar. The only entertainment is an old Jukebox filled with songs from the seventies and eighties, but the drinks are nice and strong. Lucy and I love the place.

"I don't know," she hesitates. "My family is all in town for Father's Day."

Since Lucy's mom died her family has gotten really close and always seems to be around for holidays, no matter what they are. I totally understand, but still, I haven't really gotten a chance to talk to Lucy all week.

"Please. Just one drink. I really need it."

"Why don't we just have a drink here?" she suggests, even though she knows it's not the same.

"Fine," I say because I'm not into begging.

Sunday mornings are always a rush to get to church, no matter what time Mass starts, and this morning is no different.

It's Father's Day, so there will be extra people filling the pews at St. Luke's and my mom seems on edge. She hovers over me while I sip my coffee.

"It's 9:*35*," she says.

She's already dressed in a lavender pants suit and cream colored blouse and looks much younger than her sixty-two years. I *really* hope I've inherited her genes.

My father comes down the steps looking sharp in a crisp white shirt and grey slacks. His hair is more salt than pepper, but it looks great on him, and he's gotten some sun over the weekend (I don't know how, since he never steps foot on the beach).

He walks into the kitchen wringing his hands. "You almost ready to go?" he asks looking at me.

I'm still wearing my yellow and white pajamas and haven't even *thought* about a shower yet. Last night was a late one, and we didn't get home until after 1:00 a.m. "I'm getting in the shower right now," I say getting up from the table. I walk across the den still holding my coffee cup. I still haven't talked to them much since the fight about Drew, but I've let the whole moving out thing go. Who wants to live with strangers anyway?

"You better hurry up or we're going to be late," my mom calls after me.

Mass doesn't start for another hour, and it takes all of five minutes to walk to church, so I have no idea why my parents are so concerned about time. I peek into Mario and Dante's room and see that they are both still asleep. Typical. No one's telling them to get a move on. That's the way it is in an Italian family though. The boys can do no wrong, and the girls get dumped on.

Pietro comes out of his bedroom, wearing dark jeans and a blue polo shirt. He absolutely *refuses* to dress up during the weekend, saying that he wears enough suits during the week. He's wearing sneakers, which I'm sure Gina will veto once she sees them.

"Gina's in the shower," he says as he passes me. "She should be out in a minute."

"Nice sneakers," I mumble and walk to my room.

I decide on a pale blue cap sleeve dress and brown wedge sandals. We're going to brunch in Atlantic City after Mass and I'm not sure if I'll have time to change before work. This dress is versatile enough to wear to brunch and work.

My parents were right. St Luke's is packed with families. There are new fathers holding tiny infants in hand, young fathers with rows of small children dressed in their best, and mature father's like my own, who enters the pew followed by his four tall sons, wife, daughter, and future daughter-in-law.

Fr. Jim gives a wonderful homily about the importance of fathers as role models for their families. As he talks, I look at my brothers, each one so different, yet they all seem to know what they want in life. They all have direction. Whereas the only thing I know is that I have no clue what I want to be when I grow up. At eleven, this would be a problem, at twenty-seven it is a disaster.

By the end of Mass, we're all hungry. The ride to Atlantic City takes about forty minutes and we arrive just in time for our 1:00 reservation at the Hilton.

You'd think that we are big foodies since we have two restaurants in the family, but the truth is, we don't get out to each too much. You wouldn't either if you owned a restaurant. Most of the time, when we do go out, we're disappointed and wished we'd just stayed home.

The exception to this is Atlantic City.

My parents are secret degenerate gamblers.

Ok, maybe not *degenerates*. They never lost a *house* or anything.

But the point is, they love to gamble. And they spend big bucks at the Hilton, their favorite spot in AC. Which means one thing: they get lots of comps.

So usually, when we go out to eat, it's in a casino, and today is no exception.

We take our seats at a long alcove table, which is perfect for my family. It gives us the right amount of privacy, since we have a tendency to get a little loud. It seems like there is always something to scream about, but today, we can just enjoy each other's company and the delicious food on the buffet table.

Gina places her Louis Vuitton clutch on the seat next to mine before getting in line with my brother. I wait for my parents and walk with them.

Typically, buffets are crass, especially brunch ones, which usually serve dried out eggs, soggy hash browns, and greasy sausage links, but *this* buffet is different.

Solid ice sculptures line the tables and fruits and vegetables are transformed into colorful flowers filling giant vases along the buffet. There are three carving stations serving prime rib, French cut lamb chops, and porchetta, which my mom lines up for first.

Tuxedo clad servers man the chafing dishes, which are filled with different kinds of pasta, but none of us will get in that line.

Two chefs work the omelet station while another serves fresh Belgium waffles hot off the press. The faint smell of brandy hits me and I see the flambé station. I make a mental note to save room for Bananas Foster.

Dante makes his way towards the salads, where servers are tossing torn romaine leaves with house made Caesar dressing. He lifts his plate to receive some.

Mario and I tackle the raw bar, where a chef freshly shucks the oysters and sets them on our plates. I scan the ice packed shrimp cocktail and take three jumbo pieces then move towards the red slivers of Ahi tuna. I take a cup of soy sauce for dipping.

Back at the table, Gina patiently waits for everyone to sit. Her plate is full of greens dressed in raspberry vinaigrette, grilled vegetables, and one thin slice of prime rib. She's been off dairy for a month now, saying it's better for the skin, and, I have to admit, she is glowing. Maybe I'll try to give up dairy. I don't eat too much of it anyway. Except for my morning cappuccino. And the occasional gelato. Oh, who am I kidding? I'd rather have raging acne than give up cheese.

"Champagne?" the waiter behind us asks.

We both look at each other and smile. "Yes please," I say.

The waiter proceeds around the table and once everyone is served, my father stands to make a toast. "To my family," he says raising his glass. "May we always love and respect one another, no matter what the future brings."

We clink glasses but I can't help feeling this toast is ominous.

I look at my mother, who nervously picks at some French toast, then at my father, who is working his way through king crab legs.

Something's up.

My second round at the buffet is for dessert, and I proceed to the flambé table for my Bananas Foster. The chef sautés the bananas and then adds the shot of brandy, making a large red flame in the pan. My stomach turns as I watch it burn.

Somehow, I can't shake the feeling that my life is quickly going up in flames. I mean, I am twenty-seven with no career path and worse, no boyfriend.

As soon as I take my seat, my dad stands up again, and clinks his fork on his wine glass. Pietro and Gina kiss, as if practicing for their wedding.

Honestly, sometimes they're *too* much.

"Your mother and I have an announcement to make," Dad says.

My heart begins to pound.

I knew it. Something's wrong.

Instantly my mind reels and I start thinking of the worst-case scenarios.

I can imagine it already. They're getting a divorce. After thirty-nine years of marriage my father's taken a girlfriend, and he's about to break the news. Of course, my mother will play it cool and act like she's okay, but later on tonight, I'll have to feed her chocolate cake and vodka while she cries. Come to think of it, that's not really likely.

Oh God. My dad is sick. He's probably got some incurable illness that can't even be treated. I'll have to drop out of school to care for him. Wait, I graduated college five years ago.

Has it really been five years? It seems like just yesterday I was walking down the steps of Keating Hall surrounded by my closest friends. I really need to figure out my life. What have I been doing for the past five years? I mean, look at Julie. She's built a career while I've been wasting the time away, slinging spaghetti and meatballs…

The sound of my dad clearing his throat knocks me back into the moment.

I close my eyes. Here it comes.

"We want to thank our wonderful children for all the hard work that you've done over the years at La Cucina and now, at Lorenzo's," my dad begins.

He stops to look at each and every one of us with a smile.

Tears are welling up in his eyes.

Oh God. I *knew* something was wrong. I *knew* it. I've always had a sixth sense about these sorts of things…

"Your mother and I appreciate all the years of sacrifice that you've put into the business. When we first opened La Cucina, your mother was scared that it would tear the family apart. Instead, we've both been impressed at how it's made all of us stronger."

My mother smiles and squeezes my father's hand. They lock eyes and she nods for him to go on. "But your mother and I are tired. We want to enjoy our old age."

"And grandchildren!" my mom pipes in, winking at Pietro and Gina.

"So that is why we've decided to sell La Cucina," my dad says with a sigh. "We wanted you all to be the first to know."

My father keeps talking but I'm not listening.

He can't be serious.

My brothers and I have invested so much of our time into the restaurant. It seems crazy that my parents would even *think* of selling it.

This is *worse* than an incurable disease.

Ok, I don't mean that. But still, this is bad.

Slowly, images of the restaurant start filling my head like leaves falling from a tree. I see the first day we opened, watching my parents cut through the ceremonious red tape over the front door. Then I flash to Lorenzo and I playing war in the storage room, then, years later, stealing drinks from the bar. I literally grew up in that place, and just the thought of it closing is too much to handle. How could they do this?

"How could you do this?" Mario echoes my thoughts.

"It was time to sell," my dad responds as if he is talking about an old car.

"When did you decide this?" Mario asks. He looks flustered and I don't blame him. He's the general manager of the restaurant. How could my parents make the decision without even telling him first? I mean, talk about pulling the rug right out from under ya.

"A buyer approached us about a month ago," my dad says remaining calm. He takes his seat and reaches for an apricot tartlet. "And he made us an offer we couldn't refuse." He winks at his own reference to *The Godfather*. I image Luca Brasi holding a gun to my dad's head, while Don Corleone assures him that either his signature or his brains will end up on the paper. Clearly he was pressured into it.

We don't have to stand for this. I'll go to the feds if I have to. Rat out whatever goon was behind this.

"So you already sold it?" Mario asks just as I'm imagining myself as Connie smashing all of her dishes. It's always been a secret fantasy of mine to be able to recreate that scene. Minus the whole husband beating the hell out of me part.

My parents look at each other. "Yes. He wanted a fast deal," my mom explains. Her voice sounds as if she's pleading with Mario. She knows her son well.

Mario stands and throws his napkin on the table. He moves to leave the table.

"Mario, sit down," my father says standing up but my brother doesn't listen and walks right out of the restaurant. My father follows him.

The rest of us just sit there in shock, and I'm pretty sure not even this dessert is going to make me feel better.

Recipe: Bananas Foster (for when your life goes up in flames)

Yields 4 servings

This is a simple version—your life is complicated enough. But trust me ladies, you'll love this one.

1 stick butter
1/2 cup light brown sugar, packed
4 firm bananas (peeled and cut into 1/4" rounds)
1/4 cup dark rum

1) Melt butter in a large saucepan over medium heat.
2) Add brown sugar and stir until dissolved.
3) Add bananas and cook until caramelized (about 5 minutes).
4) Add the rum and, using a long lighter, ignite the flambé. (Be careful, the flame will rise pretty high.)
5) Let the flame die down on its own, then spoon the bananas in individual bowls and serve with vanilla ice cream.

Chapter 6

Ok, just to recap. It's July 1 and in exactly fifty-nine days, I'll be twenty-eight. Which wouldn't be such a big deal if I

1)Had a fiancé

2)Had a job.

But since both prospects are out the window (It's been three weeks and Drew hasn't called once. And to make matters worse, my parents really are selling La Cucina, which means that come Labor Day when Lorenzo's closes, I'm jobless), I've hit freak-out mode.

I just keep telling myself to calm down.

There are *plenty* of jobs I can do.

Plenty.

I mean, I went to college for God's sake. That has to count for *something*.

I've been trying to think of this rationally, once the initial shock wore off and all. Pietro and Dante have made me see that this is a *good* thing.

An *opportunity*.

Granted, neither one of them depends on the restaurant like I do, but there's no need to panic. I mean, if my brothers can get decent jobs so can I.

Maybe I can get a job at Pietro's law firm. I know I'm not *exactly* a lawyer, but I'm sure I can do something in the office. Like file. And type things.

I'd probably be very good at that. And I'd get to wear classy suits and kitten heels.

Not that I really like suits or kitten heels (they make my legs look really short).

And I've never actually worked in an office. Or filed anything.

Hum.

Maybe I can be a teacher like Dante. That way I'll have summers off to come back to work at Lorenzo's.

If Lucy can do it, I certainly can. And who cares that St. Iggy's is all boys. I'm used to that. I have four brothers.

Yes, perfect. I'll become a teacher.

I can even ask Luce what to write on my résumé. I'm sure she'll find some way to finagle it.

It'll be great. Luce and I can have lunch together in the teacher's lounge every day! And I can get a cute pair of glasses (not the matronly librarian kind). Of course, I'll have to practice my handwriting on a chalk board, but there's plenty of time to do that.

My brothers were right. This is a good thing. An *opportunity*.

I just wish Mario would see it the same way.

He hasn't said a word to Dad since Father's Day, and I worry that their relationship is permanently damaged. Lorenzo and I talk about them a lot, and even though he's upset as well, he respects my parents' wishes.

"It's their place," he says, and I agree.

Lorenzo is surprisingly not that worried. He actually seems happy about La Cucina closing. He's been wanting to open a small restaurant in Philadelphia, but hasn't been able to leave La Cucina. He's thinking that this is his big opportunity. He even drove back to Philly to start talking with real estate agents.

Again, my twin is showing me up. But that doesn't matter. I'm going to be a teacher or something.

About a week after Father's Day, my mother calls to tell me the exact date of the closing. La Cucina will officially close on September 30th, exactly three months from tomorrow. It's impossible for me to think that we won't have another Christmas there, or that I won't be working on New Year's Eve.

Lucy tried to be optimistic about it and even suggested we go up to New York City for New Year's this year. But as much as I complained about working all those years, I love ringing in the New Year with a restaurant full of regulars wearing cardboard party hats and throwing paper streamers in the air. They were like an extension of the family, and partying at some lame bar in New York just doesn't feel right.

To avoid thinking about La Cucina and Drew, I throw myself into work and with the Fourth of July right around the corner, that's pretty easy to do. This year, the holiday falls on a Wednesday, which we thought would be bad for business, but as it turns out, it's ideal. Both this weekend and next are jam-packed. It's nice to know that we're in high demand, but I do wish we had some slots open, since I'm the one who has to deal with the phone calls.

Since today is Friday and the kick off to a busy weekend, I'm here earlier than normal. I don't mind it though; there's something peaceful about an empty restaurant. And I get full range of the kitchen, even though I almost always make a salad. Did you really think I eat restaurant food every day? I'd be 800 pounds by Labor Day.

In the kitchen, I'm in a zone, dicing roasted red peppers and tomatoes to add to my salad bowl. I've been dreaming of an arugula salad with jumbo lump crabmeat all morning. Just as I walk towards the fridge to get the crabmeat, I hear a knock on the back door.

"Come in," I yell stooped over by the fridge. Usually we don't get deliveries until a little later, but I can check the order and sign for it, no problem.

"Hey Stella."

I turn towards the door and almost drop my salad bowl. Roberto Lancetti is standing in the doorway carrying a large bag of bread. My eyes flicker over him because, even though I'm sure it's him he looks completely different than the Roberto that I remember, or the one I imagined. The Roberto standing before me looks confident and strong, his skin is sun kissed, his hair is a controlled mess, and his smile teases me. A large scar travels diagonally from the left corner of his bottom lip to the base of his chin, making him look rougher than I remember. And sexier. For a minute, our eyes lock and I forget all about Drew. If I were comparing the two on looks alone, Roberto would win, hands down.

Not that I'm interested or anything; obviously, I have Drew (sort of). Besides, Roberto is so not my type. He might be smart, but if you ask me, he totally wasted his talents. I mean honestly, a PhD in Latin? I can see him now, standing in front of a classroom wearing ripped jeans and Chuck Taylors, trying desperately to be a non-conformist while teaching a bunch of half-wit college freshman how to conjugate verbs. It's a shame really, because Roberto is the heir to the Lancetti bread company, which supplies the best Italian rolls to restaurants in the tri-state area. He'd be walking on easy street.

Now Drew, on the other hand, went to Wharton for his MBA and, given the opportunity that Roberto has, would take the bread company and make it a global sensation. They'd be eating that bread in China, Chile, and even Italy for God's sake.

"I have your delivery." He smiles and places the bag on the work station. He reaches around to hug me and I awkwardly reciprocate. His arms pull me in close enough to smell the cologne on his neck. It is a mixture of spicy musk and lemon, which smells both exotic and familiar at the same time.

"You look good," he says pulling away. Yeah right. I smile but can feel my face getting hot. I look down at myself. I'm wearing blue running shorts, a yellow tank top, and purple flip-flops, the official uniform of a fifth grader. I couldn't be more un-sexy if I tried. And the worst part is, my scoop neck Theory dress is hanging in the waiters' station; I was going to change as soon as I finished lunch. Not that it matters.

The only comfort I have is the fact that he's wearing a similar outfit of dirty Nikes, a white t-shirt, and yellow mesh shorts. Still, on him it somehow works.

"Come in," I wave. "Do you still need that reservation for this weekend?" I ask, remembering that he never called back.

Roberto makes his way into the kitchen and looks at me again. "Na, she cancelled on me."

"Sorry."

He keeps looking at me but doesn't say anything.

"So, what have you been up to?" I ask because I'm suddenly flustered and can't think of anything else to say.

"I just got back from Rome. I finished my PhD actually."

"In what?" I ask though I already know.

"Translation. I translate ancient poetry." He smirks at himself, and I can't tell if he's cocky or what.

"Sounds interesting."

"Yeah, I'd tell you all about it, but it'd probably put you to sleep." He laughs. "What are you making?"

"A salad," I reply, and before I can stop myself I ask if he wants one.

"Only if I can help." He grabs an apron off the rack and ties it on. I can't help but laugh at him.

"What? You don't think I can cook, Stella? I was in the kitchen before you were even born."

"Ok Dad," I mutter and stick my head in the fridge. He laughs. Lorenzo put the crabmeat on the bottom shelf, right next to the sauce. "Do you like crabmeat?" I ask.

"I thought we were having salad."

I close the door of the fridge. "What kind of operation do you think this is Lancetti? We're in a restaurant, I'm not going to give you some mixed greens and call it a lunch."

He laughs. "Ok, get the crabmeat. Got any filet mignon?"

"Ha ha." I walk towards the stove and grab a sauté pan from the rack on top. I turn up the heat, pour some olive oil in the pan, and once it gets hot, throw in the garlic.

"Not too much garlic, I have more deliveries to get to."

"Oh, and I guess you pick up a lot of ladies in your bread truck?"

Roberto laughs.

"Make yourself useful and plate those salads." I sound just like Lorenzo in the middle of service.

Once the crabmeat is done sautéing I spoon it over the two salad plates and drizzle a little balsamic reduction on top.

"Perfect," I say.

"Almost perfect," Roberto replies and walks over to the bread bag. "We need a little Lancetti on this plate." He grabs two rolls and gives me a wink.

I ignore him and carry my plate into the dining room. He follows me to the back table, closest to the waiters' station. We both sit, still wearing our aprons.

"This is delicious," he says after just one bite. "You should write a cook book."

"Yeah right," I roll my eyes and stab a piece of crabmeat.

"I'm serious," he insists. "You could be 'the salad chick' or something catchy like that."

I entertain the thought for a minute and envision myself on the cover of some girly cookbook, wearing a frilly pink apron and a fake smile, holding an oversized bowl of mixed greens and chopped veggies. But the thought is ridiculous. Even the most remedial home cook knows how to throw a salad together. See, this is exactly the difference between Roberto and Drew; Drew has foresight and brilliant ideas, while Roberto studied a dead language and has dead-end ideas.

"So how'd you get stuck delivering bread?" I ask trying to change the subject. "Shouldn't you be translating something?"

He looks at me and laughs. "Well the job market for a Latin translator is a little slow right now, so I'm helping my family. I thought of all people you'd understand that."

"I just don't get it," I say. "Why would you get a PhD in a dead language when you have a bread empire all to yourself?" I wave a roll in the air to dramatize my point. I'm not sure why I'm asking him this. Honestly, it's not like I care or anything.

"You sound like my mother," he says and takes a bite.

"Seriously though," I continue. "Latin?"

He sighs. "When I graduated college I was *expected* to run the family business. But I needed a change. So I packed up and moved to Rome for a year and got a job bartending." He looks at me, and forks a piece of crabmeat, then pops it into his mouth.

"And the other bartenders spoke Latin?" I ask.

He laughs. "No, I realized that I wanted something different. And I'd always been interested in Language. So I enrolled in a PhD program and got a degree."

"In Latin?"

"In translation. I had to study Latin, Greek, and Italian."

"So what are you going to do now?"

"I don't know. Maybe I will take over the family business. Or maybe I'll get a job doing something else. Who knows?"

I roll my eyes. He makes the future seems like a simple thing, when instead, it's so very complicated.

As we're finishing lunch the phone rings. "Lorenzo's," I say. "May I help you?"

"Hello, my name is Shirley Johnston and I'm calling from the Villa Hotel and Casino."

It's unusual that we get a concierge calling from Atlantic City. This reservation is probably for a high roller.

"Ok." Out of the corner of my eye, I see Roberto cleaning off the table. He picks up the plates and disappears into the kitchen like he belongs here.

"I'd like to speak to Mr. Lorenzo DiLucio if possible," says Shirley, bringing me back to the conversation.

So she really is making a VIP reservation. They *always* ask to speak to the owners when they're dealing with a VIP.

"He's not in at the moment, may I take a message." I reach for a pen and paper and write her name down.

"Who am I speaking with?" she asks.

"This is Stella DiLucio. I'm the manager here."

"Then perhaps you can help me. I'm calling in reference to Mr. Charles Verton."

My head starts to spin. Mr. Charles Verton? Chuck? She's calling about Chuck?

She continues, "How long has he been employed with you?"

Then her words click. This is a reference check.

"Where are you calling from?" I swallow.

"The Villa Hotel and Casino in Atlantic City. Mr. Verton applied for a position with us and I just need to check his references."

"Ok" I say. Damn, the Villa is nice.

"How long has Mr. Verton been employed at your establishment." The way she says it makes it seem like she *knows* her job is better.

"He's worked with us for three years." I can barely speak.

"And what does he do there?"

Roberto walks up to the hostess stand, carrying the keys to his delivery truck. I hold up a finger, motioning him to wait.

"Chuck's the sous-chef and is in charge of all the pastries as well. Can I put you on hold for a moment?"

I click the hold button and look up at Roberto. "Sorry, this is a pretty important call."

"It's okay. I have to run, actually." He smiles at me. "We should grab a drink sometime."

I'm caught off guard and before I can stop myself I blurt out something about having a boyfriend.

For a second, he looks taken aback. Then he flips his keys around his finger and smiles. "Oh, I thought I heard you guys broke up. Sorry." He turns to leave and I roll my eyes. I am such an idiot.

The hold button beeps. Thankfully.

"All right Bella Stella. Thanks for lunch," he says looking back at me.

I give him a wave as he walks towards the kitchen. I click back to the phone call.

"Sorry to keep you on hold."

"No problem. How would you rate Mr. Verton's performance over the last three years?" she asks.

Where can I even begin? Chuck has been a dedicated employee, an amazing chef, and a great friend. He's never missed a day, and until this moment, has been loyal to my family. My eyes start to fill with tears.

"Hello?" Shirley says.

"He's great," I mumble.

"So you would recommend him?" she asks.

"Yes."

When I hang up the phone, I call Lorenzo, and ask him to come to the restaurant early. I need to talk to him before Chuck arrives.

The back door opens about twenty minutes later and I hear Lorenzo turn on the kitchen ventilation system before entering the dining room. Maybe I don't need to tell him. I should just leave it up to Chuck.

"What's up," he asks sitting down. Since my parents made their big announcement, he's been more willing to talk.

"I got a weird phone call this afternoon," I blab.

"From who?" he asks, suddenly suspicious.

"A lady from the Villa. She was calling about Chuck."

"Yeah," he says sitting down. "So what?"

So what?

"She was doing a *reference check* on him." I can just imagine Lorenzo flipping out and throwing things all over the kitchen. God, it'll be a nightmare.

Lorenzo doesn't look concerned. "It's probably for the fall."

"Then why would she be calling *now*?"

"I don't know," he says. "Chuck wouldn't leave in the middle of the summer."

"You should ask him."

The phone rings and when I stand up to answer it Lorenzo goes into the kitchen. I look at my watch. Chuck will arrive in about five minutes. He's never late.

The night goes smoothly despite the tension in the kitchen. Everyone has picked up on it. Lucy asked me three times if everything was okay, and even Frankie seems on edge. I'm the only one who knows what's going on, and I still don't know when Chuck is leaving, or if he even is. All I know is that the kitchen is quiet, there are no jokes tonight, no one laughing or shouting, no music blaring from the speakers.

The restaurant is full of regulars, which makes it easier. With regulars, there are never any complaints, and even if the service is a bit slow, like tonight, no one seems to notice.

Joe and Diane Shefferd, a couple in their late sixties who always come in for eggplant parmigiana, are among the first guests of the night. They are always quick to smile and seem to be excited to eat out, though they come in at least twice a week. They greet me with a hug and follow me to their favorite table in the back of the restaurant, close to the waiters' station, or "the action" as Mr. Shefferd puts it.

The Hermans are sitting in the front window with their five kids, calmly eating ravioli and laughing together. They remind me a lot of us when we were little. Our parents taught us to be well behaved at restaurants and in church. We knew to sit quietly, talk in low voices, and not play with our food. None of us would ever dare to throw anything on the floor of a restaurant any more than we would have at home, so it always shocks me when customers let their kids run wild here. The Hermans would never do that.

Mr. and Mrs. Moore sit at the table closest to me. They are not the kind of couple who sits at a restaurant without talking. Instead, they really enjoy each other's company. They even flirt with each other, which is reassuring given the fact that they've been married for so long.

Looking at them makes me think of Drew. What went wrong? We were supposed to be that couple. I shake the thought from my head and channel my inner Gina. We will be that couple. If everything goes according to plans, we will be that couple.

As if on cue, my cell phone vibrates in my pocket so I step out front of the restaurant. It's so loud in there that it would be impossible for me to talk on the phone, plus, if it is Drew, I want to hear everything he has to say. I take a deep breath and look at my phone. It's my mother.

"Hello," I say.

"Hello," she shrieks. I hold the phone away from my ear a bit. "What's wrong with your brother?"

"Which one?"

"Lorenzo. I just called him to tell him we're not coming down this weekend and he almost hung up on me."

"Why aren't you coming down?"

"Your father doesn't want to deal with traffic. We'll be down on Tuesday. What's wrong with your brother?" she repeats.

"He's not having a good night."

"Why, what's going on?"

"I think Chuck is leaving us," I say.

"What?" she screams.

"Mom, I'm not sure. I gotta go. I'll call you when we finish up."

At the end of the night, after I pay all the waiters and the dishwashers have mopped the kitchen, Lorenzo comes out of the kitchen. Lucy and I are sitting at our usual table, drinking the leftover wine from the night. I told her about Chuck, so she understands when my brother plops down in the chair. He's taken off his chef coat and his t-shirt is soaked with sweat.

"How many people did we do?" he asks.

"One fifty-seven." I say. "Tomorrow we already have one sixty-four on book."

"Great," he says sarcastically.

"What did Chuck say?" I ask.

"He got the job at the Villa. They called him right before he came into work."

"When's he leaving?" Lucy asks the question I'm scared to. I smile at her and take a sip of my wine.

"Tomorrow's his last night."

I can barely swallow. "What?"

"Yeah, they need him to start right away. He has to."

"That's so messed up," I say in shock. "He should at least give two weeks' notice. That's standard."

Lorenzo looks at me as if I should know better. There are no standards in the restaurant business. Still, it's hard to be mad at Chuck since he's been such a good employee.

"He has to take the job," Lorenzo says. "It's good for him. Steady all year round. Plus he gets health benefits and paid vacation."

One of the hardest parts of having a seasonal restaurant is finding consistent help. No one wants to only work for three months out of the year, so you run the risk of having a revolving kitchen door, hiring chefs for only one season, meaning you have to train someone new each year. We've heard horror stories of restaurants having to break in new chefs, only to realize, mid-July that they're not any good. So far we've been lucky that Chuck has stuck with us. In the winters he's helped out part-time at La Cucina. He didn't say much when we told him my parents sold the place, but I guess that's what prompted him to look for other jobs. Still, I'm scared of how the rest of the summer is going to go.

"What are you going to do?" I ask.

"I guess I'll ask the Russian guys if they know anyone. I can train someone fast."

Every summer, a group of students from Russia comes to the Island to work. We always hire a great crew from Russia to wash the dishes and bus tables, but we've never had a Russian kid in the kitchen. It doesn't seem like a good solution to me, but for now, it's the only one we've got.

"I'm sure it'll all work out," Lucy says looking at Lorenzo.

"Whatever." He stands. "I'm going home. I'll see you guys tomorrow."

"See ya." I wait until I hear the back door shut. "I'm worried," I say to Luce.

She takes a deep breath and sighs. "I know. It's going to be really hard without Chuck."

"Who's gonna do the cakes? Lorenzo can't train a Russian guy to do those."

"Do you have the recipes?" she asks.

"Yeah, they're all written down in a binder in the office."

"So why don't *you* do them?" She flashes me a smile.

Lucy knows me better than anyone in the world, and knows how much I love baking. I'm always the first one to bake a birthday cake for my friends, or cookies for customers on Halloween; it all ties into Food Therapy. But baking for fun is one thing. Doing it professionally is a whole different ball game. "I'd never be able to."

"But some Russian kid can?"

We both laugh picturing Ivan in an apron, whisking eggs and sugar together.

"Just try it Stella. What's the worst that can happen? You fail. Who cares? You can easily buy some good cakes to serve. But if you're good at it, this could be something big for you. It can be a career."

I smile and take a sip of wine. Why is it that a best friend can bring out the potential in you? "You're right. I'll try it."

We sit for a few more minutes, finishing our wine. "Want to get another bottle so we can sit on the deck," I say getting up. I collect all my paper work and put it in my bag.

Lucy looks down. "I'm actually gonna stay at my aunt's tonight."

Ok, she *definitely* didn't mention this before.

"My cousins texted during the night. They're all down."

"Oh," I say disappointed. I guess that makes sense. It is Fourth of July weekend. Sort of anyway.

Lucy waits while I gather my papers from the office. I slip the binder full of recipes into my bag just before shutting off the light. After I lock the front door, we go in separate directions. I don't know why, but it bothers me that she didn't invite me to hang out. She's such a big part of my family, yet I barely know hers. I think of calling Drew, but stop myself before I can. Instead, I call my mom and tell her all the details about Chuck as I walk home.

Mario shows up early the next morning. "I'm here to save the family business," he says as he opens the door to our house. I've barely had two sips of my coffee and can't handle his sarcasm. I knew he was coming though. When I called my mom last night and told her the situation she thought it best to send Mario down. Out of all of us, he is the only one who could help Lorenzo in the kitchen. Even though he didn't go to culinary school, he knows the menu inside and out, and can easily prepare any dish on it.

I can tell Mario's *already* unhappy about the situation, so I try to remain positive.

"Want some coffee?" I ask.

"How about a valium?" he says and lugs his suitcase up the stairs.

I roll my eyes and continue flipping through the recipe binder. I remember typing all of these up after our first summer, when Lorenzo handed me various scraps of parchment paper with recipes scrolled all around. We figured if we catalogued them it would be easier to train the kitchen staff. The pictures of all the food proved to be a great help to the wait staff as well. But there are fewer recipes in it than I remember, and I try to get a mental picture of our dessert tray to see if everything adds up. There's the chocolate cake, crème brulee, tiramisu, cannoli, and ricotta cheesecake. I wonder what kind of desserts Chuck'll make at the Villa. I hope they give him set recipes to follow and stifle his creativity. I close the binder and turn on my computer, searching for some new desserts to introduce to the restaurant.

That'll show Chuck.

By eleven a.m. I'm dressed (in an actual dress, not gym clothes, you never know who can pop in) and on my way to the restaurant. Tomorrow starts my new career as pastry chef extraordinaire, so I want to pick Chuck's brain before he goes.

Recipe: Ricotta Cheesecake

Yields 12 servings

Just one of the many desserts I know I can make.

Don't be scared to try this one ladies, if you mess up, who cares? You can always buy something to serve.

3 pounds whole milk ricotta
1 quart whole milk
10 eggs
2 cups sugar
1 lemon zest
1 orange zest
1/4 cup flour
1/2 cup graham cracker crumbs (finely ground)
butter for greasing the pan

1) Preheat oven to 400 degrees.
2) Grease a 12" spring form pan and dust with graham cracker crumbs.
3) In a large bowl, beat together ricotta and sugar until smooth. Slowly pour in the milk.
4) Beat the eggs in a separate bowl, then slowly pour into the ricotta mixture.
5) Add citrus zests and flour to the ricotta mixture. Stir to incorporate.
6) Pour the batter into the prepared pan.
7) Wrap aluminum foil around the sides and bottom of the pan so it doesn't drip in the oven. Place on a baking sheet.

8) Bake at 400 degrees for 30 minutes, then lower the oven to 350 and bake for an additional 30 minutes.
9) Give it a light shake, if the cake still appears too liquid bake for an additional 10 minutes.
10) Remove from the oven and allow to cool completely before removing from the pan.
11) Refrigerate until ready to serve.
12) Dust with powdered sugar immediately before serving.

Chapter 7

Mario is a terror in the kitchen. He questions everything that Lorenzo says and the two of them have already gotten into dozens of fights (three of which were loud enough to be heard in the dining room. Granted, it was before service, but still). Honestly, I don't know how Lorenzo is dealing with it. Every night it's like I'm holding my breath, waiting for Lorenzo to throw him out. Of course, then he'd lay into me in the dining room. He's already started to micro-manage my wait staff.

And if that wasn't bad enough, the temperature outside reached 102 degrees and has stayed that way for the past three days. I read in the newspaper yesterday that it's the hottest it's been at the beach in forty-seven years. The air is on, but it's already warm in the restaurant and no one's even here yet. I can only imagine what it'll feel like with sixty people crammed in here. I fan myself with my hand.

Truthfully, I think the heat might be radiating from me. I've been so miserable lately.

There's been no word from Drew and we're going on four weeks now. I've stuck to my guns and haven't called him (unless you count the other night when I was frazzled and accidentally reached for the phone and called him. It was like an automatic response to stress or something, but I hung up before he could answer, and anyway, it was an *accident*).

Lucy thinks my plan to get Drew back is ridiculous, but what does *she* know about relationships. Let's be honest here. Lucy's never really had a boyfriend so she's not one to be dishing out advice.

"Will you just forget him?" she says when she comes into work. "You're miserable and it's not making it easier on any of us."

This infuriates me.

Why do *I* always have to be the happy one around here?

Why does Mario get to waltz in and be the big mean boss?

How come Lorenzo gets away with yelling at the waiters?

I'm not hurting anyone. I'm just not smiling like normal. At least not until the guests come in.

If there's one thing I've gotten to be very good at over the years it's acting. My father taught me to *never* let the customers know you're upset. "If they see that," he says, "the dream is over."

My dad has this theory that people go out to eat to escape their problems, their worries, and their everyday. When they enter a restaurant, they step into a dream world where they're kings and have complete control.

It makes sense if you think about it. At a restaurant, you get to choose what you want to eat, have other people prepare it, serve it to you, and clean up after you.

Which is exactly why I'll plaster a smile on my face from 5:00 to 11:00 tonight.

Even if Drew doesn't call me.

Some therapists might call this "repression," but I call it getting through the night, and if that means I'll be lying on a couch in a few years, talking about my childhood while some shrink takes notes, so be it. Lucy thinks that one day I'll just explode, but that's not likely.

I can't even imagine the look on people's faces if I just started screaming and throwing pasta in the middle of the dining room one night.

Not that I would ever do that or anything. Talk about ruining the dream.

"What are the specials tonight?" I ask entering the kitchen with a pen and paper in hand. We open in ten minutes, so the waiters need to know this info, like now.

"We only have one," Lorenzo says with a smile. "Penne all' arrabbiata. Angry penne, just for you."

He and Mario laugh and I storm out of the kitchen.

Stupid brothers. They think they're so funny.

I fume as I stand by the hostess podium. I get nine more minutes to brood and I'm using every last second.

"Did you get the specials?" Dante asks. I look to see the rest of the waiters gather by their station, pens in hand. They've sent a family member to try to talk to me.

"Get them yourself," I snap. Dante scowls and walks past me. I watch him enter the kitchen. A few minutes later he's in the back, telling the waiters the specials of the night. As soon as he finishes, he switches on the music and dims the lights, signifying that we are now open for business.

I take a deep breath and smile.

As the night drags on, the heat continues to rise. I've lowered the air down to forty degrees, but the meter is still reading eighty-two. That's twenty degrees cooler than the outside air, but still not enough to make a comfortable dining experience. Each year, about a hundred thousand people gather on the Island for the Fourth of July, and everyone uses their air conditioning on full blast. This year is the worst yet, as the temperature is forcing the electricity into overdrive.

At around 7:00 the lights flicker. It's just a momentary lapse of power but is enough to send a hush through the noisy restaurant. I look around and see people fanning themselves with their cloth napkins, wiping sweat from their brows. I don't think anyone has ordered the penne all' arrabbiata; who needs the extra heat on his plate?

That'll show Lorenzo for trying to make fun of his only sister. His *twin.*

But I start to worry that maybe it's too hot. Last year, Mario suggested back up air conditioners, but the project was too expensive so my parents decided against it. They should have listened. Instantly, I imagine a customer revolt, where people decide to all walk out together, and the restaurant is left empty. The phone rings.

"Stella," Stacy, the owner of Sea Breeze says. She sounds frantic.

"What's going on?" I ask.

"Is your power out?"

"No, it just flickered a little but it's back on."

"Ours has been out for forty minutes," she says in a panic. "I think we need to close."

Every restaurant's biggest nightmare is losing power during service. Not only will they lose the business of the night, and get a bad reputation for canceling their reservations at the last minute, but they'll also most likely lose all of their inventory. I know they have a huge walk-in fridge and matching freezer, probably stocked with thousands of dollars' worth of food.

"If you need to use some of our ice, feel free to come by and take it from the machine," I say. Our ice machine is located in our refrigerated storage off the kitchen. It has a separate door to it so they could come in, unnoticed. "I'll unlock it for you."

"Maybe I will, at least for the expensive stuff," she says. I imagine her making a mental list of filet mignons and king crab legs. "There's one more thing," she continues. "Our best customers, Mr. and Mrs. Klean, are coming in twenty minutes. They're with a party of six. Can you squeeze them in?"

It's strange that I never heard of the Kleans. We generally share the same clients since our restaurants are only three doors apart. I scan my reservation list. I'm actually overbooked, and squeezing in a six is nothing like squeezing in a two. But I feel bad, imagining what would happen if we had to cancel on our best customers at the last minute.

"Ok," I sigh. "You can send them over. I'll figure something out."

"Thank you so much," she says, sounding relieved.

I try to reorder my reservation list and tell the waiters to rush everything along. If they move quickly enough, and if people don't linger, I should be okay. I'm nervous because we have no waiting area, so if things don't work out tonight, people will have to wait outside in the sweltering heat.

The Kleans arrive to find their table all set. They're in their early fifties and look like Island Royalty. He's tall with sable hair and not a speck of grey. His skin is bronzed and he wears casual khaki pants and a light blue polo shirt. She's petite, just slightly taller than me, and embraces her height by wearing flats. Her peach Capri pants offset her deep tan, and her silky blonde hair is pulled into a tight bun. She wears a tight white t-shirt and a yellow cashmere sweater tied over her shoulders despite the heat.

"It's warm in here," she says under her breath.

Take off the cashmere, girlfriend.

The rest of their party is dressed similarly in Ralph Lauren Polo. One man wears navy blue shorts with tiny whales embroidered all over them, thus proving that money certainly doesn't buy taste. Honestly, there should be a law saying that no male over the age of six is allowed to wear shorts like that.

As I collect their menus Mr. Klean raises his eyebrow and looks at his friends. Do I have something on me? "Your table is right this way." I flash them a big smile.

They follow me to the back of the restaurant. Table fifteen is the last on the right, before the waiters' station. They don't look too happy with it, but since the restaurant's packed, they don't have another option. Brittany is their server, so hopefully her bubbly attitude will rub off.

People just love her.

Whenever we have new guests in the restaurant, I try my hardest to impress them. Usually people love the food, and are used to the tight atmosphere. Most shore restaurants pack their guests in like tuna in a tin.

At best, people finds this cozy and intimate.

At worst, they complain about the noise and having the waiter reach over them to serve the table.

I agree that it's not exactly fine dining, but we try to make it work.

Tonight, however, the heat is an added insult to the tight seating.

The waiters are doing a great job pushing tables along. Some tables are in and out in less than an hour, and it's working out perfectly. The most people have to wait is about five minutes and so far people seem to be dealing well with the heat. I've noticed a lot of salads being ordered, which is not the best for sales, but at least people are happy.

You can't expect people to eat too much when they're dripping with sweat.

I'm so focused on seating my guests that I almost don't notice Brittany standing next to me with tears in her eyes.

"What's wrong?" I ask her. I can only handle so many disasters in one night.

"That guy is *such* an asshole. He *humiliated* me in front of the entire table."

I assume she's talking about Mr. Klean, because the rest of her tables are regulars who would never do such a thing. "What did he say?"

"He keeps calling me Barbie," she explains. "And when he needed more bread, he told me to 'shake my tail' and go get him some."

I hate to admit it, but *it is* kind of funny. Brittany does look oddly similar to the famous doll, especially now with her deep tan and sun bleached hair.

Still, his remarks are rude.

"Don't let him bother you. I'll check them out in a minute," I assure her.

She walks away and I notice, for the first time, how she does put a little shake in her hips as she moves. I'll have to talk to her about her walk another night.

A small group of diners gathers at the door. They must be the 8:00 reservations.

"Excuse me," a voice to my right says. I turn to look and Mr. Klean is staring me in the face. "My friends and I would like some towels."

The crowds have moved in and are waiting at the podium. "Oh I'm sorry, did something spill? I'll send the bus boy over right away."

"No, nothing spilled. It's just that it's so hot in here we feel like we're sitting in a fucking sauna."

My eyes widen. The other guests look appalled.

If ever there *were* a time for an explosion, this would be it.

No. Try to keep calm.

"I'm very sorry about the heat sir. It's usually not like this in here, but it seems that the power is waning tonight. Sea Breeze had to close," I remind him.

"I don't care what the excuse is. It's way too hot." He storms off without giving me a chance to respond.

I look down and see my hands trembling a bit.

"Nice guy," the guest in front of me says and I smile.

"I'm sorry. I know it's hot in here," I apologize.

"It's hot everywhere, at least we're not cooking at home," the wife chimes in. I seat the couple and move back to the hostess stand to seat the rest of the reservations.

Lucy comes running up. "There's a guy in the waiters' station fiddling with the air conditioner," she says.

Before she can even finish, I feel something inside of me snap. I walk through the dining room in a rage and glare at Mr. Klean.

"Who do you think you are?" I yell. "You have no right to touch our air conditioner, or anything else in the restaurant." At this point I don't even care that service has stopped and people are starting to stare. I've had enough of this shit.

"This says it's eighty-three degrees in here. That's ridiculous!" he screams.

I take a deep breath. "Have you eaten dinner yet sir?"

"No, we're waiting for our entrées."

"Well then you can march back to your table and tell the rest of your party that you're being kicked out before dinner. We don't need your business here."

He turns pale and storms off to his table. Michele laughs but I'm not in the mood. To be honest, I'm in utter shock. I imagine the Yelp review already. *Zero stars, we complained about the heat and the bitchy manager kicked us out for no reason. Don't go there!!!*

Mrs. Klean approaches the waiters' station sans sweater. "I apologize for my husband's behavior," she says to me. "He's having a bad night. We'd appreciate it if you allowed us to stay and eat dinner."

I soften. "Fine. But keep you husband under control."

Mrs. Klean smiles and returns to her table. I watch her reach for her wine and shoot a nasty look at her husband. Somebody's sleeping on the couch tonight.

Imagine having to deal with a husband like that. Poor lady.

The rest of the night goes smoothly. To make amends Mr. Klean leaves Barbie a big tip, so she's smiling as she does her check out.

Everyone is buzzing around, doing his or her side work but for some reason, I'm still feeling frazzled. Between breaking up with Drew, my parents' big news, the heat, and the stress of the business, I just want to crawl into bed. Thankfully tomorrow is the Fourth and we're closed.

"Want to go to the beach tomorrow?" I ask Lucy as we are folding napkins.

"I don't know what I'm gonna do," she replies distantly.

What's *with* her lately?

"Is your family down again?" I snap.

"Yeah, they actually are." She stands to put her stack of napkins away. "I'm meeting them out tonight."

I don't believe her. All of my anger comes back. "Oh yeah? Where are you going?"

She looks put off. "I don't know, I'll call them when we finish."

It's already 1:30 a.m. but the bars are open until 4:00 a.m., and should be fun, especially on the night before the Fourth.

I wait for her to invite me.

Instead, she takes her money off the table and grabs her bag. "Everything's done."

The other waiters pick up their money and head for the door. Lucy moves along with them and waves goodbye as she exits.

"What's up with Luce?" Mario asks. He enters the dining room just as the waiters are leaving.

"I don't know," I say. "Her family's down."

"Don't they usually rent out their house until the end of August?" he asks sitting down.

He's right. They've never spent a full summer here. This makes me even madder than before. Then it clicks. Lucy has a boyfriend. I know it.

But why would she hide him from me?

"Want to grab a drink at Bob's?" I'm practically begging my brother to hang out, because honestly, I just don't feel like going home.

"Stella, I'm beat. If I even have a sip of wine, I'll probably pass out." He stands. "Do you mind waiting for the dishwashers to finish up? I want to go home."

"Where's Lorenzo?" I ask. Usually he waits for the kitchen staff to finish.

"He left already. He said something about going out with friends tonight."

Again, I'm hurt. My best friend is being shady, and now, even my family doesn't want to hang out.

"Fine," I say. "I'll wait."

"Oh yeah, I forgot to tell you. Gina and Pietro are down for the night, so you need to sleep on the couch."

Lovely.

I hear the Russian pop music blasting through the kitchen doors so I figure they're mopping the floors by now. I take the time to think about Drew and before I know it, my eyes start to mist.

Why hasn't be called?

I mean, honestly, how can you go from loving someone for three years to just totally shutting them out?

This is craziness and it has to end.

I see Ivan the dishwasher's cell phone on the table and reach for it. Before I can stop myself I dial Drew's number and hit send.

My heart pounds as the phone rings once, twice…

"Hello," he says. Just hearing his voice makes my heart leap up into my throat. He answered! I knew he would answer! "Hello?" I can hear really loud music in the background and it's obvious that he's out at a bar. Well, good for him.

"Hey Drew," I say hesitantly.

"Stella?" he asks as if he's not sure. Has he forgotten my voice already?

I hear some muffled noise in the background and some high-pitched laughter.

"Yeah, it's me," I reply calmly. "How are you?"

"It's almost two a.m." He sounds angry. It's not like he's in bed or anything. "Christ."

This is so not going as planned. For a minute I contemplate hanging up, but that would just be weird. "Sorry. Am I disturbing you?"

"Well it is July 3rd. I'm at a party." I hear more laughter in the background and what I think is some girl calling Drew's name. She sounds like a slut.

I'm about to ask what his plans are for tomorrow, when I hear the music in the kitchen shut off. Stefan and Ivan come out, their shirts drenched in sweat and dishwater. "We are done," Stefan says in his thick Russian accent. I just stand there paralyzed holding Ivan's phone in my hand. Then, in one swift motion, I click it shut and place it back on the table, and pretend that I was only looking at it.

The Russians look at me as if I'm nuts.

Which I probably am.

"Ok." I walk towards the doors hoping they'll follow me. "Have a good night." Out of the corner of my eye, I see Ivan tentatively pick up his phone and follow me. I hold the door open while they exit.

“Happy Fourth of July,” Ivan says. I smile because I think I’m in the clear. This is their first American holiday and they’re very excited about it. Earlier in the week, Stefan told me about the barbeque they’re planning to have on the beach. All of their Russian friends are going. I know I shouldn’t but I can’t help feeling pathetic. Even the Russians have plans, while the only thing I’ve got going on is the Lancetti’s stupid barbeque.

Recipe: Penne all' Arrabbiata

Yields 4 servings

The name of this pasta translates to "angry penne" and honestly, it is. Even though Lorenzo and Mario were making fun of me with this one, it was really fitting. I was mad. No, in fact, I still am.

1 lb penne
1/4 cup extra virgin olive oil
2 cloves of garlic, minced
1 28oz can of crushed tomatoes
1 tablespoon crushed red pepper flakes (as hot as you like them)
2 tablespoons basil, chopped
salt to taste

1) Bring 10 cups of salted water to boil. Add pasta.
2) While the pasta is cooking, heat the olive oil in a large saucepan over high heat.
3) Add garlic and cook until golden.
4) Add the crushed tomatoes, pepper flakes, basil, and salt. Lower the heat and let the sauce simmer for 10-15 minutes.
5) Drain pasta and toss into the sauce.
6) Top with grated cheese and more pepper, if desired.

Chapter 8

It's not even 9:00 a.m. when I hear my mom and Gina talking about the wedding.

Not that I don't love wedding talk, but seriously, isn't there anything *else* to talk about?

I try to roll over into a more comfortable position but it's no use; the couch is as old as the house, and every way I turn, I'm hit by a different spring. I get up and walk into the kitchen.

"We need to buy a new couch," I announce bitterly.

Mom and Gina look up at me as if I have three heads. "Good morning," my mom says. "Did you sleep well?"

I shuffle towards the coffee pot and pour myself a cup. "No."

"Well you can sleep on the beach," Gina replies. "I bought these beautiful beach towels at Saks. They're amazing."

"I think I'm just gonna stay in today." I rub my eyes.

They both stare at me. "Are you serious?" my mom asks. She knows how much I love sitting on the beach long into the evening hours, and this is the only chance I'll have to do that until September.

But somehow, the thought of sitting on the beach with my entire family is not appealing. Not after everyone abandoned me last night.

"Yeah. I just don't feel like it."

"Siete tutti pazzi," my mom mumbles. Whenever my mother wants to badmouth her children, she does so in Italian, even though we all understand exactly what she's saying. Today, apparently all of her children are crazy, not just me. This makes me feel better.

"What's going on now?" my dad's voice booms as he enters the kitchen.

"Nothing," I say.

"All of our children are weird." My mom starts. "Lorenzo's not coming to the barbeque and Stella doesn't want to go to the beach. Gina and Pietro came all the way down to stay with the family, and now everyone is separated."

Gina lowers her head. It's not fair that my mom threw her under the bus, but Gina should know this is one of my mother's famous tactics. Whenever she's upset about something, she tries to place the blame on someone else, instead of just admitting that she's mad. Again, it's probably another form of repression. We DiLucio's are famous for it.

I move to the couch and turn on the TV. I plan to veg out right here in my pajamas for the rest of the day. Maybe I won't even go to the barbeque. Lord knows I don't want to deal with Mrs. Lancetti force-feeding everyone carbs all night long. Plus, I'm sure Roberto will be there and I can't take the embarrassment of having to explain that I actually don't have a boyfriend.

When Gina and my mom leave, I try to call Lucy to see if she wants to come over, but her phone goes straight to voicemail.

Honestly, I'm still a little mad that she didn't invite me out last night. If she does have a boyfriend why is she keeping him secret?

Is she scared I'll judge him?

I would never judge.

Unless he's a *total* loser. But that's what friends are for right? I mean, if I started dating someone horrible, I'd *want* my best friend to intervene.

At around three, after I've watched about fifteen episodes of Judge Judy, I decide that I should go to the Lancetti's party. For one thing, if I don't I'll never hear the end of it. And for another thing, the food is usually amazing and after last night I could really go for some Food Therapy. Plus they always have an open bar stocked with plenty of top shelf stuff. Part of me wants to see Roberto too. Just for some innocent flirting to boost my ego after the blow it took last night. I still have every intention of getting Drew back, I just may need to change my strategy a bit.

By the time my family gets back from the beach, I'm already showered and ready to go to the barbeque.

While the rest of the house showers, I take time to apply make-up. The downstairs powder room is small but has the perfect mirror, and for once, I think I look good from any angle. Miraculously, my hair is set in loose waves, without even the suggestion of frizz. My face is clear despite all the milk I drink (take that Gina), and the kiss of sun brings out the deep olive hues in my skin.

As usual, Gina has brought her entire make-up kit down for the night, and she lets me use whatever I want, so I browse through the various shades of eye shadow, settling on a translucent mushroom shade called "brownstone." I like it so much that I consider asking Gina if I can keep it. After all, she can pick up a new one at any time.

I'm wearing jeans tonight, since I spend most of my days in dresses. I choose a dark pair and wear a tight white tank top, with a pearl colored chiffon shell on top. I like the effect of the cool white, contrasting with my skin. I finish off the look with extra tall wedges, gold hoops, and a Fendi clutch.

"You're wearing jeans?" my mother asks in shock when I step into the kitchen.

"Mom, I wear dresses *every day*," I whine like a twelve year old.

"Let her wear whatever the hell she wants," my dad chimes in. He winks at me.

"She'll look out of place," my mother squeals. She always has to have the last word.

Still, I don't change. I'm wearing jeans. Period.

At 8:00 my parents and I walk directly across the Island to the Lancetti's house. Much to my mother's dismay, Pietro and Gina left for New York right after the beach. Mario and Dante said they'd go to the barbeque later and Lorenzo has stuck his ground. He's not coming to the Lancetti's this year.

The Lancetti's house is located right on the 99th Street beach so we're on opposite ends of the island, but since it's only one mile from beach to bay it's a very short walk. The house is enormous and makes ours look like a shack. It's built of yellow stonewalls, reminiscent of the villa in Tuscany where Mr. Lancetti originally wanted to retire. The roof is my favorite part, because its terracotta tiles remind me of a Spanish hacienda.

As if being right on the beach weren't lavish enough, they have a large pool in their back yard, facing the ocean. I used to imagine living in that house, and spending each night in the pool, listening to the ocean in the background.

The entry way is paved in Italian tiles and the skylight in the foyer makes it seem as though you're still outside. The professional grade kitchen, with its Sub-Zero fridge and Viking range, looks like it's not used too much. I don't think the Lancettis come down the shore all that often. It's a shame to waste a house like this.

Mrs. Lancetti greets us at the door. She's wearing a flowing strapless maxi dress and has turquoise stones on her sandals. For not coming down the shore much, she has a pretty flawless tan, and the black of her dress only accentuates it. She's a classic beauty, slightly younger than my mother, though they look about the same age. The one thing I love about Anna Lancetti is that she's never confined to one look. Some women, especially women in their fifties and sixties, tend to stick with what they know, but Anna is a chameleon; each time I see her she has a new look. Tonight she's sporting a Cleopatra hairdo, complete with thick bangs cut straight across her forehead. I can't help but think how much better it looks on her than it would on me. "Come in DiLucios, come in!" She squeals, hugging each one of us as we enter her kitchen.

A small crowd is gathered around the buffet, which is set up on the island in the kitchen. They turn to look at us, and continue on with their conversations.

"Where's Lorenzo?" she asks.

My mother huffs. "He might stop by later."

"Oh, it's a shame he's not here, I have the *perfect* girl for him."

I find it strange whenever someone wants to set one of my brothers up. If the girl is perfect for Lorenzo, why not set her up with Mario? Or Dante? There's really not too much surface difference between them. Still, she doesn't offer this match to either of my other brothers, so I'm guessing the girl has been to the restaurant and tasted his food.

I'm surprised my brother is still single. Everyone knows women are suckers for a man who can cook.

Mr. Lancetti comes in from the sliding glass doors. He's a short, round man, with a big bald head and warm smile. He smells slightly of smoke and charcoal and I wonder if he's been manning the grill. Usually this is a catered event. I really hope they're not skimping this year. I only came here for the food. Barbeque ranks pretty high on the Food Therapy list.

"Antonio!" he yells and gives my dad one of those manly hugs that end with a loud pat on the back. "So good to see you all. Who wants a drink?"

Um, me.

We all follow Mr. Lancetti to the bar area, where a bartender is mixing drinks. I look around casually to see if I know anyone, but the guest list pretty much only includes well to do people in their sixties. Hopefully none of our customers are here. I secretly plan on getting drunk.

My dad orders a Bombay Sapphire martini with olives; Dante and Mario, who arrived by car two minutes after us, opt for beer; and my mom orders a white wine spritzer like the other women here. I really want vodka, but opt for a glass of champagne instead. All I need are the town gossips saying I have an alcohol problem. Plus, I can just down this and sneak back for a martini in a few minutes.

Drinks in hand, we disperse. My dad hangs back with Mr. Lancetti, my brothers go outside by the pool, and I mingle in the kitchen with my mother. I'm by far the youngest of the women here, and the most casually dressed. I feel a little childish in my jeans, and secretly wish I had put on one of my dresses.

"So Stella," Mrs. Lancetti says to me over the poached Salmon. "I heard about your boyfriend. I'm so sorry to hear that."

I shoot my mother a death look. She looks back innocently and takes a sip of her drink. "We're just taking a little break," I mutter.

The women all look uncomfortable. Some exchange glances with each other, others looks down at the salmon, and still others give me an apathetic look, as if to say "yeah right." What the hell do they know anyway? We *are* just taking a little break. I mean, we talked last night didn't we?

"My Robbie says he saw you the other day."

Now all the ladies, including my mother, turn their heads to look at me.

"Yes, he came to deliver the bread." I shrug my shoulders and pop a fried olive in my mouth like this is no big deal, but I can feel my mom staring at me.

"He's been living in Rome you know," Mrs. Lancetti says, as if she's trying to sell him.

"That's nice," I reply. "Rome is a beautiful city."

The ladies start talking about Italy and all the vacation hot spots they've been to. I excuse myself and exit through the sliding glass doors, making my way towards the grill.

My dad, Mr. Lancetti, and a few other men are smoking cigars near the pool. Dante joins them while Mario talks to some man I don't recognize. I'm sad that my brother is avoiding my father, and hope that their relationship can be mended. If there's one thing about my brother, it's that he's a *testa dura.* As stubborn as a mule.

The chef manning the grill is replenishing the stock of hamburgers, sausages, and hot dogs on the buffet. A waiter refreshes the fixings, placing new spoons in both the mustard and ketchup, rearranging the slices of lettuce, tomato, and onions, and fluffing the rice salad. This year, the Lancetti's have arranged an impressive array of bread to accompany the meats. I take a plate off the buffet line and reach for a multi-grain bun.

"Bella Stella," I hear Roberto from behind me and I can't help but turn around. "You look great," he says.

"Thanks, you too." I stand there for a minute, holding my plate. For some reason, I'm nervous and can't think of anything to say. "Great party."

"I guess," he shrugs. "It's a little lame, but I missed it while I was away." He looks down at my plate. "Did you get something to eat?"

"I was about to," I say awkwardly. There's something about this whole scene that's making me uncomfortable. I glance towards the house and see all the ladies in the kitchen staring at us. They quickly look away, but it's obvious. Suddenly I feel my face flush. I may have been dumped by my boyfriend, but I'm certainly no charity case. If Mrs. Lancetti and my mom have plotted to set me and Roberto up, they're in for a big disappointment.

I move towards the spread of meats, as if to say to Roberto that I'm done talking. Hopefully he can take a hint and realize that I'm not interested.

"So, how about that drink?" he says from across the meat table.

I'm about to throw out the old boyfriend excuse, but that would just be weird since Drew and I technically aren't together. Instead, I pretend not to hear him and focus on building the world's most decadent hamburger, topped with crispy pancetta, provolone cheese, sautéed onions, and mushrooms.

I can feel Robert looking at me, waiting for an answer. "I work every night," I mumble, and top my burger off with a thin slice of tomato. Finally, I reach for a large piece of red onion because I will not be kissing anyone in the near future.

"Well how about tonight?" he insists.

Why is he being so persistent? And why won't I just have a drink with him? He is kind of cute, and it's not like I have anything else going on. I hold up my burger and look at is as if it has the answer to all my questions. As I'm about to take a bite, I hear the clinking of glasses and the music is cut.

A bartender is passing out glasses of champagne to each guest in preparation for a toast. I take one off the tray, eager to gulp it down. Once everyone has a glass Mr. Lancetti taps on his to get everyone's attention. Thank God.

"I'd like to make a toast to my good friends Antonio and Teresa DiLucio. As all of you know, they've had the best restaurant in the Philadelphia area for the past twenty years."

"With the best bread," Mrs. Lancetti shouts. Everyone laughs.

"And now, they have decided to sell it. Let's raise a glass to them for cent'anni of happiness in their retirement."

Everyone clinks glasses. I look at my mother whose face is pale. Up until now, they haven't told anyone besides the family of their decision. Mr. Lancetti just made it public.

I scan the area looking for my dad, and see Mario, leaving the through the pool gate.

Shit.

Roberto looks at me as I place my plate and glass on a nearby table. "I have to talk to my brother," I mumble and walk towards the gate.

I exit and step onto the beach, fumbling in my wedges. Mario is nowhere in sight. He must have gone home. I take a deep breath and walk towards the water. The sky is beginning to darken and in the half-light the ocean looks completely black.

I take a seat in the sand, close my eyes, and listen to the rhythm of the waves.

"You okay?"

I look up to see Roberto holding my plate and two glasses of champagne. He sits in the sand next to me.

"I'm fine," I say though truthfully I don't feel fine.

"Have something to eat," he says handing me the plate. "It'll make you feel better."

I give him a funny look. Could he be a supporter of Food Therapy too? I reach out and take the plate from his hands and eye up the burger. It does look delicious.

"So I finally get to have a drink with Stella DiLucio," he says handing me the glass of champagne.

"I'm not really great company at the moment," I reply and take a swig of champagne. "What would you do if your parents closed the bread company?"

"I would toast their retirement. I'm not really into taking over the business. You should figure out what you want to do aside from the restaurant."

Again, he's shocked me. Here he is sitting on a fortune and he's so happy to walk away from it. Sometimes I wish it was as easy for me to walk away from the restaurant, but I'd feel so guilty abandoning my family.

"I don't even know what life is like without a restaurant," I sigh.

"You've got the perfect excuse to find out now," Roberto replies and for a second, I feel better.

Just as I'm about to say thank you, the first firework erupts in the sky.

Tonight, it sounds like a bomb.

Mr. Lancetti wasn't the only person to announce the closing of La Cucina. A few days after the Fourth, Amanda Hut, the restaurant reviewer for the *Philadelphia Explorer*, wrote a full-page article about our twenty years in business, complete with vintage pictures of the restaurant before we remodeled in 2001, and glorious descriptions of the food. She was nice enough to include Lorenzo's address and phone number in the article, so business has been booming.

My parents are also in over their heads at La Cucina. The article prompted people from all over the tri-state area to come out for one last dinner. One woman showed up with a gift certificate from 1989. Back when we were hand writing them, we sometimes forgot to write an expiration date on the back, so my mother had to honor it. We laughed about it over the phone that night.

You see all types of people in this business. That's for sure.

Amanda Hut's article placed an emphasis on our homemade items, especially the time consuming pastas and intricate desserts, so I've been getting up really early and going into the restaurant to bake, which is the perfect excuse not to think about Drew and the fact that he hasn't called.

So far, I've not been so successful.

It's okay though, because I have a plan. By Monday, it will be four weeks exactly since we broke up, and, as you know, Gina and I have formulated the perfect, get-Drew-back plan.

But never mind about that now. I have cakes to make.

And to be quite honest, making cakes is not as easy as it originally sounded.

Of course, it's nothing I can't handle. It's just a little *different* than I imagined.

I kept Chuck's amazing chocolate cake in the repertoire, and with a few instructional phone calls, was able to perfect it.

Well, almost anyway. I mean, who cares if it had a big crack down the middle. The point is, it tasted good.

The tiramisu and ricotta cheesecake also remained on the list because they are and always will be crowd pleasers.

But they're easy. I'm looking for something more complex to introduce to our tray, something that would produce a wow factor.

Something like profiteroles.

There's this amazing restaurant in New York City that makes huge profiteroles. One time Drew and I went *just* for dessert, and I'm not like that.

But seriously, profiteroles are the Food Therapy equivalent to Xanax. They'll make you numb to your problems. Which is exactly why I'm making them.

And they're actually quite simple to make.

The dough is so easy, in fact, that it can be done while making other desserts, which is exactly what I'm doing this morning. As my eggs and ricotta are combining in the mixer, waiting to be transformed into cheesecake, I drop one stick of unsalted butter into a small saucepan. To that, I add one cup of water and let them simmer together over a low flame.

Told you it was easy.

I switch back to the ricotta cheesecake, which is ready to be poured into the spring form pan. When I get back to the stove, the butter is all melted into the water, and the mixture is just beginning to boil. I drop in a cup of flour and stir like mad, making sure that all the flour cooks off.

It's supposed to "sizzle" when it's done, so I stand above the stove and wait for it.

After a few minutes, I don't hear anything.

Maybe the flame is too low. I turn it up just to speed up the process a bit.

While that's getting hot, I place the cheesecake into the oven and shut the door. Even though I forgot to preheat, I'm sure it'll be fine. It's a gas oven for God's sake. How long can it take to heat up?

Back at the stove, I see that the bottom of my mixture is almost black.

Crap.

I didn't hear any sizzling.

I look at the lump of dough and decide that I can salvage it. I tip over the saucepot and the dough plops out onto the worktable.

Oh yeah, I can totally fix this. No problem.

I grab a knife and just cut away the black parts until only about a third of the dough remains.

Who needs thirty-six profiteroles anyway? Twenty-four is plenty. Or, um, twelve.

Plus, I can always make more tomorrow.

I lay the dough flat on a plate to cool for a few minutes, while I check on the cheesecake.

It's a carefully choreographed dance, this baking business, but I love every minute of it. In the kitchen, I feel so totally focused on what I'm doing that I don't have *time* to think about Drew or my job.

What I really need is to talk to Luce about all this, but she is *never* available anymore. She sleeps at our house about once a week, with the excuse that she stays at her aunt's the other nights. I know she's lying but what can I say? I can't *force* her to be my friend.

"That looks good," Lorenzo says after opening the oven door and seeing my cheesecake. Any sort of culinary praise from him is always welcome. If he thinks it looks good, it must.

Only, is it supposed to bubble up like that?

Maybe I should've preheated the oven.

"Thanks," I say looking at him. He smiles, snaps his fingers and makes a motion like he's throwing dice.

I know exactly what he's talking about. "No." I shake my head. "I don't have any money."

"Come on," he replies. "Mario and Dante are in. You can even invite Lucy to come along."

The thought of a night out in Atlantic City with my brothers and best friend is appealing, but I doubt she'd go for it. Plus, I really don't have the money to waste, especially now that I will be unemployed come October 1st.

I'm not *worried* or anything but the other night when I couldn't sleep, I calculated all of my expenses for the year. The wedding is adding a major debt to my finances. This whole Maid of Honor thing is costing a lot.

"Don't be a loser," he snaps and puts on his apron. I take the cake out of the oven and set it on a wire rack to cool. The bubbles have left large holes in the top, making it look like the surface of the moon. Maybe when it's cut it won't look so bad.

Lorenzo keeps staring at me, as if he's waiting for me to agree.

"I'm going home to shower." The profiteroles will have to wait. Or better yet, maybe I should just throw out the dough and try again tomorrow.

"Ok, but think about AC," he calls after me.

Recipe: Profiteroles

I'll have to get back to you on this one.

Chapter 9

All night, every time I go into the kitchen, Mario and Lorenzo make an Atlantic City reference. Even though it's a Tuesday, I know that we won't be finished with work until at least midnight, then we have to shower, and drive forty minutes to get there. "It'll be too late," I protest on one of my trips in the kitchen.

"It's open all night," Lorenzo replies. "Even Chucker is meeting us."

Ok, it *would* be nice to see Chuck. I imagine the scene. It would be like our first years of the restaurant, where the crew would go gambling at least once a week after work. It didn't matter if we got home at 7:00 the next morning. We'd sleep until 2:00, shower, and go back to work.

"We can even get scallion pancakes for breakfast." Mario's eyes light up, referring to the Chinese food we inevitably get at 5:00 a.m. before the long drive home.

"No," I say firmly and leave the kitchen.

Midway through the night I pass Lucy in the waiters' station. "Are you going to Atlantic City?" she asks.

"I don't think so. Why?"

"I sort of want to go," she says with a smile.

This trip could be the perfect opportunity to talk to Lucy. I start to think more seriously about going, when the phone rings.

It's Mr. Lyndon, a regular who comes in often with his wife. Unexpected guests showed up at his house and he places a giant take-out order. I assure him that everything will be fine, and that he can pick it up in one hour.

When I hand the order to Lorenzo he makes the same throwing the dice gesture.

"Maybe." I smile.

By the time Mr. Lyndon comes to pick up his take-out, we've calmed down for the night. All of the reservations have been sat, and it looks like the flow of walk-ins has died down a bit. I look at the clock; it's only 9:45.

"Thank you so much," he says signing his credit card receipt. "You really saved us tonight. My son came in with six of his friends and my wife barely had enough food to tide them over until dinner." He smiles and closes the check presenter. "We'll see you during the week."

"Great. Thank you."

When he leaves, I open the check presenter to retrieve his credit card slip. I have to look at it twice to make sure I've read it correctly.

He's left me a $100 tip on his $97 check.

Did you hear that? One hundred dollars!

It just goes to show how appreciated I am.

"It's a sign," Mario says when I run to the kitchen, waving the credit card slip. "We're going to AC."

And just like that, I'm in.

I bet you want to know what happened, don't you?

Well, let's just say, someone (aka Stella DiLucio) had a hot hand at the craps table.

And when we left the casino at 5:30 this morning, I was fifteen hundred dollars richer than before.

That's right. Fifteen. Hundred. Dollars.

I still can't believe it.

But no matter how much money you win, mornings are still rough. Especially when you go to bed when the sun is coming up. Still, I have work to do. I'm a professional.

The only downside of last night is that I didn't really get the chance to talk to Lucy. I think about making her a mug of coffee to wake her up, but decide against it.

As I sip my breakfast I wonder when exactly I should execute the plan. I mean, I got lucky last night, maybe I'm on a winning streak. Part of me wants to pick up the phone and dial Drew right now, but the other, more cautious part of me decides against it.

To distract myself I start to think of all the possible things I can buy with fifteen hundred dollars. I'm usually very responsible with money (besides the time I bought that extra-large Louie, but that's an *investment* piece), but since I've won this, I figure I can blow it on anything I want. I've been wanting another Fendi for a while, and with fifteen hundred, I can get a nice large tote. Or, I can treat myself to a day at the Villa's spa, complete with an extra-long massage and relaxing facial. I've also been wanting a beautiful leather jacket, and with this kind of money, I'm sure I can get a buttery soft one. Pure luxury. I imagine myself walking through the streets of the Upper West Side in the fall, when the weather is crisp enough to wear leather.

Maybe I can use the money as the first month's rent for an apartment in Manhattan. Once I'm there I'm sure I can find a great job doing…well. I'm sure I can find something. Plus, this way I can live close to Drew and we'll see each other every day. It's strange but as I'm thinking of New York, images of Roberto keep popping into my head.

I take a few extra minutes applying concealer to my eyes and dusting bronzer on my cheeks, just in case Roberto stops by with a bread delivery.

By 10:00 a.m. I'm in the restaurant, already whisking egg whites into stiff peaks to mix into my cake batter. Today I'm making the Money Cake, the end-all-be-all of cakes, which my mother has made for every single one of my birthdays. I'm sure she'll be making it in August, but I can't wait until then. This is my cake and today, when I'm finished assembling it, I'll cut a thick slab and eat it for lunch. I'm that happy.

The Money Cake looks like your average Strawberry Short Cake. You know, the tall ones piled high with pound cake and whipped cream. Only this is different because the cake is Pan di Spagnia, Italy's version of Angel Food Cake. It's light and spongy with a slight hint of sweetness that makes the entire cake heavenly. Stuffed with fresh strawberries, the cake screams summer. I'm not sure why we haven't thought of putting it on the dessert list before.

I follow the recipe exactly and it looks right. This time I preheated the oven as soon as I got here, so there'll be no mistakes.

As the cake bakes, I make myself an espresso and look out towards the street. There are crowds of people walking along the sidewalks, some stopping to read our menu or peek inside the window. I smile.

The restaurant business is hard work but it's worth it. We endure the long hours and seemingly endless summer so people can enjoy themselves when they walk through our door, and sometimes, the smiles on their faces are the only thanks we get. But still, I can't imagine what my life would be like without a restaurant. Already, it will be so different with La Cucina closing. My heart pounds as I realize, once again, that I will not have a job at the end of the summer. Maybe winning that money was a sign from God, giving me a little savings before I'm dropped on my head.

Miraculously, the cake bakes evenly, and by noon, I'm finished dressing the cake and am ready to taste it. I cut myself a slice, ignoring the calories and fat in each bite, and sit down to enjoy it. I don't even take my apron off, as it feels more authentic to reap the fruits of my labor while still being dressed the part. I take a bite of the moist cake and savor the burst of strawberries in my mouth.

A tap on the window startles me out of my trance. I look up to see a teenage boy holding a large vase of flowers. Every so often, customers will have flowers sent to the restaurant for their table. This happens about four or five times a season and is usually for a table of twelve or larger. I don't remember any big parties reserved for tonight. I open the door to let him in.

"I have a delivery for Stella DiLucio," he says, awkwardly carrying the vase into the restaurant. He places it down on the hostess stand and hands me a slip to sign.

I take the piece of paper from his hand, sign it and give it back to him without a word. I'm mesmerized. The square vase is full of giant orange gerbera daisies, peach and white roses, plush amaryllis, pink snapdragons, and delicate white orchids. The signature brown and white polka-dot bow tells me they are from Dots and Bows, the Island's premier florist and my immediate thought is that this grand gesture is from Drew. He's finally come to his senses and wants me back. Good thing I didn't put the plan into action.

I tear open the card.

For the most beautiful Star on the island.

The minute I read the card I know they are from Roberto, and I have to admit, a tiny part of me is elated. At the very least, I know that if things don't work out with Drew, I have a nice back-up plan. Not that I'm giving up hope on Drew just yet.

"You look happy tonight," Mr. Godil comments as I seat him at his regular table.

"That's what flowers will do to a girl," I say. His wife smiles.

Even though I'm tempted to daydream all night, I need to focus on work. My brothers and Lucy are all sluggish, which can mean a disaster for reservations. If we don't move people in and out of the restaurant, I'll be backed up once again. I walk into the kitchen. "Who wants espresso?" I ask.

Lorenzo raises his hand.

"A double," Mario says.

I walk by the waiters' station and ask Lucy if she wants one. She's been quiet all day and barely took notice of my flowers. "No thanks." She walks past me as I fiddle with the espresso machine. I know something is up, but I won't let it get to me. Not in front of the flowers.

Back in the kitchen, my brothers are arguing about veal. Lorenzo generally serves two pieces per portion and it's one of the many things Mario is trying to change since he's been in the kitchen. I place their coffees on the line and walk back to the dining room.

By 7:45 I'm calm. Michelle and Brittany have been picking up the slack and have each turned their tables quickly, making my life a little easier. The tables for 8:00 will be available without even a five-minute wait.

The rest of the night progresses smoothly and I'm amazed at how my brothers do it all. Since the article, our numbers have jumped to almost 200 dinners a night. We're not open longer hours, so those extra people are being brought in all at the same time.

And since the money seems to be pouring in, I'm thinking of asking my parents for a raise. It's the least they can do considering they've decided to sell La Cucina.

By 11:30 I'm running on an espresso-induced autopilot. Good thing I've got this money counting thing down to a science. In the office, I swiftly divide all the bills into piles and tap the numbers into my calculator with ease.

"Do you have our tips yet?" Brittany asks coming into the office.

I hand her envelopes for her and Michelle. "What about Lucy's?" she asks.

"I'll give it to her later," I say.

"She asked if I could just get it."

"Oh." I hand over Lucy's envelope.

I follow Brittany out into the dining room and walk towards Lucy. "Want a glass of wine by the bay?" I ask.

"I'm actually going to my aunt's again. I'm really tired."

I don't understand why she has to go to her aunt's if she's tired, but I let it go. Obviously she's hanging out with someone else, and my gut is telling me it's some big-time loser.

Recipe: The Money Cake

Yields 12 servings

This is the end-all-be-all of cakes, ladies. It should be a staple in your dessert repertoire. Trust me on this one.

Pan Di Spagnia
(This cake can also be used when making Italian Rum Cake, or simply, as angel food cake.)

5 eggs, separated
1 cup sugar
3/4 cup all-purpose flour
1 teaspoon Baking powder

1) Preheat oven to 400 degrees. Line the bottom of a 9-inch spring form pan with wax paper. Set aside.
2) In a large bowl, beat egg yolks with sugar until soft yellow (about two minutes).
3) In a different bowl, beat egg whites until they form stiff peaks.
4) Sift together flour and baking soda.
5) Alternate folding the egg whites into the yolks, adding a small bit of flour after each incorporation. Repeat until all the egg whites and flour has been added.
6) Pour into prepared pan and tap the pan against the counter a few times to settle any air bubbles.
7) Bake for 25-30 minutes or until a toothpick inserted in the center comes out clean.
8) Cool completely before removing from the pan.

To assemble the Money Cake:

1 quart of heavy whipping cream
8 tablespoons powdered sugar
1 cup simple syrup
2 pints strawberries, sliced

1) Whip the heavy cream and powdered sugar together until it forms stiff peaks. Set aside in fridge.
2) Cut the Pan Di Spagnia in thirds lengthwise. Pour simple syrup onto each layer to moisten.
3) Starting with the bottom layer, spread whipped cream over the inside of the cake, add sliced strawberries.
4) Top with the next layer and repeat. Don't worry if the layers are crooked, it gets sliced anyway.
5) Place the top layer over the cake. Spread whipped cream over the entire surface of the cake, smoothing with a spatula. Place remaining strawberries on top.
6) Refrigerate until ready to serve.

Chapter 10

The bridesmaids' dresses are in. When Gina called and left me a message about it last week, I scheduled an appointment at Bella Sposa's to get my first fitting. But when my dad calls to remind me this morning, I completely blank.

"Your dress appointment is today," he says when I answer.

"Oh God," I say fumbling for my clock. It's 6:30. "I'll be on the road in twenty minutes." I get out of bed.

"Drive safely."

My dad is so cute sometimes. Despite being busy at the restaurant, he's offered to drive me to Maryland, where my dress is waiting. Even though there are many dress shops in Long Island, Gina chose to get her dress at Bella Sposa's in Townsend, Maryland, because the shop is owned by two of our good customers. She was skeptical at first, but when we drove there with our mothers in March and she saw their selection, she knew it was the best shop around. And Maria and Charlene, the owners, fawned over her just enough to convince her of the right gown for her. Even the sample dress was stunning. When she walked out in a satin Amsale ball gown, my mother teared up. It didn't matter that it was three sizes too big and pinned tight in the back; we could all envision her as she'll be in October.

Luckily, Gina allowed me to have a say in the bridesmaids' dresses and we decided on a delicious chocolate brown silk gown, with a slight mermaid shape. I love the low V in the back, and envision wearing my hair in a low bun to highlight the cut of the dress. I may be short, but I've got a great back.

I make a fast stop at Quick Mart for a twenty-ounce coffee before heading home to meet my dad. It doesn't make sense to drive north only to go south, but there's no way to get to Maryland from the shore, and this way my dad can do the bulk of the driving.

On the road, I think of the flowers. After analyzing the situation through multiple text messages to Gina and Julie, I realized that Roberto sending me flowers was the best thing to happen to me all summer.

"Stella," my dad greets me as I pull into the driveway. "You ready for some Baltimore crabs?"

Now I know the real reason he offered to drive. My dad is a sucker for crab cakes. "Sure," I say. "But let me try on the dress first. I don't want to be bloated for my first fitting. It'll throw everything off."

He gives me a look like he has no idea what I'm talking about.

Within minutes, my mom is trying to feed me. It's just before nine and she's headed to the restaurant to start the day. Unlike Lorenzo's, La Cucina is open for lunch, which means her hours are much longer than ours. I can't help but notice how tired she looks lately, and even though I don't want to admit it, maybe selling the restaurant really is the best thing.

She thrusts an English muffin in my face. "You don't eat enough," she says. Ironically, she's right. I tend to slim down in the summer because Lorenzo is not as generous with his food as my mother. He could care less if you're fed or not.

I take the toast out of her hand and reach for the raspberry jelly on the counter. I take a seat at the breakfast nook and butter my toast.

"Are you ready?" my dad asks, coming into the kitchen.

"Yep," I jump off the barstool, ready to roll.

We get to Bella Sposa's just before 11:00 a.m. Maria and Charlene greet us at the door.

"How's my girl," Charlene asks giving me a hug.

"You're going to die when you see this dress!" Maria exclaims.

Charlene leads my dad to the couch in the lobby and talks to him about the drive while I follow Maria upstairs to the dressing rooms. My dress is waiting in its plastic garment bag. She unzips it. I take off my top and fold it neatly on the chair.

"You've lost weight." She scans me with her eyes.

"I'm down the shore. There's no time to eat."

"That's funny," she says walking towards me with the dress. "Whenever I walk into your restaurant I gain five pounds. It's those damn gnocchi. They're so good though, I don't even care."

The gnocchi at our restaurant are legendary because they're handmade and unlike any you'd buy. I laugh. "Well I don't get to eat those too often." She slips the dress over my head and lets it fall dramatically to the floor.

"Beautiful. You look beautiful." She's right. Besides the length, the dress is an almost perfect fit and won't require much work at all. I step onto the platform for fittings and realize I've forgotten my shoes.

"Crap," I whine. "I didn't bring my shoes."

"Cinderella, you came to the right ball. What size are you?"

"Six."

"How high were your heels?"

"About six inches," I say. She raises her eyebrows. "I'm short; I can get away with it."

"I don't want you dancing around the reception in flip flops because your feet hurt."

Does she know who she's dealing with?

"I won't," I reply with a smile. "Trust me."

She shakes her head and goes to fetch me a pair of shoes. I turn to look at myself in the three-way mirror. The dress accentuates all the right places, making my bust look big, my hips small, and my butt round. I envision Drew and me dancing at my brother's wedding, and then suddenly, Roberto comes to my mind.

Eva the seamstress comes in to start pinning me, and Maria watches her approvingly. "If your dad wasn't waiting, I'd bring up some wedding gowns for you to try on." She winks.

I smile and refocus on getting Drew back.

"It's only a matter of time before that hot little boyfriend of yours pops the question."

I relax my shoulders. My thoughts exactly.

Vince's crab shack is packed with a lunch crowd. People are rushing by us and the hostess doesn't greet us when we walk in the door. She seems frantic and stressed. My dad and I look at each other and smile. She's broken the dream, but luckily, we're pros. We don't dine for the ambiance, or the service like others, because that will almost never satisfy us. We dine solely for the food and Maria assures us this place serves the best crabs in Baltimore.

We both order crab cake sandwiches and unsweetened iced tea. My dad and I are so similar that sometimes it's scary. I stare at the servers in their workstation and think about the long night ahead of us. My dad reaches over and squeezes my hand.

"What are you thinking about?" he asks.

"Nothing. The business."

He nods his head, as he understands.

"Your mother is excited to finally retire," he says. I look at him and can see that he is also excited by this. It's strange to think of my parents without the restaurant. I wonder what they'll do with all of their time, but more often, I worry about what I'll do.

"It's weird to think about not having the restaurant," I say.

"I know, but it's too much damn work. Besides, you have the shore."

"But what am I going to do the rest of the year? And what about Lorenzo and Mario?" Without even meaning to, I'm getting angry.

"Lower your voice," my father says sternly.

"Sorry."

"Your mother and I talked about that, we know it's going to be hard for you guys but you're young. You'll figure something out."

Is that really his explanation? We'll figure something out? That hardly seems fair.

"What if I don't?"

"You will. You're exactly like Grandmom Stella. You've got her spark." My dad's eyes moisten. "You can do whatever you want Stella. You'll always be a success."

I've never heard my dad talk like this and I feel myself getting emotional too.

Our food arrives just in time. We eat quickly, and in silence. I'm comforted by my dad's words. I just hope he's right.

On the way back to the shore, I decide to ditch my master plan and just give Drew a simple call. The last time we talked wasn't so successful, but my dad is right. I can do whatever I want. Which means that I don't need some elaborate scheme to get Drew back. I just need to be my amazing self.

The phone goes right to voicemail.

I try three more times during the drive, and each time is the same. Honestly, you'd think a big marketing executive would keep his phone turned on.

On my last try, I decide to leave a voicemail. "Hi Drew," I say casually. "It's Stella. I just wanted to say hi and see if maybe you wanted to come down the shore. It would be so great to see you. It's been so long and I think we have a lot to talk about since that night…"

Damn. The voicemail cut me off.

I call right back and leave a second message. "Hey. I must have gotten cut off or something. Anyway, give me a call."

That could have gone a little better, but oh well.

Even though it's a Wednesday, there are twenty-seven messages, so by the time I finish checking them and returning the calls, it's past five and people are starting to come in.

I seat the first two top in the front section, and then walk towards the waiters' station to talk to Lucy. She's not there.

"Where's Lucy?" I ask Ryan.

He points towards the bathroom so I walk back to the hostess desk. The smell from the flowers is so strong that it's making my head spin. Funny, I didn't notice that yesterday.

By 5:30 there's already a crowd at the door. The restaurant fills up quickly, and I'm running around trying to make sure everyone is fed, happy, and working efficiently. Lucy has been sluggish and avoiding me all night, but I'm too busy to care.

"Can you rush the entrées to table thirteen?" I say to her as we pass each other near the desserts.

"I'll try," she says and hurries into the kitchen. I follow her to make sure she's calling in their order.

She walks right past Lorenzo on the line, and moves through the kitchen like a whirlwind. In the dish area, where Ivan and Stefan are scrubbing pots and pans, she leans into the trashcan and throws up. They cringe and look away.

I don't believe this. If she wants to have a boyfriend and not tell me about it fine, but I'm also her manager, and I won't tolerate her showing up hung over.

Stefan runs to fetch water and by the time he gets back, Lucy straightens up. She accepts the glass from him and wipes her mouth with a towel.

"Nice," I snap sarcastically. "Drink too much vodka last night?"

She shakes her head and bends towards the trashcan again, ready for round two.

I leave her there and walk through the kitchen. "Fire Lucy's table thirteen," I yell to Lorenzo. "And when she's done vomiting I'm sure she'll pick it up." I walk past the line and out to the dining room floor.

Her three tables are all at different stages of their meals. Table eleven is eating appetizers, table thirteen is waiting for entrées, and table fourteen is ready for dessert. I pull Brittany aside. "Do you have a minute to show table fourteen the dessert tray?"

She shakes her head and continues walking. "Sorry."

I rush to the dessert area and grab the tray out of the fridge, slamming the door a bit too loudly. I take a deep breath, collect myself, and walk towards the table. They decide on cannoli, which are, of course, the most complicated dessert, and as I walk the tray back to the fridge I get even madder. I fill their cannoli with sweet cream in seconds, piping it into the shell with precision and speed. Then I dust powdered sugar over the pastries and deliver the dish. "Enjoy your dessert." I smile before storming back to the kitchen.

Lucy is sitting on a dish rack, a wet kitchen rag on her head. Lorenzo is standing next to her, talking to her in a low voice.

"Are you done?" I ask.

She looks at me with watery eyes.

"Can you deliver the food to table thirteen?" my brother asks me.

"Sure. I'll do it because Lucy is too irresponsible to do her own work. Anyone else need me to do something? Why don't I just start cooking too?"

I grab the hot plates off the line and nearly burn the skin off my fingers. "Shit," I scream.

"They've been sitting there for five minutes," Mario snaps.

I grab a napkin to guard my hands. "Yeah well if someone wasn't *hung-over*, I'm sure they'd be out on the table by now."

I kick open the swinging door and walk towards the table.

"These plates are extremely hot," I say placing the food in front of the guests with a smile. "Please be careful."

The man asks for cheese and I tell him it's on its way. I motion for Frankie to bring some and walk back into the kitchen.

Lucy is standing up, walking towards the back door. Lorenzo is still with her.

"Where's she going?" I yell.

"Home. She's sick," my brother answers.

"What the hell? You're just going to walk out on the restaurant?" I say to Lucy.

"She's sick," Lorenzo yells at me. Why is he defending her?

"Well you better go to your aunt's then," I scream at her. "Because I don't want any of your germs around my house."

I walk back into the kitchen and through the swinging doors to the waiters' station. "Brittany, I need you to pick up table thirteen, Ryan you take fourteen. Lucy went home sick."

"Great," I hear Ryan mumble. Even though he's worked with us for three years, he's not accommodating and not that fast. He's on thin ice as far as I'm concerned. I would give Michelle an extra table but she already has the biggest section of the night, and I can't load her down. Instead, I take tables ten and eleven. Somehow I'll manage to juggle the phones, the door, and wait on two tables.

The rest of the night is a blur, but I survive.

We all do.

The restaurant looks like it's been through a battle, but when you're one man down, you don't worry about keeping clean. The waiters' station is strewn with linens falling haphazardly out of the hamper. The bread bags are spilling crumbs onto the floor, and one empty coffee pot is burning on its warmer. The dessert area is even worse. The cakes, which I normally cut for the servers, are either broken or toppling and there's chocolate sauce all over the tiles and grout. Espresso grinds spill from the grinder and all the plates need to be restocked.

I sigh heavily. We're in for a long night of cleaning, which is the last thing I want to do after the day I've had.

Now that all the guests are gone, I have a minute to think. Was I too hard on Lucy? We used to show up hung over all the time, and we'd always cover for each other. Still, she never left before, and her walking out tonight was a bleak reminder of her new attitude this summer. Obviously she doesn't care as much about our friendship as I thought she did. Now I'm convinced. She has a boyfriend and she cares about him more than me.

I scrub the tiles with a hot wet rag but the chocolate just smears into the grout even deeper, making brown streaks. I walk to the kitchen to get some soap. Lorenzo's standing near the stove, counting the tickets from the night. He looks up at me.

"Why do you always have to be such a bitch?" he asks.

"What was I supposed to do? Be happy that a server walked out on the restaurant?"

"She was sick. Do you want her throwing up in the dining room?"

"She wasn't sick, Lorenzo. Don't be dumb. She was hung over."

"You don't know that."

"Yes I do. She doesn't stay at our house anymore. She probably has some loser boyfriend and stays with him every night. I can just see it. She's probably out drinking until four in the morning."

"You don't know what the hell you're talking about," my brother says and throws his tickets in the trash. Why does he keep defending her? Doesn't he see that a *real* friend would never walk out on the business?

"How do you know?" I snap. "She's my best friend."

"Really?" he shouts. "Then why don't you act like it? If my best friend treated me the way you treated Lucy tonight I'd never talk to him again."

"Yeah, well, I'm sure your best friend wouldn't treat you the way Lucy has been treating *me* all summer." I turn my back to exit, forgetting about the soap.

"Ok, Stella. You're always right," my brother says as I exit through the swinging door. "No wonder Drew didn't want to marry you."

Why am I at fault here? Suddenly, I'm the bad guy? *I* wasn't the one who drank too much and then threw up in the kitchen. *I* wasn't the one who walked out on her friends and their business. No, instead, *I'm* the one who picks up the messes, who reorganizes, who keeps a smile plastered on her face so the customers don't know how hard it is to play hostess, waitress, and manager all at once. Tears are falling from my eyes in fat wet drops that fall on the tiles I'm trying to clean.

Out of the corner of my eye, I see the flowers sitting on the hostess desk and suddenly everything becomes clear. These weren't a nice gesture; they're pity flowers. I think back to the Fourth of July and remember the look in Roberto's eye. He feels bad for me. I walk towards them and sweep my arm across the table, knocking them off. The glass vase shatters on the floor and the flowers, once beautiful, look twisted and old among the water and shards of glass.

Recipe: Maryland Crab Cakes

Yields 8 large or 20 mini

1 pound jumbo lump crabmeat
2 eggs
1/4 cup mayonnaise
2 tablespoons Old Bay seasoning
1 tablespoon Dijon Mustard
2 teaspoons Worcestershire sauce
1/2 teaspoon crushed white pepper
3/4 cup breadcrumbs

1) In a large bowl, beat together the eggs, mayonnaise, Old Bay seasoning, Dijon Mustard, Worcestershire sauce, and white pepper.
2) Gently fold in the crabmeat and breadcrumbs (add the breadcrumbs 1/4 cup at a time. If it looks too dry, don't add all of the breadcrumbs).
3) Shape the mixture into balls.

For fried crab cakes:

1) Roll the crab cakes in breadcrumbs to coat.
2) Heat 4 cups of vegetable oil in a large pot. To make sure the oil is hot enough, drop a pinch of breadcrumbs into the mix. If it bubbles up, you're go to go. If not, wait a few minutes and test again.
3) Gently drop 3 crab cakes into the oil. Fry until browned on all sides. Lift them out and place on a paper towel lined plate to absorb excess oil. Repeat until all the crab cakes are fried.
4) These are ideal for sandwiches.

For Baked crab cakes:

1) Let the crab cakes rest in the fridge for at least 30 minutes before cooking.
2) Preheat oven to 400 degrees.
3) In a medium sauté pan heat 1 tablespoon butter and two tablespoons extra virgin olive oil.
4) Gently sauté the crab cakes until lightly browned on all sides.
5) Place crab cakes on a baking sheet.
6) Bake for 10-15 minutes, until warmed through.

These are ideal as entrées.

Chapter 11

I don't talk to Lucy for the next seven days. She calls Lorenzo to say that she's still sick, and he tells me to schedule another waiter, which I gladly do. Maybe I was wrong about her being hung-over but what was I supposed to think? She's been so shady this whole summer that I could only assume the worst. I'm pretty down about our fight, but still won't call her to apologize.

She should be the one to call *me*, since she's been acting weird lately.

Since the fight with Lucy, everyone has been acting pretty strange. Lorenzo won't even talk to me, Mario is quiet, and the other waiters are all looking at me as if I might explode at any minute. I must've shocked them all when I threw my flowers on the floor. I still don't know what came over me, but honestly, it felt good.

To make matters worse, Drew never called and after a week, it's pretty obvious that he's not going to. When I called Gina and told her what I did, she told me I basically ruined all chances of getting him back according to our plan.

But what the hell does Gina know anyway? Just because she's engaged doesn't make her the freaking Dali Lama of dating, for God's sake. There must be something else I can do to get Drew back.

This whole mess is my dad's fault. He pumped me up with his bullshit pep talk about me being like my grandmother. In truth, I'm nothing like her. If I was, I'd have it all figured out by now.

To avoid reality, I'm here at the restaurant, throwing myself into this whole baking thing.

Believe it or not, it is the highlight of my day. I love the hours between 9:00 a.m. and 11:00 a.m. when I'm here, in the kitchen making pastries by myself. When I'm engulfed in work, I do a great job of not thinking about Lucy, or Drew for that matter. As far as I'm concerned, I don't ever need to see either one again.

Ok, maybe I do miss Lucy, a little. But if she doesn't want to be my friend, then we must not have been so close to begin with.

And as for Drew, well, I'll deal with him later.

Every day as I bake, I listen to music off my brother's greasy iPod, which has been in the kitchen since we opened the doors, with speakers hanging around the kitchen area. Lorenzo loves his music, and he's got a great collection on this thing. Today I've chosen Ligabue, Italy's most beloved Rock and Roll icon.

Or at least, he's my favorite.

I blast the Italian rock, sure that none of our deliveries will arrive until at least 11:00. It's only 9:30 so I know I have a few hours to myself.

One thing I love doing when I'm alone is dancing. I'm pretty horrible at it, but that's the fun of it. It doesn't matter if I look crazy when I'm all alone. And thank God I'm alone today because in my cut off jean shorts, white tank top, and red bandana, I must look like a cross between Daisy Duke and Axl Rose. My apron, which hangs past my knees, completes the look with its smeared chocolate stains.

The song "Piccola Stella Senza Cielo" – "little star without a sky" – comes on and I turn the music up. Sometimes I feel like this song was written for *me*. I am exactly that, a little star without a sky, especially now that I pretty much have no future.

In college, I was an English major with an Italian minor, which almost ensured that I'd be jobless at twenty-seven. Plus, the fact that I haven't done *any* work in my field since graduation five years ago doesn't help my case. If I saw my résumé in an inbox, I'd delete it too. So I'm stuck in the restaurant business, which is, ironically, exactly what I've been trying to escape all my life. The whole reason for *going* to Fordham was so that I wouldn't end up waiting on tables, yet the minute I graduated, I went back to work for my parents, donning my famous black apron and non-slip work shoes.

And now here I am on the other end of the spectrum, all alone in a kitchen. If you want to know the truth, this is the real restaurant life. It's not pretty dresses and smiling guests; it's just a girl, a stick of butter, and a cup of flour.

I've mastered a few of Chuck's cakes, and even invented some of my own, but I just cannot call myself a pastry chef until I've mastered these profiteroles. They're sort of haunting me. But I'll show them who's boss. I'm all prepped and revved up. And I spent two hours watching profiterole demos on YouTube last night. That's right, I'm armed with knowledge from Julia, Wolfgang, and even Anthony Bourdain (my kitchen crush).

I dice the stick of butter and add it to a small saucepan. When all the butter melts I add a cup of water and a cup of flour and stir the hell out of it.

The music is so loud that I don't hear the knocking on the back door, or the swing of the spring as it opens. I'm singing along at full volume when I hear someone yell, "Hello?"

I jump back, a little startled. And then I see him. Roberto Lancetti is standing in the kitchen holding two brown bags full of dinner rolls. Oh God.

"Hi," I say coolly. "You can put the bags over there." I point to an empty work table and then turn back to my batter, which has totally thickened.

"I didn't expect to see you here," he smiles. He sets down the bags and moves towards me.

I try to give him the cold shoulder but he can't take a hint.

"You like Ligabue?" he asks and points to the iPod.

"Yep" I'm trying to hear the dough sizzle against the sides of the saucepot, but it's not happening.

"Do you understand the lyrics?"

"You're not the only person in America who understands Italian," I snap.

"Whoa. Sorry." He turns to leave and instantly, I remember the flowers. That was pretty sweet of him, even if they were out of pity. And let's be honest, Drew never sent me flowers and we dated for three years.

"Hey wait," I shout. He stops and turns toward me. "Thanks for the flowers."

He shoots me a puzzled look. "What?"

"I said thanks for the flowers that you sent. They were nice."

"I didn't send you any flowers," he says and walks out.

Well then who the hell did?

Wednesday nights are strange. Since it's high season at the beach, every night feels like a Saturday. People are on vacation; they don't mind eating late. But for some reason, Wednesdays tend to be a little slower. You'd think people would want to go out in the middle of the week, but I guess there's no need to break up the monotony of a vacation.

By 8:45 p.m. all the reservations are seated, but I still have no clue who the hell sent me the flowers. I leave the hostess stand for a minute to go into the kitchen. I'm craving pasta tonight; I think the carbs will help me solve the mystery. The carbs and a quick call to my mother.

"Can you make me pasta with marinara?" I ask in the kitchen.

Lorenzo nods and drops some spaghetti in his boiling water. "Just wait for it," he says. The great thing about restaurants is all the prep work the kitchen does ahead of time. Each afternoon, right before we open for the night, Lorenzo cooks off some pasta. He leaves it slightly under cooked, so that it can finish off when he adds it back to the boiling pot he keeps on the stove. This reduces the cooking time from ten minutes to about two.

As I wait for the pasta, I call my mom.

"How was business tonight?" she asks before even saying hello. She and my father are on the Island so she probably can't figure out why I'm calling since I'll see her back at the house.

"Good. Steady." I shift the phone to my other ear. "Hey Mom, who sent me those flowers?"

"Roberto. Wasn't that nice of him?"

"He said he didn't send them." I wait a few seconds for her to respond.

"He's probably just lying," she says with a little laugh, which is a telltale sign that she's lying.

"Who sent them, Mom?"

Lorenzo pours the steaming pasta into a bowl and tops it with a ladle of marinara sauce and hands it to me under the heat lamp.

I douse it with hot pepper flakes, just like my father, and cover the top with a layer of cheese. My mom doesn't answer.

"Mom?"

"Alright, fine, I'll tell you. Anna sent them. We both thought of it."

"What?"

"We saw you and Roberto talking at the barbeque so we thought we'd just set things in motion a bit." She sounds so casual and flippant that instantly, I want to scream.

"How could you do that?"

"Stella, it's no big deal."

"No big deal? It's humiliating, Mom. Now not only does Roberto think I'm crazy, but my own *mother* thinks I'm pathetic."

She starts to speak but I hang up the phone. There's nothing she can say to right this situation.

I carry the bowl out to the front of the restaurant, where I can sit at a corner table and brood. On the way, Brittany rushes by me with a stack of plates and bumps my hand. Some of the pasta slashes out onto my shirt.

"Oh no. I'm so sorry." She reaches into her apron and grabs a cloth napkin.

"It's fine," I snap taking the napkin. After all, I'm the biggest loser on the Island, I may as well have a big stain on my shirt. I place the pasta down and rub the sauce off my chest with a napkin. As I'm trying to remove the stain, my cell phone rings.

"Leave me alone, Mom," I bark into the phone.

"Stella?" I hear Julie on the other end.

"Hey Jules," I perk up and take a seat, placing the pasta bowl in front of me. "You won't believe what my mom did. She—"

"Stell, I need to tell you something," Julie interrupts. She doesn't sound good. Since I've known Julie, there's been a major crisis at least once a year, but somehow I'm always able to help her through it. Today, she seems to need me more than ever. I shift positions in my chair.

"Tell me everything."

I can hear her lighting a cigarette and inhaling deeply. "Ok, I was at this party last night," she begins and then stops. "I really don't know how to tell you this."

My heart races. This seems really bad. "Just say it. It'll be okay."

She takes a deep breath. "Drew was there."

"What party?"

"It was this thing for this new Vodka company. It was at the rooftop bar at the Hudson. They invited the press."

"How did Drew get in?"

"I guess Connective reps the company or something." She inhales again. "Anyway, he was sort of with someone."

My heart stops and my mind flashes back to July third. The bimbo that I heard on the phone is Drew's new girlfriend? This can't be happening.

"What did she look like?"

Julie doesn't respond, which only makes me think Drew's new girlfriend is a freaking supermodel or something.

"Jules, what did she look like?"

"It's someone you know actually."

My heart races. This is the exact moment where everything is going to fall apart. I brace myself.

"It's Trisha Motley."

For a minute, I'm stunned. Drew is dating Trisha Motley. Trisha Motley who has a beautiful house on 100th Street and comes into the restaurant all the time. I mean, I don't think Drew would actually come into the restaurant with her, but still, I'm sure they'll be on the Island together. Which means that I might actually bump into them. Together.

I try to catch my breath, but I feel like the wind has been knocked out of me.

"Stell, there's more," Julie says exhaling another puff of smoke. She takes a deep breath. "They're getting married."

Instantly I feel like I'm going to pass out. "How do you know?" I mumble.

"I saw the ring."

Images start flashing in my mind. Trisha asked me if Drew and I were getting engaged. He had a Tiffany's catalogue in his apartment. That's my ring. The bitch stole my ring.

Ok, Calm down and think about this rationally. There must be some explanation for Drew and Trisha getting engaged.

Engaged.

How the hell did this happen?

I know Trisha and Drew have known each other for years but I didn't think they still talked. Or that they'd start dating for God's sake. I bet she tricked him into the engagement. I mean, how else could this be possible?

Or maybe she's pregnant. It's probably not even his child, but she knew that Drew was kind hearted enough to marry her, so she lied and said it was his. Nine months from now he'll be in for a big surprise.

Serves him right. The bastard.

But maybe I can save him before it's too late. If I can only expose Trisha for the fraudulent slut that she is, then maybe Drew will see how much better I am. Of course, he'll have to buy me a new ring. I don't want sloppy seconds on an engagement ring, even if it does come from Tiffany's.

I hang up with Julie and I run into the kitchen to ask Mario to cover for me. Thankfully, he doesn't ask questions, and doesn't try to follow me when I run out of the back door. As soon as I get to the street I start to cry.

It's only 10:30 so the streets are still full and as I walk towards the beach I'm praying that I don't see anyone I know.

"Stella?" I hear a familiar voice. Obviously God wasn't listening to my prayers. I put my head down and ignore it. I try to pick up my pace.

"Stella?"

The voice seems closer to me now, so I stop and turn around. "What? What do you want?" I blurt out.

Roberto looks at me with what can only be described as pity. "Are you okay?"

"Do I freaking look okay?" I scream. I just stand there in the middle of the street, tears running down my face. "No, I look pathetic don't I?"

"What happened?" He moves closer to me and I step back.

"My ex-boyfriend is engaged to some else. Engaged. And we broke up a month ago."

He looks down but doesn't say anything.

"What's wrong with me?" I yell the question I've been avoiding since Drew broke up with me. "Why am I so un-loveable?"

"Are you kidding?" He moves closer and tries to hug me. "You're so beautiful."

I back away. "Please. That's why your mom is sending me flowers and pushing you to date me?" I turn around and start walking.

"What are you talking about?"

"Just leave me alone Roberto. I don't need your pity or anyone else's."

I pick up my pace and, thankfully, he doesn't follow me.

I've been sitting on the beach at 101st Street for a while now, just thinking about the mess of my life. But I don't really feel like sitting here anymore, so I get up and start walking. I look at my watch. It's 4:30 a.m. I know I should just go home but I really don't feel like talking to anyone.

I need to make soufflés for tomorrow night, and there's no time like the present. Besides, baking will do me good, at least it will take my mind off this mess.

As soon as I start walking towards the restaurant, I feel a huge blister on the back of my heel. Sand has gotten into it and it really burns. For some reason, this makes me cry even harder. I take my shoes off and start walking barefoot down Third Avenue, mascara running down my face.

A police car pulls to my left. I turn to see two officers looking at me strangely. That's the thing about living on the Island, there's never any privacy when you need it most.

They roll down the window. "Rough night?" the officer in the passenger seat asks. I peer into the car and realize the driver is Officer Manning, a regular at the restaurant. He doesn't recognize me.

"Hi Officer Manning," I say and get his attention.

"Stella, what are you doing walking the streets at this hour?"

Walking the streets? He makes me sound like a hooker. Excuse me, my name is not Trisha Motley.

I look down at myself and realize that I do look a little bit like a hooker, especially with make-up smeared all over my face.

"I locked myself out of my house," I lie. "So I'm going to the restaurant. I've got that key."

"Do you want us to call your house or anything?" the other officer asks.

"No, I don't want to wake anyone up."

He doesn't say anything, but gives me a half smile and waves good-bye. Does he think I'm lying?

They remain parked on Third Avenue and watch as I unlock the door and enter the restaurant. I lock it behind me and walk to the kitchen in the darkness.

There, the kitchen mats feel strange against my bare feet. I turn on the lights and walk to the office, where I know I've stashed a pair of flip-flops. Once I locate them, I get down to business, opening the first aid kit and tending to this blister. The last thing I need is an infection or gangrene on my foot or something. That's totally unsexy. As I'm working, I spot the bottle of Sambuca I keep in my office for good customers.

Perfect. I'll just take a little sip.

I unscrew the black top and take a swig right from the bottle. I've never been a fan of the dark licorice flavor of Sambuca, but right now, it tastes so good to me that I take another swig and nestle the bottle under my arm. I grab a fresh apron and place it over my head, then move to fetch the chocolate out of the dry storage.

Instead of using precut chocolate, I prefer to order big blocks and cut it myself, so I take the entire block of semi-sweet chocolate, and the entire block of bitter chocolate off the shelves and plop them onto the workspace.

I search through the various gadgets until I find our kitchen scale, and I line up large stainless steel bowls to hold the chocolate once it's been cut.

Then suddenly, as if by magic, I'm able to forget everything.

I focus only on the task at hand, making the batter for chocolate soufflés, and as I prep the chocolate by cutting it into tiny slivers, I realize that, for once, I'm at peace.

The time passes quickly, and I've almost forgotten that it's past 5:00 a.m.

I feel better already, so I focus all my attention on the soufflés, buttering and sugaring the ramekins and melting the chocolate into the roux.

Then, of course, there are the eggs. I skillfully separate the yolks from the whites, and drop the whites into the bowl of the Kitchen-Aid mixer. I'm particularly slow, because I know that when I finish baking, I'll have to return to the real world and think about what happened tonight. Drew's engaged.

I take another shot of Sambuca, hoping to wipe the thoughts out of my head.

By the time I finish making the batter and filling the ramekins, I decide that he's totally not worth it anyway. The jerk.

Really, after three years of being together he gives *my* ring to another woman.

All this work and stress have made me pretty hungry and instead of actually making something, I figure I'll just eat some of the soufflé batter.

I mean, what could be more comforting than a warm chocolate soufflé?

Not that I'm going to *cook* it or anything. But still, the flavor is the same cooked or raw.

I pop all of the ramekins except one into the dessert fridge and am about to shut the door when I spot the cake.

Of course!

The perfect cake for a heartbreak.

I reach my fork directly into the dessert case.

The bitterness of the chocolate hits me hard, and I realize that this will taste *so much better* with some more Sambuca. I grab the entire cake and take it with me.

On my way to the kitchen, I stumble a tiny *tiny* bit.

But it's okay, no one is here to see me.

I settle on the floor of the waiters' station, I take a sip of liquor and chase it with a forkful of cake. I was right. It *is* better with Sambuca. I proceed that way, alternating between sips and bites, until I'm scrapping up the last remnants from the bottom of the serving dish.

The problem is, I don't really feel better.

In fact, I actually feel a little worse.

Maybe I was wrong about the cake.

I look over at the Sambuca bottle and see that it's almost half empty. It wasn't full when I opened it was it? No, it couldn't have been.

My stomach starts to really hurt, so I figure I should lie on it for a while. I lay my face on the cold tiles and feel more refreshed than ever before.

Now *this* is comfortable.

I'm surprised more people don't sleep on floors.

Don't they do this in Asia?

Maybe I should move to Japan. Or China. I *do* like Asian food. I start to envision myself as a world traveler, speaking fluent Japanese….

Somewhere between thinking of how I'd look in a kimono and wondering how much plane tickets cost, I must have fallen asleep, because when I wake up, it's already light outside. I move to stand and it feels like my head was hit by a baseball bat. Then my stomach flips and I realize I'm going to vomit. I crawl into the bathroom and just make it to the toilet.

I feel so much better when I finish that I decide to just lay on the ground again and sleep it off.

The next time I wake up, I hear Mario screaming at me.

"What the hell are you *doing*?"

"Huh?" I say. I look around and realize I'm on the bathroom floor. I should ask him what *he's* doing spying on me in the women's room. I actually move to say this, but before I can talk, I scoot myself up near the toilet and throw up.

"That's lovely," Mario says. "My sister's got real class."

I don't feel like talking to him, but he makes me so mad. "What, you've never been hung over before, Mr. Perfect?" I realize how bad this looks, but still.

"Not in the restaurant."

"Well who cares where I am?"

"Mom and Dad care, actually. They've been up all night trying to call you. Mom wanted to call the police. But I said I'd find you." He pauses and gives me a dirty look. "I just didn't know you'd be like this."

"Can you get me some San Pellegrino?"

He sighs and walks towards the waiters' station. I hear him open the fridge, then grab a glass off the shelf. When he returns, he hands me a glass of water.

I try to sit up straight and can feel that I have vomit in my hair. I don't even want to look at myself in the mirror.

"You better clean up before Mom and Dad see you," he says, shaking his head.

"What time is it anyway?"

"It's just after nine."

"Can you call Mom and tell her where I am."

"Fine," he says and reaches into his pocket for his phone.

When he steps out of the bathroom, I try to stand again, but instead, I throw up. I don't even want to think of Sambuca again in my life.

I finally stand and walk over to the sink. I run the water and splash it on my face, trying to scrub away the remnants of the night.

Dark circles hang under my eyes and it's obvious I've been crying. I take a deep breath. The last thing in the world that I want to do is face Mario right now, but I know I need to start explaining myself, so I think of what I'm going to say.

When I walk into the dining room, I see him sweeping up the broken glass. I vaguely remember knocking over some glasses last night. It's still hard to place myself time wise, but as I glance out the window and see all the morning shoppers going into Beautiful People next door it all clicks.

"What happened?" he asks when he sees me.

I don't believe Mario *actually* cares, but at this point, I just let it all out. "Drew's engaged. We dated for three years and he didn't want to marry me, but after only one month with a new girl he's engaged." I slump down in a chair and realize that, no matter what plans I can come up with, it's really over. Drew didn't want to marry me. He wants Trisha Motley.

Mario puts down the broom and looks at me. "Other guys will want to marry you."

"Yeah right," I say. Suddenly it's clear. I'll never get married and I'll end up in a small apartment with seventeen cats. "I'll die alone."

"You just need to calm down."

Ha. That's easy for him to say. He's never been dumped on his ass.

By the time I get home it's almost 10:00. Mario was nice enough to go get his car so I wouldn't have to do a walk of shame across Third Avenue.

Thankfully, my parents don't ask any questions as I pass them and make my way up the steps. Mario must have filled them in when he came to fetch his car, so they just smile at me as if I'm a psych patient who just escaped from the ward. I don't mind it though, because honestly, it's better than having to explain why my head is pounding and there's dried vomit in my hair.

Of course, the first thing I see when I get into my bedroom is a stupid picture of Drew and me from last Christmas. Spare me the lecture. I know I should have taken it down a month ago, but give a girl a break, will you?

I place it face down on the dresser, take my cell phone out of my bag and set the alarm. I really need to be in the restaurant by 2:00 at the absolute latest. I figure I'll just take a little nap before I need to shower and make my way back to Lorenzo's.

My mom comes in and sits on my bed before my alarm rings at 1:15. When I open my eyes, I see her smiling at me sympathetically. She pats my head and brushes my face with the palm of her hand. "How are you feeling?"

"I'm ok," I say sitting up. Man my head still hurts. Who would have thought a little Sambuca would do such damage. I reach for my phone on the nightstand and see the picture lying face down where I left it. "Drew's engaged to Trisha Motley." Even though I'm saying it out loud, I still can't believe it.

"I know."

"Did Mario tell you?"

"No, Anna did."

Anna? Mrs. Lancetti? How the hell did she know? I give my mom a puzzled look. "Honey, she's friends with the Motleys."

I feel like my world is crashing down. The Island is too small for me. Now the entire town knows about my love life. I'm a laughing stock.

"Stellina" my mom says, which makes me sadder. She only calls me that in dire situations. "There's someone out there who's better for you."

"Yeah right," I say. "All men are assholes."

My mother shoots me a troubled look, but I'm convinced. That's it, I'm giving up men. What I'll probably do is devote my life to others. I'll become a nun and move to a little town in Peru. The children of the world will be my children. It'll be like *The Sound of Music*, only without the lederhosen.

My mom sighs. "Listen, I think you should stay home tonight. We can manage at the restaurant."

I shake my head. There is no way I am staying home.

"Stella, you look awful, and you're stressed out. Just take the night off and rest."

Nope. Not gonna happen.

Even though I feel like a bus leveled me, I *need* to go into the restaurant tonight. I need to see people and solve all the problems that arise. No one can do that like I do. Without me the restaurant will practically fall apart. "Mom, I'm going into work," I say and fling the covers off my bed. She moves slightly to let me out.

"Whatever you want to do Stella," she says with a frown.

I walk past her and into the bathroom. I step into the shower and let the water run over me. Before I can stop myself I start to cry. It's really over. Drew is marrying someone else. There's nothing left to do but get over him.

As I shampoo my hair I start thinking back to our relationship, and suddenly everything becomes clear. Drew wasn't the man for me. When I was with him I compromised myself, and always did what he wanted. Without even realizing it, I let him control me. How could I have let this happen? I feel like a fool, and I never want to feel this way again.

Recipe: Chocolate Souffle

Sorry, I can't even *think* of chocolate right now!

Chapter 12

My phone rings at exactly 10:30 the next morning.

"Hello?" I say without looking at the caller ID.

"Stella, it's Lucy."

I knew Lucy and I have ESP. Just last night I was thinking about how I needed her now more than ever, how she'll be able to make sense of this whole mess and put it into perspective for me. Before bed I started sending her subliminal messages, and she got them.

I just knew she would.

She sounds drained. "Is everything all right?" I ask.

"Yeah, I just… I miss you." I hear her beginning to cry and tears well up in my eyes too.

"I miss you too Lucy. You have *no* idea. I'm so sorry for flipping out at you."

"No, it's okay. I admit I was being shady."

I can hear her clinking things in a kitchen, and I wonder where she is.

"Want to get some breakfast at Cindy's?" I ask.

Cindy's is our favorite breakfast spot, right on the bay, and it's a tradition for us to eat there whenever we need to talk about serious issues. Today I need a thick stack of pancakes and my best friend.

"No," she says and instantly I'm disappointed.

Doesn't she get that I need her?

Maybe her ESP is out of whack.

I'd be able to tell if *she* was having a crisis.

"I do need to talk to you though. Can we meet at the restaurant?" her voice snaps me back to reality.

"Sure." Why does she want to meet there of all places? Why doesn't she just come here?

"Can you be there in a half hour?"

I get to the restaurant a few minutes early, planning on making myself a cappuccino, but Lucy's already there, sitting on the bench out front. She looks sleek in skinny jeans and a tight red tank top. Her long hair is pulled into a low ponytail, and she's wearing the Tiffany's open-heart necklace I got her for her twenty-fifth birthday. She smiles at me and stands.

God, I missed her.

I can't wait to tell her *everything* that's happened.

"Luce, I'm so sorry," I say giving her a hug.

"Me too, Stella."

I move to unlock the door and Lucy follows me into the dining room. She sits at the table closest to the door. "You want a coffee?" I ask.

"No, I'm good."

"I need one. I had *such* a rough night." I move towards the espresso machine and turn it on. As it heats up, I cut a slice of strawberry short cake, and another of almond amaretto cake. I plate the desserts and walk them over to the table. "Breakfast." I smile and place them down. "I made these myself."

Lucy looks at the cakes but doesn't move to take a bite.

"Do you want a different cake?" I ask. I walk back over to the espresso machine to check if it's warm enough.

"No. I'm not hungry actually."

I'm not sure if Lucy is mad at me, or if she's really not hungry so I make a quick espresso that comes out luke warm. I heat some milk and pour it over the coffee then return to the table. I sit across from her. "So what's going on?"

Lucy takes a deep breath.

I've known my best friend for four years and she's never nervous.

Something bad must have happened.

She looks straight at me and I prepare for the worst. She's ending our friendship, I know it. I can imagine it already. She probably has all of the stuff she ever borrowed from me in a cardboard box in her car. She'll leave it out by the front door and I'll have to scramble to collect everything while running after…

"I'm pregnant," she sighs.

What?

Pregnant?

As in, with child?

The words seem to float around in my brain but don't sink in.

Lucy leans forward and I can tell she's waiting for my reaction, but honestly, I don't know how to respond. I can't tell if she's happy or sad about this news. I still don't know who her *boyfriend* is, for God's sake. "Oh my God," I manage to say.

"And I'm getting married." She looks down at her lap.

"Lucy," I nearly yell. "Who's the guy?" My heart is racing. This is too much.

Lucy stays silent but I can see the corners of her mouth tighten.

She doesn't want to tell me.

Why wouldn't she want to tell me?

Oh God.

It's one of *my* ex-boyfriends.

I flip through the list of my previous boyfriends. I hope for her sake it's not Tom. Anyone but Tom. None of them were exactly *winners*, but Tom was the worst of all. But Tom's from the Bronx, why would he be in New Jersey?

"Lucy, you know you don't have to get married." I hear myself saying. A baby is a big enough deal, she doesn't need *marriage* to a guy she hardly knows thrown in the mix.

Especially if it's Tom.

"Stella, I want to. I'm… *we're* in love."

Love?

I swallow hard. Ok, Stella, be tactful. She's obviously hormonal. It's critical to be supportive in situations like this.

"How the hell did this *happen*?"

She looks at me as if she's about to explain human biology. She opens her mouth and then immediately closes it. She sighs.

"Does your dad know?" Lucy's father is stricter than mine. I can only imagine how he reacted.

"Oh God, no. He's going to flip out. You're the first person we've told."

Since she refers to her boyfriend, I assume he knows about me. It must be one of my exes. "Who is this guy Lucy?"

I'm bracing myself for the worst. If it's Tom, I'll have to smile and tell her how wonderful he is.

She takes a deep breath. "Lorenzo."

I feel as though I've been slapped in the face.

My brother?

My twin brother?

There's no way.

This isn't happening.

"Stell, I wanted to tell you from the beginning but I couldn't. We both thought it was best not to say anything until the summer is over."

"*Lorenzo*?" I say, stunned.

"Stell, don't be mad."

"I'm not… mad."

I'm shocked.

I had no idea they even *liked* each other.

Oh God. My parents. They're going to die. "This is crazy."

"I know, I know," she says. "I didn't mean to be shady about it all summer but we had to. Now we're in this mess, but we've talked about it. We're getting married."

"When? How did this all happen?" Even though I'm sitting down, I feel dizzy. "Wait, I don't want details of *that*," I say with slight disgust. I do not want to imagine my brother and Lucy.

Ew.

"Stell, I've loved him since the day I walked into this place for an interview. I remember he was standing at the hostess stand, looking over inventory, and you were there waiting for me. The first thing I thought was that I belong here. But not just as a worker. As family."

I look at her strangely.

This was *not* supposed to happen.

He's my brother and she's my best friend. They are *not* supposed to get together, ever.

Ew.

When her words finally settle in my brain, I start to feel a little used. "Were you only friends with me to get to my brother?"

She looks hurt. "Come on Stell, that's not fair. You know you're my best friend regardless of anything."

I take a deep breath.

Thinking back to our history, I do believe her, it's just that this is a lot to take in all at once.

"Where's my brother?" I ask. He should be out here talking with us.

"He's in the kitchen, waiting for us to come in."

Now it makes sense why she wanted to meet in the restaurant. I stand up and feel like my knees have turned to rubber bands. Lucy gets up and starts walking towards the kitchen. I follow her through the swinging doors.

Lorenzo is sitting on one of the prep tables, swinging his legs back and forth. He looks like he's about ten years old, and suddenly, I remember our childhood as if it were yesterday.

When we were six, our neighbor, Mrs. Stewart would baby-sit us. She had this amazing tree in her back yard, and one afternoon we had a contest to see who could climb the highest. I've always been short, but that didn't stop me from getting way up in the tree, and when I looked down, all I could see was how high up I was. I was paralyzed by fear and started to cry, but instead of leaving me there, Lorenzo climbed all the way up and sat on the branch with me. Neither one of us could get down, but at least we were together.

Seeing my brother sitting there fills me with compassion. He needs me now, and even though I'm not sure what to do, or say, I can sit here with him and Lucy.

He looks up at us. "Did you guys talk?" he asks jumping off the table.

"Yeah, I told her everything." Lucy walks towards him and takes his hand. I look at the two of them and wonder why I never realized that they're in love.

"I'm happy for you guys," I say honestly.

"We're getting married," Lorenzo beams. "I already talked to Fr. Jim."

"When are you gonna tell Mom and Dad?" I ask.

Lucy and Lorenzo look at each other. "We aren't going to until after the wedding," he says.

"What?" I yell and immediately my heart starts racing again. As much as it will kill my parents to know that Lucy is pregnant, it would be a million times worse if they got married in secret. "Why not?"

"I don't want to put your parents through that kind of stress." Lucy looks at me. If she is going to be part of my family, she's going to have to learn the rules.

"If you guys don't tell them they'll be way more stressed. Look, they're not going to stop you. You're *pregnan*t." I say this with a slight change in tone that makes it sound judgmental. I look at Lucy who is looking at the ground. Oh crap.

"I'm sorry."

"Stella, we're not telling them," Lorenzo says. I can't believe what he's saying. He knows it'll kill our parents to be left in the dark.

"No, you have to."

"She's right," Lucy says firmly. "It's much worse if we sneak around. We need to tell you parents *and* my dad."

My brother feels outnumbered and I wonder if he thinks it'll always be like this. He is marrying his twin sister's best friend. He should have seen it coming. "All right," he sighs.

"Don't worry. I'll help you." I move to hug them both and throw my arms around them. Even though the situation is hard, I'm really happy for them.

Lucy starts to tear up and before I can say anything, Lorenzo cups her face in his hands. "Stay calm, babe," he says and kisses her nose.

Ok, now I'm officially in shock.

Lorenzo looks at me. "You hungry?"

"We have cake," Lucy says. "It's out front."

"No," he shakes his head. "My baby is not eating cake for breakfast."

Ew. I really hope he's talking about the *actual* baby and not Lucy.

"Go out front and relax. I'll make you girls a frittata. I think you have a lot of catching up to do."

I turn to her. "How have you been feeling?" I ask.

"Like shit."

"Me too," I smile.

Lucy looks at me as if she knows all about Drew being engaged. "Let's talk about the home wrecker," she says and leads the way into the dining room.

By the time Lorenzo steps out with the frittata, Lucy knows all the details. "Slut," she says. "I never liked that girl."

I shrug my shoulders. For some reason, Lucy's situation has helped me to see even more clearly that Drew is not the right guy for me. Or maybe Trisha really is pregnant, and Drew is the father. Honestly, I can't deal with this fertility rush right now.

"Here ya go," Lorenzo says placing the eggs in front of us.

I'm so hungry that it's the most beautiful sight I've ever seen. Golden slices of caramelized onions and potato slivers are surrounded by the fluffy eggs. Tiny flecks of green parsley are scattered throughout, and a crumbly layer of blue cheese is browned perfectly on top. Lorenzo has already cut it in slices for us, and drizzled white truffle oil over it. And to think, I was just going to eat a slice of cake.

"This looks incredible." I reach my fork out to stab a slice. But before I get it on my plate, Lucy is up and running towards the bathroom.

Lorenzo and I look at each other.

Oh boy, here we go.

Recipe: Potato and Onion Frittata

Yields 2 servings

So this might not be the best pregnancy food, especially if you're nauseous, but I obviously don't need to worry about that. Not until I'm married at least, and the way things are going, who knows when that'll be.

5 large eggs
1/2 cup sour cream, or plain Greek Yogurt
1/2 cup flat leaf Italian parsley, chopped
1/4 cup Parmigiano Reggiano cheese, grated
1/4 cup extra virgin olive oil
1 potato, peeled and sliced into 1/8" slivers
1 large Spanish onion, diced
1/4 cup gorgonzola cheese
1 tablespoon white truffle oil

1) In a large bowl, whisk together eggs, sour cream, parsley, and grated cheese. Set aside.
2) Heat olive oil in a large oven-proof sauté pan. Add the onions and cook until translucent.
3) Add the potatoes and flatten them over the base of the pan. Cook until potatoes start to brown.
4) Pour the egg mixture into the pan. Lower the heat and cover tightly.
5) Cook until eggs have set.
6) Top with crumbled gorgonzola cheese and place the pan under the broiler until cheese is golden brown.
7) Before serving, drizzle with white truffle oil.

Chapter 13

I've never been so nervous in my entire life.

After we talked, Lorenzo and Lucy decided to tell my parents this weekend.

Last night, instead of coming right home after work, I stayed at the restaurant until 3:00 a.m. baking chocolate chip cookies.

I'm secretly hoping that they'll put everyone in such a good mood, that when Lorenzo and Lucy tell my parents today, my mom will applaud them and my dad will stand up, cookie in hand, and give them a toast.

You never know. From a Food Therapy perspective it is quite possible.

Anyway, the arrangements are all set. Fr. Jim agreed to marry them next Friday night, and afterwards we'll all go to dinner in Atlantic City. Lucy asked me to be her maid of honor (obviously), but told me I could wear whatever dress I wanted. She's not buying a wedding dress, or even getting her hair done. She just wants to marry my brother and doesn't care about all of the hoopla like invitations, cakes, flowers, and dresses.

But I have a strange feeling that it's all sort of an act. Like she's putting up a wall.

In fact, I know it. I *know* Lucy wants something nice, but since her father's not speaking to her, she feels bad about celebrating.

I just hope my parents take it a little better than Mr. Caulden.

But if they don't… well, I'm not even going to think of that.

"We'll mail the invitations next week," Gina says as I walk into the dining room. I know weddings are a big deal and all, but honestly, she could learn a lot from Lucy.

"Hello," my mom chirps. "We're finalizing the guest list for the invitations." She throws me a glance that says she's in total agony. Damn Gina and her stupid plans.

I smile and shuffle into the kitchen, pour myself a cup of coffee, and try to think of a way to change the subject.

"Do you think Lucy will bring a date?" Gina asks when I walk into the dining room.

I'm caught off guard and nearly spit out my coffee. They look at me. "I think she might."

"Oh, is she seeing someone?" my mom asks, genuinely interested. Lucy's never had a real boyfriend before, so this is big news.

"Um, I'm not sure," I lie. I can feel the sweat beading up on my head. "I mean, it's a wedding, everyone brings dates."

"So true." Gina starts flipping through pages of her yellow legal pad.

That was close.

Unlike most normal brides, Gina is not looking to cut down her list, but instead, she's looking to *add* people. She promised the Botanical Gardens that at least 300 guests would show up, and now they have to pay for 300 regardless. When my mother told them to go low, Gina didn't pay any attention. Now she looks at her guest list and seems unsure. "Who are you bringing?"

They both look at me. I reach for a cookie.

Honestly, I hadn't really given it any thought. I mean, until last week I thought I'd be there with Drew, and the whole night we'd be talking about what we wanted at our wedding. Now I've joined the ranks of the pathetic bridesmaids who don't have a date and are forced to dance with the bride's middle-aged cousin all night. Oh God. Gina is from Long Island, which means that her single cousins are extra guidos.

They're still waiting for an answer.

"No one." I shrug it off as if it doesn't matter.

Gina sighs and flips through her list. "Can't you bring someone?"

"I'd rather not." I reach for my second cookie of the morning. Damn these things are good.

"What about Roberto?" my mom interjects.

I wrinkle my nose. I want to explode on her, but I know I can't. Not with Lorenzo and Lucy's big announcement coming her way this morning.

"He's already on the list," Gina sighs, exasperated. "According to Martha Stewart only seventy-three percent of your invited guests will actually attend. That means that to get three 300 people, I need to invite 411. Right now the list is only at 382." She looks as though she might cry.

"For God's sake, Gina. Calm down. It'll be fine. What does Martha Stewart know anyway?" my mom blurts. She's not as good with this wedding stuff as I am.

Gina looks as though her head may pop off. "Martha Stewart is the queen of weddings!"

"She's divorced," my mom adds the last word the way we DiLucios know how. Martha Stewart may be the queen of weddings, but she couldn't hold her marriage together, so my mother discredits everything she says.

I smile and take a sip of my coffee. "We can start inviting customers," I say jokingly.

"That's a great idea. Who can we add?" Gina lights up and grabs her pen.

"Are you crazy?" my mom asks, shooting me a look. "None of our customers even *know* you. Pietro never worked a day in the restaurant. And now that we're closing it will look like we're begging for friends."

Gina throws her pen on the pad. "I guess we'll just have to pay for empty seats."

Before my mom can start her "I told you so" tirade, I jump in. "What about the photographer's dinner? And the wait staff? Their meals can come off head count." I know exactly what I'm talking about because I've read so many restaurant management books.

Ok, maybe not so many. But I've read a few.

"Yes!" Gina squeals. She counts the crew who will pull the wedding together and starts writing their names on the list.

"How was last night?" my mom asks, eager to change the subject.

"It was good. Where's Dad?"

"He went shopping off-shore. I think he's at Wal-Mart."

My father is addicted to shopping at low-end chain stores. He likes to browse through the aisles slowly, looking at all the potential savings. Usually he only buys small things, like shampoo or crackers, but he's been known to make a large dent in the credit card bills. One time he spent a whopping $900 on various household products, replacing our old toaster and microwave with lesser models, which only lasted a year. Still, he loves a bargain. He could be shopping for hours. I look at the clock. It's already 9:30. Lorenzo and Lucy will be over in one hour.

This was *not* in the plan.

I eat another cookie. I've always been an emotional eater, eating more when I'm stressed or worried, or even bored. Lucy is just the opposite. She runs to get her frustrations out, though she's been feeling too sick to lace up her sneakers lately. I think of running upstairs to call her, but I don't move. I don't want to look suspicious.

Pietro and Dante come downstairs. "Good morning," they say and walk into the kitchen for coffee.

God, why is everyone up so early?

Dante sits at the table and takes a cookie. "So, I just got an email from the headmaster," he says looking at me.

What do I care about his headmaster?

"Is everything OK?" my mom asks. Even though my brother has tenure at Philadelphia's top private school, she still worries about job security.

"Yeah, they actually got notice that one of the English teachers is leaving. The headmaster asked about Stella."

I can barely swallow my coffee. How does the headmaster even know I was an English major? "Why did he ask about me?"

"He wanted to invite you to apply."

My mother's eyes light up. "That would be amazing, Stella. You could teach during the off season!" I guess she's excited at the possibility of me actually using my overpriced college degree.

"I don't know," I say. "I never even thought about teaching."

"Well start thinking," Pietro says. "St. Iggy's is the best school in Philly. You won't get an opportunity like this again."

It annoys me when my brothers think they know what's best.

"But maybe I don't want to teach," I snap.

"Why not?" my mom snaps back. "Siete tutti pazzi."

The last thing I wanted to do was to start my mom on *that* number. Especially when Lorenzo is coming in with huge news of his own.

But now I'm upset. I hate it when my family gangs up on me.

"Think of how great it would be to work with Dante and Lucy," Gina chips in. Now *she's* telling me what to do? She's not even family yet.

"Yes, that would be amazing!" my mom adds.

"There's no harm in applying," Dante says. "You can always say no after the interview if you don't want the job."

I know he's right, yet somehow, I feel that if I did interview and were to say no, it would look bad for him. "I'll think about it," I say, hoping to end the conversation.

"Think about what?" Mario says walking into the kitchen. "What's everyone screaming about?"

"Your sister is going to be a teacher!" my mom says getting up to get him coffee.

"Teaching what?" Mario asks sarcastically.

"English," I say defensively. Two seconds ago I was unsure and now I'm defending myself. What's going on this morning?

Lorenzo walks through the door first. "Hey," he says as we all turn to look at him. Lucy follows close behind. "We have something to say."

My heart begins to pound. Are they going to do this right now? In front of everyone? I shoot him a look but he doesn't see me. This is *not* at all how we planned things. They were supposed to speak to my parents alone. I was going to stay close by so that I could step in if needed. This is totally different. My dad isn't even here.

"Why don't you guys have a seat? I made some cookies," I say hoping he'll get the hint.

"What's going on?" Mario asks. He's the only other person who saw Lucy vomit in the kitchen that day, and now I think he suspects something. Maybe I'm just being paranoid.

"Maybe you should wait until Dad gets home," I reply before Lorenzo can even say a word.

"What is it?" my mom asks.

Damn it.

"Lucy and I are getting married." Lorenzo takes her hand. He smiles widely and I'm happy that he's so confident in his decision. Lucy looks a little green.

The room goes silent. I hold my breath, waiting for the big explosion.

"I didn't even know you were dating," says Pietro casually. He really doesn't mean anything by it; since he lives away he misses some things.

"They're not." My mom stands. She looks visibly distressed and I know she understands what's going on. For someone who's so old fashioned, she sure catches on quickly.

I want to jump in but I know it's not my place.

"We've been dating for a few months now," Lorenzo says and looks at everyone. "We just wanted you to know. The wedding is next week."

"What?" Gina says a bit too loudly. She realizes this and looks down at her list of invites, trying to fight off tears.

"What's the rush?" Dante asks. God love him, he is so naïve when it comes to these things.

Everyone in the room is silent and you can cut the tension with a knife.

"Lucy's pregnant." Lorenzo squeezes her hand. He looks at her with love and I can tell that he's excited about being a father.

My mother stoically walks away from the table. We all watch as she walks up the stairs in silence.

We're stunned. It takes a lot to silence my mother. We've never seen her like this. We hear the creaking of the floorboards as she walks to her bedroom, then the boom of her door slamming.

It seems like I have a thousand steps to climb before I reach my mother's bedroom. The door is still closed and as I knock on it, I feel like I'm a little girl who had a nightmare in the middle of the night. "Go away," she screams.

"Mom, it's me."

"Stella I don't want to look at anyone right now."

I take a deep breath. "Mom, open the door."

I wait for her to move but she doesn't, so I turn the doorknob. I open it to see my mother lying face down on top of the bed. She looks up at me. Her eyes are puffy from crying and black mascara is streaked down her cheeks.

"Never in my life would I think one of *my* sons would do this," she says as I walk towards her.

I sit on the bed and put my hand on her back. "Mom, they really love each other. They're getting married."

"Please," she says as if the thought of it sickens her. "That little *puttana* trapped him."

I'm shocked to hear my mom call Lucy a tramp. "Mom you love Lucy. You wanted her to date Dante."

"That was *before* I knew her *true* character," she says. "She had me fooled, and you too."

This is worse than I thought.

"Mom, she didn't fool anyone. And she's *still* my best friend."

My mother looks at me as if I'm crazy. "That's the kind of friend you want? One who uses the entire family, and traps your innocent brother? She's been calculating this one for years. And she goes after Lorenzo because he's the most successful." My mom starts sobbing.

She's lost it. Seriously, she's over the deep end.

"And you act as if you're happy for them!" she screams at me. "Your twin brother! His life is over."

I stand up. "Calm down, Mom."

"You calm down, Stella. My son, my youngest son is marrying a *puttana*. How can I be calm?"

"Mom, they love each other. They're getting married. They're having a bab…"

She puts her hand up to stop me. "I don't even want to think about it. My first grandchild, a bastard."

"You're being ridiculous," I say and turn my back.

"Stella. I'm worried about your father. This will kill him."

"Then you better start dealing with it in a different way," I snap, my heart pounding. "Because it's happening Mom. There's nothing you can do to stop it."

I close the door behind me and instantly regret being so harsh to my mother. Instead of smoothing things over, I pushed her away.

Still, she's being unfair.

Lucy sniffles. "How's your mom?"

"She'll be fine," I say swiftly, though I'm not so sure.

We hear keys in the door and for a moment, we're all paralyzed. Mario stands. Pietro and Gina take Mario's hint, and they all walk out towards the bay.

"Good luck," Dante mutters and follows them.

My dad opens the door and smiles at us. He's carrying five Wal-Mart plastic bags, and I see that he's bought two kinds of soap, bug spray, and some toilet paper. I can't tell what's in the other bags. "Hello," he chirps, taking his keys out of the door.

"Hi Dad." Lorenzo starts walking towards him. "We have something to tell you."

"Where's your mother?" my dad asks in a panic. He can see that Lucy's crying and Lorenzo looks on edge.

"She's upstairs," I say quickly.

"Is she okay?"

"Yeah, she's… fine."

"What's going on then?" my dad asks placing the bags on the dining room table. He takes his wallet and cell phone out of his pocket and places them next to the bags.

Lorenzo doesn't waste any time. "Dad, Lucy is pregnant," he says as if ripping off a Band-Aid.

My dad steps back for a minute. "Lucy." His eyes soften as he looks at her. "Are you all right? Can we help with anything?"

Oh God. He doesn't understand.

She nods her head and looks at Lorenzo.

"Who's the father?" my dad asks looking at me. He expects that since I'm her best friend, I'll have the answers.

"I am," Lorenzo says quietly.

"What?"

"I am, Dad. Lucy and I have been dating for a few months now." He goes and stands next to her chair, placing his hand on her shoulder.

"Dating?" my dad booms.

Lorenzo speaks calmly. "Dad, we really love each other. We're getting married."

Dad sits in the chair next to Lucy. He looks pale.

I feel like I should leave the room but I can't.

"We already talked to Fr. Jim. He agreed to marry us next week. We've been doing Pre-Cana with him in the mornings."

My dad looks at Lucy and then up at Lorenzo. He takes a deep breath. "Let me go and check on your mother."

We wait in silence for my father to return. Lucy continues to cry and I take her hand. "Luce, don't get yourself all worked up. They'll come around." I squeeze her hand.

"I wrecked everything. Your parents hate me and my dad won't even speak to me."

My heart breaks for her. Instead of feeling joyful about her marriage and baby, my best friend is suffering inside. "Be strong," I say though I wish I could think of something else.

Lorenzo paces back and forth nervously.

About an hour later, my father comes downstairs. "I need to ask you both to go. Your mother doesn't want to see you."

Lucy stands, her head down. She walks out of the kitchen and through the screen door.

"This is total bullshit." Lorenzo yells. "After all I do for the family this is how I'm treated?"

"Lorenzo, go," my father demands.

"You know what? You guys can have fun cooking in the restaurant tonight because I'm not doing it." He walks out of the door, slamming it as he exits.

Recipe: Chocolate Chip Cookies for Good Karma

Yields 3 dozen

Even though things didn't go exactly as I planned these cookies are still damn good.

Maybe if my parents would have eaten a few more, they wouldn't be so angry with Lorenzo.

2 1/4 cups all-purpose flour
1 teaspoon baking soda
1 teaspoon salt
1 cup (2 sticks) butter, softened
3/4 cup granulated sugar
3/4 cup packed brown sugar
1 teaspoon vanilla extract
2 large eggs
2 cups chocolate chips

1) Preheat oven to 375 degrees.
2) Combine flour, baking soda, and salt in small bowl.
3) Beat butter, granulated sugar, brown sugar, and vanilla extract in large mixer bowl until creamy.
4) Add eggs, one at a time, beating well after each addition.
5) Gradually beat in flour mixture. Stir in chocolate chips.
6) Drop by rounded tablespoons onto ungreased baking sheets.
7) Bake for 9 to 11 minutes or until golden brown. Cool on baking sheets for 2 minutes.
8) Place on wire racks to cool completely.

Chapter 14

Despite my attempts to call him, Lorenzo doesn't answer his phone. It's 2:30 p.m. and as of now, we have no chef. The phone is ringing off the hook with reservations and I don't want to take any more. But it wouldn't matter anyway. It's Saturday; we're already booked.

Mario is good, but there's no way he can handle all the reservations for tonight.

Maybe I can help. Ok, so I'm not exactly Wolfgang Puck, but I can hold my own. That's it. I'll just ask Lucy to come in and hostess, and I'll don an apron and help Mario out.

Just as I'm about to call Lucy, I see my mother walking towards the restaurant. She's wearing her chef jacket and kitchen clogs. She takes all her frustrations out on the door as she swings it open.

"Does he think I can't handle the kitchen?" she screams at me. "I taught him how to cook!"

She walks past me and through the swinging doors to the kitchen. Her head is held high and her back is straight. She's all business and ready to tackle every order of the night.

The phone rings.

"Hello Lorenzo's, how can I help you?" I say, my eyes still on the kitchen door. I wonder how Mario is taking this one. She'll probably micromanage him the entire night.

"Is this Stella?" a man's voice says knocking me back to reality.

"Yes. Who's this?" I look at the caller ID but the information is blocked.

I wait for a minute.

"Hello?" I'm getting ready to hang up.

"It's Roberto. Lancetti."

Ugh. This is *so* not what I need right now. I wait for him to say more.

"I heard about Lorenzo and I was wondering if you guys needed some help. I'm not doing anything tonight."

How the hell did he hear about Lorenzo? I swear this town taps its phone lines or something.

"We'll be all right," I say and twirl the phone wire around my finger. For a second, I think of telling him to come on by. He can cover the front for a few hours while I smooth things over with my brother. Plus, if we add a third party to the mix my mother will be less likely to explode. But just as quickly as the thought enters my head, I push it away. The last thing I need right now is his pity.

"Ok, well if you need anything, just give me a call."

When I hang up, I can't help but think how kind he is. I mean honestly, Drew would have never offered to roll up his sleeves and pitch in. Still, I'm fairly certain that Mrs. Lancetti has something to do with this. After the whole fiasco with the flowers, I can't really trust her or my mother.

The waiters file in, one by one. Dante comes in last, buttoning his shirt as he walks into the dining room. "How's Mom?" he asks.

"I don't know."

I follow him in the kitchen and we see my brother Mario looking like a seven-year-old who's been scolded. She must have unleashed her fury on him. Thank God for soundproof doors.

My mother methodically slices tomatoes for bruschetta. She and Lorenzo are exactly the same.

"How are you doing?" I ask her.

"I am fine. Can you give me the breakdown of the night?" she snaps. Is she mad at me or something? What the hell did I do? Besides try to hold this damn family together.

By 6:00, I can already tell that the kitchen is slower than normal. I glance around the restaurant and see tables that have been here an hour only just eating salads. That's not good. If it stays like this I'll have crowds of angry people at the front door by 7:00, complaining about the wait time on their reservation. And to be honest, I can't handle that. Not tonight.

The phone rings. I reach for it, hoping it's Roberto offering to help again.

"Hello Lorenzo's."

"Stella, honey, it's Dad." He sounds tired.

"Hi Dad. How are you?"

"I'm doing good. I talked to Lorenzo."

I sigh happily. My dad cannot stand fighting with his sons. Since Mario won't let up, my dad was forced to make peace with Lorenzo.

"He'll be coming there in a few minutes. He just left now."

"Really?" I'm delighted.

"Yeah, just make sure your mother doesn't kill him until all the orders are served."

Like clockwork, my brother arrives a few minutes later. He comes in the front door and sees the crowd of diners eating slowly.

"Thank you," I say to him.

He smiles at me and I know that my dad patched things up. Lorenzo walks into the kitchen and I can't help but follow him. I need to see my mom's face.

She doesn't look up as Lorenzo takes a spot next to her. My mom is normally hard to please, and she's so mad at him that Lorenzo's peace offering is not going to be enough.

He reaches for a ticket and scans the burners. When he sees that it's already been started, he reaches for a different ticket and starts the order.

No one says a word, and I wonder if they'll ignore each other all night.

I return to the hostess desk to see a line of people. I smile at the man in front of me.

"We have a reservation for Johnson," he says leaning over my reservation book. He points to his name, as if I am illiterate.

Doesn't he know that I have a degree in English? I'm almost a teacher for God's sake.

"Ok sir, it's just going to be a few minutes for your table."

"How much is a few. It's already 6:*35*."

I peak around the corner and it looks like we're backed up about fifteen minutes. I know that is way too much for this man, but I really don't feel like flirting. I take a deep breath, reach out my hand and lightly brush his and say, "About five more minutes. Maybe ten maximum."

His wife looks at me as if I'm trying to steal her husband.

"Did you just touch my husband's hand?" she asks coldly.

"No, no, why would I do that?" I stumble for words. "I was swatting away a fly."

She looks unsatisfied.

I give her a huge smile. "I love your…" I look at her and try to find *something* to compliment. "Bag," I say with a grin. She's carrying a faded black carryall, more suitable for a workday than a dinner out with friends.

She huffs as he turns to his friends. "Let's go wait outside, it's too crowded in here." The six of them move out the door. Her husband turns back to look at me and gives me a wink.

Oh God. I'm *never* flirting with an old man again.

Once they're seated, I greet the next couple in line and lead them to a table right next to the dessert case.

"These look amazing," the girl coos and I realize she's talking about the cakes.

"Thanks," I mumble and start to turn away. I glance at the cakes and I have to admit, they do look pretty incredible. Not to brag or anything, but I've gotten really good at the whole baking thing. It's like the worse things are in my life, the better focused on baking I am. It's Food Therapy without the calories (although, I do splurge on a piece of cake every night, but that's for quality control).

"Where do you buy them?" she asks.

I smile, proud of myself. "I make them actually."

“Oh wow,” the girl says. “I can’t wait to try a piece. What’s your favorite?”

I think for a minute and then tell her about the Money Cake, pointing at it for emphasis. Then I smile at her and make my way back to the crowd at the hostess stand.

When they finish their meal the woman approaches me.

“That cake was amazing,” she squeals with a big smile on her face, thanks to my cake and Food Therapy. “Can I order a whole one for next week”

By 10:30 the dining room has slowed down, and when I look at the reservation book, I’m amazed at how many people we’ve served. I go into the kitchen, to see my mother waving tongs at Lorenzo.

“No matter what you’re still my son,” I hear her yell.

“We’re dealing with it. You don’t control my life, Mom,” he shouts back.

“You made that clear this morning.”

“Mom, seriously, what else do you want him to do? What’s done is done,” Mario pipes in.

“You should talk, Mario. You’re crucifying your father for the decision to sell the restaurant. Now he wants to back out of it. But if we do, we’ll lose a lot of money.”

“He does?” Mario asks.

“Yes, because he can’t stand *you* being mad at him.” She’s flailing the tongs around like a crazy woman. I can only imagine what the Russians think. “But I told your father today that we’re selling the restaurant no matter what. I’m going to be a grandmother.” She turns towards Lorenzo. “Who else can help you babysit that baby?”

He throws his arms around her and I can see her start to cry. “I’m still mad at you,” she says. “But it’s not the baby’s fault. And Lucy is going to need help, poor girl. She doesn’t have a mother of her own.”

“Thanks Mom,” Lorenzo sighs.

“And you,” my mom points to Mario. “I’m tired of your bullshit. Go make up with your father.”

Slowly, Mario takes off his apron and walks out the door.

When we lock up the doors to the restaurant at night, my mother links her arm through mine. "I still can't believe Lorenzo and Lucy," she says shaking her head. "I'm really disappointed in them."

I loop my arm around her back. "Thanks for making peace, Mom."

"He's my son. What else can I do? And that poor girl. I'm her only hope."

I widen my eyes. "Well she has a great best friend."

"A sister," my mom corrects me.

I like the ring to it. I always felt that Lucy was my sister anyway, but now, in one week, she really will be.

"Let's throw her a bridal shower," I say without thinking.

My mom looks at me as if I'm nuts. "I don't think your father would want any of our friends to know about this, until after they're married."

"I'm not talking about inviting *other* people. I'm just talking about Lucy, us, and Gina. We can have a little lunch and maybe buy her a few things. We can even do it tomorrow, so Gina's still here."

My mom thinks for a minute. "That would be nice. She needs to relax. She's had a rough day."

As we walk the rest of the way, we plan to take her to Cindy's for brunch. I want to make her some zuccherini cookies, because no Italian bride can get married without them.

The next morning I wake up early to get started on those cookies. The pillow-like confections topped with fluffy coconut flakes are the perfect cookies for a bridal shower, even if there are only four women attending. When we got home last night, we informed Gina of the plans. She got the idea to bring her laptop so Lucy can look at Saks online to choose a few gifts for us to buy her. "It'll be like she's registering," Gina said. Her face lights up at the thought of anyone going through the wedding planning process, even a rushed one.

I'm excited to get started and I reach for my phone to text Lucy. Before we plan all of this stuff for her, we may as well make sure she's free this afternoon. I shoot her a text.

Me: Are you free at 1 today?

Luce: Sure what do you want to do?

Me: *Meet me at Cindy's, we'll do brunch.*

Luce: *Ok. See you at one.*

I still can't believe we pulled all this together in one morning. As I was baking the cookies, Gina and my mother went to order the flowers. Then they both went off shore to buy a small gift bag full of home stuff that you'd normally give a bride. When they called to say that they found the cutest kitchen towels and matching mugs, I almost squealed with delight.

I rush to meet Lucy at our restaurant. My mom and Gina will be going right to Cindy's and should be there when we arrive. Lucy is going to be so surprised when she sees my mom and Gina sitting there. But here we are, the DiLucio girls—for better or for worse.

I sit in front of the restaurant and catch a glimpse of myself in the reflection from the window. My hair is pulled into a high bun, and my turquoise dress is neatly pressed, but I look like I'm faking something. As I look at my façade I start to wonder what I'm really made of.

Who is Stella DiLucio?

Sometimes, I'm not quite sure.

"Hey Stella!" Lucy waves as she walks towards me. "You look so cute!"

I look up at her and see that she's also dressed up. She's wearing a pale yellow tea-length skirt and white tank top. She still wears the Tiffany's necklace that I gave her, and her hair falls in loose waves around her shoulders. "You look great too."

"Thanks, we had to meet with Fr. Jim before Mass this morning. We had the last of our PreCana sessions today. This was the only thing that didn't make me look like a cow."

She can't be serious. Lucy is the skinniest pregnant girl I've ever seen.

"How were they?" I say changing the subject.

"What?"

"The PreCana classes?"

"Oh. They weren't that bad. We thought it would be weird since Fr. Jim knows I'm pregnant, but he's been really cool about the whole thing."

I smile. "You ready to go?"

"Yeah, I can't wait for a short stack."

"Get the large one, you're eating for two," I laugh.

She laughs. As we cross the street a tiny flash catches my eye. "Is there something you want to show me?"

Oh my God, yes," she squeals and holds up her left hand. My brother has given her a beautiful diamond solitaire ring. I take her hand and inspect it.

"Stunning," I say. "Did you pick this?"

She laughs. "No, Lorenzo did a good job. I wasn't expecting a ring at all actually."

For some reason, the ring reminds me of Drew and for a minute, I think I might cry. I take a deep breath. "I'm so excited for you." I smile and open the door to Cindy's.

Cindy greets us as we enter the restaurant. "Your table is all set girls," she says giving me a thumbs up. I smile at her.

Lucy walks ahead of me and stops when she sees my mom and Gina at our table. She looks at the balloons, the flowers, the cookies, and the giant gift bag and starts to cry.

"Surprise," Gina and my mom say.

"You guys are amazing."

She's right though. It *is* amazing that my mother could change so quickly, but that's the way my family is. We stick together no matter what, and now Lucy is a part of that.

My mother stands and gives Lucy a hug, which makes her cry even harder.

"Lucia, I am happy to have you as my daughter. You always were anyway."

"Thanks," Lucy says and wipes her eyes.

"Welcome to your bridal shower." I take a seat next to her.

"Thanks guys, you really didn't have to do this."

"Yes we did, you're the bride," Gina squeals.

The waitress approaches our table and we all order pancakes. My mom and I get blueberry, Gina gets chocolate chip, and Lucy orders hers plain.

"I hope I can keep these down," she says when the waitress leaves. She's already looking a little green.

"Try drinking a glass of whole milk," my mom says. "It really helped me when I was pregnant."

"Did you get morning sickness?" Lucy asks.

"Ha, I had it so bad with the twins. They started giving me *agita* their first week of life." My mom looks at me. "And twenty-seven years later, they haven't stopped." She sticks out her tongue.

"Hey," I say. "I am an *angel* compared to Lorenzo."

Lucy laughs because she's seen me at my worst.

The waitress passes by and Lucy orders a glass of whole milk.

We must look funny celebrating a bridal shower on the back deck of Cindy's instead of in some mansion like we did for Gina, but the truth is, I like this much better. My mother is relaxed and making jokes, Gina looks like she's having fun, and Lucy is so overwhelmed with our surprise that she flips between laughing and crying. We all laugh at her.

"With all those hormones you'd better watch out. You might be having twins," my mom warns.

"Can you imagine?" Lucy says dreamily. She looks off in the distance and I see her face get sad. I wonder if she's thinking about her mother.

"Open your present!" I order and thrust the bag in front of her.

Lucy smiles and pulls the tissue paper out of the pink gift bag. She removes canary yellow dishtowels with an embroidered

D stitched in blue on them. “Oh,” she coos. “They’re so cute. I love yellow.” She laughs.

“We know you better than you think,” my mom says and pats her on the shoulder.

Lucy takes out two sunny porcelain mugs and smiles. “Prefect for our morning coffee,” she says. “Thanks guys.”

“There’s one more thing,” Gina says reaching into her bag. She takes out her laptop and starts typing, then flips the screen towards Lucy. “You need to select something wonderful from Saks.”

“No, I can’t,” Lucy says, embarrassed.

“Please, do you *know* what kind of a discount I get?” Gina insists. “Now pick something nice, a stunner.”

We watch as Lucy scrolls through the items on the screen. She clicks on a few images to make them bigger, and then finally decides on an extra fluffy feather bed. “I’ve always wanted one,” she beams.

“It’ll be yours by next week,” Gina says. “From me and Pietro.”

Lucy gives her a hug. “Thank you.”

“Ok, one more thing.” My mother pulls an envelope from her purse and hands it to Lucy.

I had no idea she was planning something else. Am I the only one who didn’t get Lucy something special?

Lucy opens the card and reads the message that my parents have written her. She starts to cry and dabs her eyes with a napkin. “Thanks, Mom.”

“We’ll go shopping for it after the wedding.”

“For what?” I ask.

“A washer and dryer,” Lucy says. “So we don’t have to go down to the basement of Lorenzo’s building.”

An awkward moment passes, where we’re all realizing that this is really happening. Lucy and Lorenzo are getting married.

Gina steps in. “Tell me about your dress.” She looks at Lucy with a sparkle in her eyes.

"I don't know what I'm wearing yet," Lucy replies. "I guess I'll go buy something new."

Gina looks appalled and I can tell she's itching to say something. Luckily my mom jumps in. "Whatever makes you comfortable, Lucia."

Just like that, an idea hits me.

"You know what happens after a bridal shower right?" I ask with a twinkle in my eye.

"What else can happen? I'm getting married in six days?"

"You can't get married without having a bachelorette party," I explain. My mom and Gina both look at me as if I've lost it, and Lucy stares at me blankly.

"Make yourself available on Tuesday." I say. "All day."

Recipe: Zuccherini Cookies for an Italian Bride

Yields 3 dozen

Ok, so maybe Lucy's not really Italian. But she's going to be part of our family now, and no DiLucio girl can have a shower without these cookies. Even if you're not Italian, you can make them for a bridal shower. They're pretty much the perfect cookies.

1 1/2 sticks of butter
1 cup of sugar
6 eggs
1 teaspoon vanilla
3 tablespoons of baking powder
3 1/2 color cups flour

for the icing:
3 cups powdered sugar
1 stick of butter (softened)
2 teaspoons lemon juice
2 tablespoons milk

1 bag of shredded coconut

1) Preheat oven to 425 degrees.
2) Cream the butter and sugar, then add eggs one at a time. Beat well.
3) Add the vanilla and mix well.

4) Slowly add in the flour and baking powder. Mix until incorporated.
5) Drop teaspoons of dough onto a greased cookie sheet 2 inches apart.
6) Bake for 6 minutes or until the bottoms are slightly golden.
7) Place on a cooling rack to cool completely before icing.

For the icing:

1) Mix powdered sugar, lemon, butter, and milk together in a large bowl until smooth.
2) Divide the icing into a few separate bowls and add a few drops of food coloring into each bowl. My mother usually makes one pink bowl of icing and one pale green. She leaves the last one white for a nice array of color.
3) Ice cookies and top with shredded coconut.
4) Place cookies in an airtight container and they will last 4 days.
5) You can also freeze the cookies in an airtight container and defrost them at room temp two hours before serving (or you can eat them frozen like I do. That's Food Therapy at its finest).

Chapter 15

Tuesday can't come fast enough. I wake at 6:00 a.m. and I *know* the day is going to be great. My best friend and brother are getting married in four days, and all the plans are set.

I pick Lucy up at Lorenzo's at 7:00 a.m. She's been staying there openly since the big news hit, and though my parents are not pleased with them living together before the wedding, they've kept their mouths shut. At this point what can they really say?

I honk twice.

Lucy walks out of the apartment wearing slim fit jeans, a long gold tank top, and brown flip flops. Her hair is pulled off her face, and big hoop earrings hang from her ears. She looks at me as she gets in the car. I'm wearing a pale grey pencil skirt and a black tank top. Of course, I'm in heels.

"Am I dressed okay?"

"You look beautiful, mamma." I smile as she gets in the car.

"So what kind of wild and crazy stuff are we doing at 7:00 a.m.?" she asks sinking into the seat.

I start laughing. "Don't worry about it." I pull the car out of the driveway.

"Can we at least stop at Quick Mart? I need some breakfast."

"Of course," I say and turn the car around.

Lucy buys a large bottle of whole milk and a granola bar. I opt for a large coffee with French vanilla cream.

"Your mom's trick really worked," Lucy says as we get back into the car. She opens the cap to her milk bottle and takes a sip. "I think the milk coats my stomach."

"Well keep drinking it then, because we have a long day ahead of us."

"Where are we *going*?" she whines and stamps her feet. Lucy's acting about five years old. She's going to be a *mother*?

"Relax. The only thing I need you to do is pick some music." I hand her the leather CD case from the console. "Something upbeat."

She decides on Beyoncé as I pull onto the Garden State Parkway. We car dance for a few hours, laughing and gossiping like old times.

That's the thing about best friends. No matter what happens between you, you'll always be able to brush it off and, eventually, laugh.

We make it to Bella Sposa's just as they open at 11:00. When I called Maria to ask her about a dress, she suggested we get there early, so that Eva will have time to make any alterations before we leave tonight.

When Lucy sees the back and white-striped awning she looks at me. "You took me here to pick up your bridesmaid's dress? That's not exactly a fun bachelorette activity."

I open the car door. "Get out. It's time for you to pick your wedding dress." I step out of the car and into the August heat.

"What are you talking about?" she says shutting the door. "Even if I *wanted* a wedding dress, I won't have time to order one."

"That's exactly why we're here. I have pull with the owners. We're getting you a sample." I start walking to the front door.

Lucy remains near the car. "Stell, I don't have money for one of these dresses. We're trying to save every penny for the baby," she frowns.

I look at my best friend. "Which is why *I'm* buying you the dress."

She shakes her head. "No, Stella, you won't have a job after September. Plus with Gina and Pietro's wedding, you'll be broke by Christmas."

I walk towards her. The morning sun is already hot, and if we stand out here much longer, she'll be all sweaty. You can't try on wedding gowns if you're sweaty. It's against the rules. I'm sure Martha Stewart would agree.

"Lucy I *won* the money in AC. It's play money," I say grabbing her arm. "Come on."

She tries to resist, but I can see that she's excited. "I can't let you do this."

"It's already done. Come on."

She lets me pull her until we get to the doors, then she smoothes out her tank top and follows me inside.

"Look at this beautiful bride," Charlene coos as she greets us in the entranceway. "With a body like this, we'll have plenty of options."

Maria scans Lucy up and down then looks at me. "You didn't tell me your best friend is a model."

Lucy laughs.

"Who do you think I roll with?" I joke.

She laughs and motions for us to follow her. "Come sit down. Let's talk about styles."

Lucy looks around the room as if in a trance. Bella Sposa's sitting room is so luscious with its soft leather couches and marble floors that it's easy to get swept away.

"What kind of bride are you?" Maria asks professionally.

"I have no clue. I was going to go to the BCBG outlet in Atlantic City to look for a dress. I didn't expect this."

"So you're an easy one to please, huh? Follow Charlene upstairs while I pick some gowns for you. We'll go from there."

In the dressing room, we sit on the small bench and wait for Maria. "I don't know how to thank you, Stella," Lucy says as tears fill her eyes. "I never imagined I'd have to get married so quickly."

"But you want to, right?"

"More than anything. It's just that, I wish I had more time to plan things. I mean, it would be nice to do things like Gina." She looks down for a minute, and then adds. "Not that I deserve those things."

My heart breaks a little. "You deserve even more, Luce. Why would you even say that?"

"My dad isn't even *talking* to me, Stella. And I caused problems in your family too."

"You didn't cause any problems," I lie.

"Stella, I saw how your parents reacted."

"Yeah but my parents always freak out, Luce. They love you." I get up to hug her.

"Thanks," she says. I can see tiny drops forming in her eyes.

"I'm glad we're here, getting you a proper dress."

"You're the best," she says and hugs me tight.

Maria arrives with five dresses. "We'll start with these. While we're trying them, Charlene is gathering more. We'll look for a style you can take home today."

Lucy is beaming as she steps on the platform. Maria unveils the first dress: a wondrous satin mermaid style gown with a long train, spaghetti straps, and plunging V-neck. I hold my breath. It's gorgeous.

"I love it," Lucy coos and Maria slips it over her head and lets the dress fall. The satin wraps around her body, hitting every curve in all the right spots. Even though she's pregnant, Lucy's stomach is flat as a board. She doesn't even need Spanx.

I put my hand to my stomach and feel it's softness. I really need to start working out.

"My boobs already started to grow," she shrieks and looks at her chest in the mirror. "I have cleavage!"

"And you can work it, girl," Maria says. She pins the straps tight, adjusting the drop of the neckline and making the dress look even better.

Lucy turns to look at the back view in the three-way mirror. "I love the train." Maria fans it out so we can get a full view. The satin is cut to reflect the light, and it seems to create an aura around her.

"Now dance around a little. Go and sit. See if you're comfortable."

Lucy steps down and sits on the bench next to me. "What do you think?"

"You're absolutely beautiful." There's nothing more to say.

She stands back on the platform. "I love it. I'll take it."

Maria laughs. "How many wedding dresses have you tried on in your life?"

"One," Lucy replies still looking at her reflection.

"Then you can't possibly decide rationally. You're love struck. Take the dress off and we'll put it in the yes pile."

"No, I don't need to try on anymore. I want this one."

The way she says it, full of conviction, makes everyone take notice. I can't help but be jealous of Lucy because she is getting everything she wants. I thought I knew what I wanted when I was with Drew, but that all blew up in my face. Now, as much as I hate to admit, I'm thinking of Roberto in the same way. Could I possibly have a future with him? Does he even genuinely like me or is it just his mom trying to fix us up? And am I just thinking of him because I desperately want to get married?

"This girl knows what she wants," Maria says snapping me out of my thoughts. "That's a good trait for a bride."

We all smile but Maria's words hit me differently. What do I want? I just feel lost. And confused. I try not to let the familiar feelings of dread sink in. I won't let them.

"Ok, time for the veil," Maria says, ushering the appointment along. Lucy is wearing her dress and glowing. "And shoes. I'll be right back with some samples. What size are you?"

"Ten," Lucy says and Maria raises her eyebrows.

"I'm assuming you want a little heel, right?"

"Not too high though, Lorenzo is only two inches taller than me."

I can't help but laugh. Lucy's main criteria for a boyfriend was that she always wanted to be able to wear heels with him. Lorenzo, her future husband, just makes the cut.

Maria shuts the door behind her.

"Do you like this one?" Lucy asks.

"It's perfect. It really is."

Maria returns with a long veil and places it on Lucy's head. She pushes the blusher in front of Lucy's face and I almost start to cry. Lucy is getting married.

"Wow," Lucy says. "This is it. I love it."

"Me too," I agree. My friend looks stunning. She beams as Eva starts pinning the dress, marking where she needs to adjust it.

"Now Stella, how about we get you in a few dresses, just for fun?" Maria asks me.

For a minute I'm caught off guard, but then I realize that if I'm going to get over Drew I need to face the facts. "I'm not getting married anytime soon."

"You never know," Maria says with a smile.

"Oh, I know. My boyfriend broke up with me." I try my hardest to say this without any emotion.

"You can get him back." Maria winks at me.

I sigh. "Even if I wanted to, I can't. He's already with someone else."

"A total slut," Lucy adds and we all laugh.

"Well then the guy was a loser anyway," Maria adds. "Any new ones in the works?"

Lucy perks up. "One of Lorenzo's friends is totally in love with her."

I shoot Lucy a look. "He's a family friend and he's so not in love with me. Our mothers are trying to set us up."

"Is he cute?" Maria asks.

"He's totally hot," Lucy responds. I shoot her another look. "What? He is!"

"Regardless, I'm just not interested," I lie. It's better not to get my hopes up anyway.

It's 12:30 when we step out of Bella Sposa. Maria told us to go to lunch, and hang around Towson for a while as Eva makes the adjustments.

I want to take Lucy to Vince's crab shack, but she's not up for fish, so we go to a diner instead.

As soon as we step into Chubby's, the place feels right. The restaurant is decorated in a 1950s style motif, with black and white checkered floors and red vinyl seats.

We take a booth in the back and start flipping through the menu.

"Do you think a milkshake will coat my stomach just like milk does?" Lucy asks after a minute.

"Yeah," I say, looking down at their milkshake list. "I just wouldn't go for the peaches and cream." I look at it again. "Or the Monstrous Mint."

She laughs." "I was just thinking vanilla."

"That's pretty boring," I say. "Look at this list, there's like fifty to choose from."

"I'm a girl who *knows* what she wants." Lucy repeats Maria's words and suddenly, I feel sick. Why don't I know what *I* want.

"I need a milkshake too," I say folding my menu and placing it on the table.

Before Lucy can respond, a waitress comes to our booth. Lucy orders a vanilla milkshake and a grilled cheese, and I follow her lead, and order a grilled cheese too.

"Something to drink?" the waitress asks me.

I take a minute to scroll down the list. "I'll take a Death by Chocolate milkshake."

When all else fails, I turn to chocolate.

Recipe: Death by Chocolate Milkshake

Yields 1 serving

For when you're facing a million options and your life seems to be spiraling out of control.

So it's not exactly chocolate cake, but trust me ladies, there's nothing as pleasant as chocolate when you're stressed. I should know. You know how stressed I've been lately.

1 cup chocolate ice cream
1/2 cup hot fudge
1 shot of espresso
1/2 cup milk
2 cups of ice

1) Place all ingredients into a blender.
2) Blend until all the ice is crushed.
3) Drink your problems away.

Chapter 16

On August 10th we'll do something we've never done before. We'll close the restaurant on a Friday night. Luckily, when Lorenzo and Lucy told me their plans a week ago I didn't have to cancel too many reservations. People understood, especially when I told them we were having a family emergency and needed to close. In a lot of ways, this wedding feels like an emergency, and I'm just hoping we can all get through it without any major blowouts.

Lucy wakes up around 11:00 on the day of her wedding. She's never been a late sleeper; being a teacher she's used to getting up at the crack of dawn. I wonder how she'll manage during the school year.

"Morning Mrs. DiLucio," I say when she opens her eyes.

She smiles and stretches. "I'm still a Caulden for the next couple hours."

I throw a pillow at her and she swats it away. "Good thing you woke up," I say. "I'm starving."

"Me too, I need a huge breakfast. Dinner won't be until nine."

I stand up and Lucy follows.

"Give me five minutes and I'll be ready to go," she says ducking into the bathroom.

Cindy's is packed for a Friday but, of course, she doesn't make us wait. She knows what a big day this is for Lucy and my brother, and wants to do everything she can to make it special.

We follow her out to the deck and take a seat at our usual table. As we settle into the white plastic chairs, it hits me that this is the last time Lucy and I will be sitting here.

Everything will change after her wedding. She'll spend more time with my brother; they'll raise a family; buy a house together.

And where will I be?

I don't even know what I'm going to do for a job.

Worse, I don't even know what I *want* out of life.

My chest begins to tighten.

Oh my God. I can't breathe…

The waitress comes to take our order and miraculously, I catch my breath.

"Two short stacks?" she asks. We're regulars, and any good waitress would remember our order.

I nod my head.

"I think I'll get an egg sandwich," Lucy says looking up at the waitress. "With extra bacon."

I feel my eyes widen. Lucy is *changing* her order?

The waitress nods. "Do you want the bacon extra crispy?"

"That would be great!" Lucy squeals as if she's acting normal.

I can't help it; I start to tear up.

"What's wrong?" Lucy asks when the waitress walks away. She can always sense when I'm about to freak out.

"This is our last time here together," I say and as the words come out of my mouth, the tears begin to roll.

"I'm getting married, I'm not going to die," she laughs.

"I know, but *everything*'s changing."

"Is this about the egg sandwich?" she asks sincerely. "I read that pregnant women need extra protein, if you want I can change my ord…."

"It's not about *that*," I interrupt.

"Well what the hell's wrong then?" She takes a sip of milk.

I sniffle. "You and Lorenzo will have a family and I'll still be single and alone." I wipe away a few tears. As much as I can, I try to push the thought out of my mind, but somehow, it keeps coming back to me. So much for getting my spark back.

Lucy gets up and puts her arms around me. "It'll all be fine Stella."

"No it *won't,*" I say firmly. "Everyone is getting on with their lives and I'm stuck."

"Who's everyone?"

"You. Lorenzo…"

"Ok, me and Lorenzo are a different case. This just *happened.* If I weren't pregnant we wouldn't be getting married so soon. And besides, I'm the one who's stuck." She pats her stomach. "When this little one arrives I'll be a stay at home mommy."

This is news to me. "What about your teaching job?"

"I'm giving it up. Besides, Lorenzo and I have a new project in the works."

I look at her, confused. "What?"

"We're opening a place in Philly. Lorenzo found a small restaurant and signed the lease last week. We're telling everyone tonight."

My heart leaps a little. I'm sure they'll ask me to be the manager. This solves everything.

I can imagine it already. I'll be featured in *Philadelphia* magazine as the most stylish manager in the city. For the photo shoot I'll be wearing a one of a kind Marc Jacobs dress…

"Mario partnered up with us actually. He's going to manage," Lucy explains.

"What about me?"

"You hate managing the restaurant." Lucy looks shocked. "You always say you're just doing it for your family."

"But what am I supposed to do? I need a job." I look down at the table because I know that if I look at her I'll cry.

"You'll figure it out," she says. How is this a logical response? Why does everyone keep saying this to me? Just as I'm about to break down, Lucy continues. "And if you don't figure it out, you can just live with us and babysit your godchild."

"You want me as a godmother?"

"Only the best for my baby," Lucy replies.

I'm moved. "What would I do without you?"

"You'd be a freakin' mess." She smiles. "But I'd be a bigger one without you."

At 5:00 p.m. my mom, Gina, and I gather in the master bedroom to help Lucy get dressed. Our hair is all curled and set with millions of little bobby pins, lacquered with hair spray and gel. (After finding the perfect dress, Lucy decided we needed to get our hair done. Thank God we have connections in this town).

As I unzip the garment bag containing Lucy's dress Gina and my mom light up. They haven't seen it yet and if they like it now, I can't wait to see their reactions when she puts it on.

Helping her into the dress is a three-woman job. Gina holds her veil to make sure it doesn't tangle in the fabric. My mom holds the dress open low to the ground so Lucy can carefully step into it and I hold her hand, keeping her balanced. I give her a squeeze and she looks up at me full of bliss. She straightens up and smoothes the fabric.

"Belissima," my mom says and hugs Lucy. "You're so beautiful, Lucia."

Lucy beams.

"Girls," my dad yells from downstairs. "It's time."

We look at the clock in the bedroom. "Crap." I am still in my bra and underwear. I reach into the closet to get my dress and step into it. This light peach number is so hot that I almost wish I had a date. "You guys start going, I'll be down in a second."

My mom and Gina help Lucy down the stairs, holding her train as they walk.

I step into my sliver stiletto sandals and take one last look at myself in the mirror. Gina did a fabulous job with the make-up. I look good. Really Good. Like trouble.

I hurry down the stairs just in time to see Lucy hugging her dad. I feel like I'm witnessing a miracle.

Deep down, I knew he'd come around.

I place my arm on my mother's shoulder. "I'm so happy he came."

"Me too," my mom whispers.

We follow Lucy and her father into the driveway as they get into the limo. My mom asks if I want to ride with her and my dad, but I'd rather walk the two blocks to the church.

I get halfway down the block when I see him.

Roberto Lancetti is walking towards me, wearing a black suit, white shirt, and skinny black tie. His hair is ruffled up in a way that looks like he spent too much time on it, and he's wearing Ray Ban aviators. I just watch him for a minute and I have to admit, he looks good. Really good. Like trouble. Still, I haven't seen him since that night on the street and I really don't feel like explaining things.

"What are you doing here?" I ask when he comes closer.

"I was invited to the wedding," he smiles. "You look beautiful."

I can feel myself blushing. "Thanks. Did my mom put you up to this?"

He looks a little hurt. "No, Lorenzo invited me."

"It was just supposed to be family members."

He winks at me. "I'm practically family, aren't I?'

I ignore the comment and start walking down the street and he strides along beside me.

"Are you feeling better?" he asks.

I sigh. "Yeah, thanks. Look I sort of just want to forget that night, ok?"

"What night?" he says with a smile.

I can't help but smile back, though I am totally going to kill Lucy and Lorenzo for inviting him. What's with my family trying to push us together

"Are you coming to the dinner too?" I ask.

"Yeah, actually, I'm your ride."

I look at him for a second to see if he's joking or not. Unfortunately he's serious.

We walk the next block in silence.

My brothers are already inside when we arrive. Roberto takes a seat as I hang outside with Lucy.

"Did you like your surprise?" she asks. I swear, if it weren't her wedding day, I would kill her.

"You shouldn't have."

The organist begins to play and my parents process, arm in arm down the aisle. I'm next and as I walk down the marble floors of St. Luke's I feel as though I'm in a dream.

Is this really happening?

Is my best friend *really* marrying my twin brother?

I see Lorenzo at the altar, anxiously awaiting his bride.

I take Mario's arm and bow at the altar, and then walk off to the side and watch as my friend walks down the aisle, unafraid of what the future holds.

The ceremony lasts about an hour, during which I go from crying (when I saw my brother Lorenzo tear up) to laughing (when Fr. Jim cracked a joke about the honeymoon at the beach) and crying again (when they finally said their vows and became husband and wife). I'm thankful that I'm standing on the altar with them.

We follow the bride and groom out of the church, and even though the only people in attendance were family members (and Roberto), there's a feeling of relaxation in the air. I hand out the small paper cones of rose petals that Gina and I made in the morning, and we all throw the flowers in the air as Lucy and Lorenzo kiss on the church steps.

Everyone claps and Roberto takes my hand in his. I feel a surge of electricity run through me, but I quickly pull away. No use getting excited over him when he's only here because my family is trying to get us together.

Roberto wasn't lying. It becomes evident that he really is my chauffer when everyone scurries to their cars without even offering me a ride. I mean, honestly. Fortunately, the ride is not awkward at all. We spend most of the time talking about Rome, and what an amazing city it is.

"I wish I could just pack up and move there," I say as we enter Atlantic City. Roberto gives me a strange look and I know exactly what he's thinking. It's a stupid idea. I should grow up and focus on my life.

By the time we pull up to the Villa it's dusk and the neon lights shine brightly in front of us. The building's façade changes from purple to green to gold, and looks more luxurious than ever on this wedding night.

The restaurant is equally as breathtaking.

Now I understand why Chuck would leave us to come work here. It's decorated with sparse, modern furniture and luscious blue suede couches fill the bar area. Blown glass chandeliers hang every few feet and low votives light the tables.

"Oh my Gawd," says Gina in her nasal voice.

"DiLucio, party of thirteen," my father says to the maitre'd.

"Ah yes," the man replies and instantly I can tell he's a little 'light in the loafers' as my dad would say, so naturally I want him as my friend and fashion consultant. "We have a private room for you, please, follow me."

My brothers glance at each other. Gina raises her eyebrows and straightens her posture. After all, there could be celebrities lurking around every corner.

"Stella," I hear Lucy call and I turn around. She is standing in the entrance of the restaurant, holding hands with her new husband. A warm glow fills me and all I can think to do is clap my hands. Other diners take the cue and start clapping as well, and Lucy's face lights up. Lorenzo kisses her and the entire restaurant breaks into applause. Some people even clink their knives on their glasses, and both the bride and groom smile so widely.

They walk towards us and most patrons continue to clap as we file into our private dining room.

The room is decorated the same as the restaurant, except a long table fills most of the room. The flowers from Dots and Bows look like they were custom tailored to this room. Gerber daisies and soft colored roses fill the bulk of each vase, and to match the décor, Dotty, the owner, tied huge navy blue organza ribbons and tucked them into each vase. Even Gina raises her eyebrows.

Votive candles run down the center of the table, and the room is so dimly lit that Lucy's white dress sticks out like a shining star. She's glowing.

To the left of the table, the cake is on display, and when I see it I can hardly believe that Chucker made such a spectacular work of art. Its three tiers are each covered with white fondant and filled different color roses, white and pink peonies and huge gardenias. The topper is two L's intertwined to form a heart shape. I *need* to see the cake up close.

The white fondant is decorated in an intricate beaded pattern all around the edges of each layer and the flowers spill out. For a moment, I think that he's cheated and used real flowers, but I touch one and see that it is actually made of sugar. Each one is crafted by hand and must have taken him hours. From up close, I can see the cake topper is made of pure sugar, and stretched to resemble transparent glass. Suddenly I feel bad for getting mad a Chuck for leaving us. He had no room to grow at Lorenzo's. Here he can really be the artist that he is.

Roberto comes up behind me. "The cake is amazing, huh?"

I turn around and my heel wobbles. Before I can stop myself, I fall in his arms, which he wraps around me. It feels so comfortable there, that for a minute, I can almost picture us together. I pull away and adjust myself, but can feel Roberto staring at me. "Sorry," I mumble.

A waiter approaches us with a tray of champagne glasses. Roberto takes one for me and one for himself. He hands me the glass and we wait for the toast. Once everyone receives a glass, Lorenzo taps on his and raises it in the air. "Lucy and I want to thank everyone for all your love and support in these past couple weeks. We appreciate and love all of you, and are so happy that you're here to share this wonderful day with us."

My brother has always been a man of few words, so his speech hits me hard. I glance at my mother who is dabbing the corners of her eyes, and I look away before I *completely* lose it.

We all clink glasses and take sips of the champagne. The sweetness tastes so good, and I realize that I haven't eaten a thing since Cindy's pancakes this morning.

Mario raises his glass. "As the best man, I need to make a toast."

We all look at him.

"I never imagined that my little brother would get married before me..."

"Neither did I," Pietro calls out and we all chuckle.

"... But I can't imagine a person more perfect for him than Lucy. Luce, you were already like a sister to all of us, and now you really are. Welcome to the family."

We all clink glasses again and I notice I've already drunk most of my champagne.

I need to slow down a little.

A waiter comes around with a tray of beef tartar on fried wontons. I take one from the tray, and a cocktail napkin from the waiter's hand. The tartar is both sweet and savory at the same time and I think they've added some soy sauce, which is typical to modern restaurants. It seems like everyone is always adding an Asian-inspired theme to everything nowadays.

I glance at my parents and can tell right away they don't like it. They're more traditional and would probably prefer clams casino and baby lamb chops. It's a wedding after all.

The next tray contains oysters on the half-shell. They've simply been shucked and topped with a spicy cocktail sauce. I'm not the biggest fan of oysters, but these are pleasant, not too briny or salty. I wash it down with the rest of my champagne and before I am even able to look around, a waiter pours more into my glass.

"Thanks," I say as he walks away. "Great service here."

Roberto looks at me and nods. Honestly, since I mentioned moving to Rome he's barely said two words to me. I know it was a stupid idea, but I was just daydreaming.

"Kobe beef," another waiter says holding a tray for me to see. "Seared rare."

My mom approaches us. "These fancy restaurants don't seem to cook anything," she says. As talented as my mother is, she's still old school when it comes to temperature and is a strong believer that all meat and fish should be cooked through. "Poor Lucy can't eat any of this."

I realize she's right and I look around to see Lucy talking to her father. She's sipping on club soda. I'm sure she hasn't eaten anything.

I grab a menu card off the table. Who planned this anyway? Did Lorenzo and Lucy forget to mention that she's *pregnant*?

Ok, honestly, it *all* sounds amazing but I'm not sure that Lucy can eat any of it. I walk towards her and wait for her to notice me. Her father turns to talk to my dad, and she looks at me. "Stell, this day has been perfect," she says and throws her arms around me. "None of it would have been possible without you!"

"I'm so happy for you," I reply and smile. "But, Luce, what are you going to eat?" I hold the menu card up for her to see.

"Oh yeah, I know there's not much I can eat. We figured it's okay, since I've been so nauseous."

"You need to eat *something*!" God, I sound more like my mother each day. But I can't help it. I envision her collapsing by 9:00, and having to be rushed to the hospital.

"I know," she says. "I'll eat bread."

"You're not having bread and water on your wedding day," I say sternly. "That's prison food!"

She laughs. "I'll be having cake too. Did you see it?" She beams.

"Yeah, it is pretty much the most gorgeous cake I've ever seen." I lean in a bit closer and whisper, "I think Gina is jealous."

Lucy giggles. "It's filled with vanilla cake and nutella."

"Sounds like a dream," I say. "I'll have to save room for dessert." I take a sip of champagne and notice I've already finished my second glass. This stuff goes down like water. It's *so* much better than André.

When I think of Lucy only one thing comes to mind. Macaroni and cheese. Since I've known her, I don't think she's gone a week without Kraft macaroni and cheese. Even when my mom tried to make her a gourmet version, Lucy preferred the boxed stuff with the powdered cheese. At one point in our friendship, I caught her buying two boxes at once, using the pasta from one, and the cheese from both to make her meal.

Even now that almost everything makes her want to vomit, she still falls back on her mac and cheese. It's perfect, Chuck can just slip out and buy her a box, then cook it up and serve it while we're eating. I can already envision her face lighting up. "I'll be right back." I stroll towards the kitchen.

"Hello," I say pushing open the winging door to the kitchen. The executive chef sees me and in a panic, looks around for a waiter.

"Someone will be right out to serve you," he says.

I walk into the kitchen and see the organized line of chefs, all men, concentrating on the tickets in front of each of their stations.

"I actually wanted to speak to you," I say approaching the chef. He looks a little confused. "I'm with the DiLucio party. We have a small problem with the menu."

The chef grabs a paper menu from the line and looks over it. "I went through this with Lorenzo yesterday afternoon. He confirmed everything." He looks away from me and back at his chefs, who are all pretending not to listen.

"Oh I know, and it really looks delicious. It's just that the bride is, well, pregnant, and can't eat anything on this menu."

"All right, we'll make her something else." He clicks his pen, flips the menu over and begins writing ideas down. "Does she like chicken?"

"She's been so nauseous lately I don't think she can eat it. The only thing she'll eat is mac and cheese."

"We have a lobster mac and cheese on the menu. I guess I can make it plain for her."

Ok, I need to be tactful here. Sometimes chefs have egos and I don't want to insult him. "Um, it might be better to just make the boxed kind."

The chef looks at me as if I've just damned him to hell. "The what?"

"You know, the kind that comes in a box with the powdered cheese. Just add milk." I smile.

"Are you nuts? Do you think I'd serve that garbage in my restaurant?" I see his face getting redder by the second.

"I know it's an unusual request, but it *is* her wedding day," I say with a smile. He doesn't look amused.

"And I *said* I'd make mac and cheese," he says. "But if you expect me to serve some boxed crap to one of my guests, you've got it all wrong."

I see that he's not going to give in, so I smile and thank him. Obviously he has *no idea* who he's dealing with. As a restaurant manager, I know the customer is always right, even if it means overriding the chef and going straight to the top.

I turn my back and exit into our private room. I see Roberto and Mario talking and I brush by them and out of the private room. I hate to admit it, but Roberto really is the perfect date. He just fits right in with my family. Plus he's easy to talk to, sweet, and, tonight especially, smokin' hot.

In the main dining room I try to locate the manager, but can't tell who's who, so I walk back to the maitre'd and give him a smile.

He ignores me. Doesn't he remember me? I'm in the VIP room.

"I'd like to see a manager," I say firmly and he quickly looks at me.

"Is there a problem?"

"Yes, and I need to take care of it *now*." Where is this bitchy side of me coming from?

He frowns at me, and then walks off. A few minutes later, a tall man in a shiny black suit approaches me. "Ms. DiLucio," he says extending his hand. "I'm Will Casper, General Manager."

"Nice to meet you," I say shaking his hand.

"Is there something I can help you with?"

I explain the situation with the mac and cheese and he softens. "Don't worry," he says. "I'll take care of it."

"Thanks," I say.

"What brand do you prefer?"

"Kraft, with the powdered cheese," I say with a smile. "Use the powder from two boxes but the pasta from one."

After the second course is served I see the chef come through the kitchen doors, carrying a platter covered with a silver dome lid. He places the dish in front of Lucy who looks up at him in surprise. "Congratulations on your wedding day," the chef says graciously. He lifts the lid and the aroma of fake cheese fills the table. Lucy's eyes light up brightly. She looks as if he just presented her the finest white truffle on earth. "Thank you so much."

I smile at the chef, who doesn't dare make eye contact with me. As he turns to leave, I see the General Manager peering out of the kitchen. I'm sure they had words, but in the end, just like at Lorenzo's, the customer *always* wins.

Lorenzo looks at me confused. "How the hell did you get the chef to make boxed mac and cheese?"

"I have my ways," I say with a smile.

Lucy digs in and I know her wedding is now complete.

After the dishes are cleared, Lucy asks if I'll help her in the bathroom. We both excuse ourselves and walk out of the VIP room. She loops her arm through mine and whispers, "Thank you," into my ear.

I help Lucy into the stall then stand outside of it, holding the top of the door, just like we used to do at grimy bars in Philadelphia.

Then it hits me.

We'll never do that again.

I feel another lump swell in my throat and I might be going for a record. How many times can I cry in one day?

While washing her hands, Lucy looks at me in the mirror. "Stell, what's wrong?"

"Nothing," I say. "I'm just emotional about the wedding that's all. You're married."

She beams. Lucy looks at me, then reaches up and puts her hands on my shoulders. "Tonight marks a new beginning for both of us." She looks me in the eyes. "Take this time to find out who *you* are Stella. This is an opportunity." She smiles at me and I can't help but smile back.

"So how's your date?" Lucy asks casually.

"It's going great, despite the fact that he was forced to be here."

"Stella, stop it. He wanted to come. He's been asking Lorenzo about you all summer."

"Then why did his mother send me flowers?"

"I don't know. But I do know that he's perfect for you."

Great, now even Lucy is in on this scheme to get Roberto and me together. Why does everyone care so much? Why can't they just leave me alone? "There's no such thing as perfect."

"Yes there is. And he's driving you home tonight." Lucy winks at me and heads for the door. As I follow her I wonder if she's right.

Recipe: Mac and Cheese for a Knocked-up Bride

Yields 1 pregnant serving

Ok, so it's not your typical wedding dinner, but when you're pregnant and nauseous, you must give in to whatever you can swallow. It was either this, or another egg sandwich, and I knew Luce would like this better. Plus, did you *see* the look on the chef's face?

I actually don't know the recipe since I've never made this stuff, but I do know that Luce uses the cheese from two boxes and the pasta from one. She likes it extra cheesy.

2 boxes Kraft Mac and Cheese
Follow the directions and serve.

Chapter 17

We pull up to 96th Street a little after 1:30 a.m. and my head is spinning. I'm not sure if I drank too much, or ate too much or what, but suddenly I realize I'm sublimely happy. Here I was thinking I'd never get married, while I had the perfect guy right in front of me.

Ever since my talk with Lucy in the bathroom, I've sort of let loose. Call it beer muscles (not that I've been drinking beer, yuck) or whatever, but I've really opened up to Roberto. In fact, this entire ride home I've been telling him all about my fears of not having a job, and my overwhelming desire to just pack up and move to Rome. I secretly wanted him to say "Let's run away together," but he didn't. Come to think of it, he hasn't said much this whole ride.

We wait at the red light, not talking. Roberto turns to look at me. "Do you mind if we sit on the beach for a while?"

"Sure," I say. "Let's go."

He makes a right and drives toward 99th Street then pulls up next to his house. We get out of the car and start walking towards the sand. I try to hold his hand but stumble a little and graze his wrist instead. He gives me a strange look. "Should we go sit?" he asks.

I nod my head and slip my feet out of my shoes. Roberto quickly takes off his shoes then starts walking up the dunes and onto the sand. I follow closely behind. When I turn to look at his house I can't help but notice that it's totally dark. "Is your family home?" I ask suddenly.

He turns toward me. "Nope."

My heart starts to pound and I muster up the courage to speak. "Roberto," I say looking right into his eyes. "Why don't we go inside?" I run my hand down his arm and feel his muscles tense up. If I were a feistier girl I'd growl or something, but instead, I just stand there with a puppy love look on my face.

He looks at his feet.

Oh God. Why did I just say that? Why?

Roberto takes a deep breath. "Stella," he sighs. "I think we want different things right now."

Suddenly, I feel like a fool. None of this makes sense. Roberto has been giving me mixed signals all night, and when I finally make a move he flat out rejects me. I don't know why I even bothered. In fact, I don't even know why I'm standing here right now. "Can you take me home?"

He nods and turns back around.

The sound of waves crashing onto the shore is usually my favorite sound, but as we walk towards the car, I barely notice it.

Roberto doesn't even bother to say anything, and when he pulls up to my house, I don't dare invite him inside. He moves to get out of the car, but I let myself out. There's nothing worse than false chivalry. If he really liked me, I'd let him open the door, but I certainly won't be a charity case. We meet in front of his car, the headlights illuminating the awkward exchange between us, and I can just imagine the neighbors looking out their windows, pining for a goodnight kiss.

We look at each other. "Thanks," I mumble.

"Stella," he looks at me for a few seconds like he wants to say something else, and then moves to give me an awkward hug, as if I'm a distant cousin or something. I pat him on the back twice and break free of his embrace.

"See you later," I say and walk up the driveway and to the front door. As much as I want to, I will not look back.

After the stress of today, all I want to do is go to bed. And that's exactly what I do.

The problem is: I can't sleep.

I had no trouble *falling* asleep; staying asleep was the hard part.

And when I wake up at 4:45 a.m. I know I'm up for the day. I take a deep breath. From my window I can see the first glimpse of sunlight yawning across the sky. I bet it's even better at the beach. I've always wanted to see the sunrise on the beach, but in all the years we've been living here, I never made it there in time. I think about Lucy's words from last night. This is a new beginning for me.

That's it. I'm going to the beach.

I fling the covers off my bed and get out of it before I change my mind. Today marks the start of the new Stella DiLucio.

I look at myself in the full-length mirror and notice how drab I look. How is it possible that I looked so good just one day ago? Did being flat out rejected automatically turn me into a spinster? It's like my body knows that I'll end up alone.

I give my body the once over in the mirror and decide that the new Stella desperately needs to get in shape.

I've never been big on exercise but this morning I want to run. Lucy used to run every morning, and look at her now. She's married!

Within five minutes I'm dressed in shorts, a sports bra, tank top, and white Nikes. I pull my hair into a ponytail as I walk down the steps, careful not to wake anyone up.

When I step outside and breathe the fresh morning air I suddenly feel at peace. I start to run at the end of the driveway and am surprised at how quick my pace is. I can't even remember the last time I went running, yet, there's something inside of me that pushes me to go on.

I run down 99th Street across Third Avenue without a problem, but by the time I get to Second Avenue I'm out of breath. I slow down and feel a stabbing pain in my side. I hold it and start walking.

I cross First Avenue still walking and can see the sun starting to rise. I need to get to the beach as quickly as possible, so I start to jog a little to get there. Soon I'm running up the sand dunes and standing on top of a small hill.

That's when I see it.

The sun seems to be coming up from the ocean in a giant ball. It moves quicker than I imaged it would, and looks like it's being thrown into the sky. Shades of pink and purple, yellow and gold fill the atmosphere, and I feel refreshed and able to start anew. No wonder my grandmother loved the beach so much.

The next two and a half weeks pass quickly. Slowly, the waiters leave us and return to college, which means we're short staffed, as usual for this time of the year. My parents have closed La Cucina until Labor Day, so my mother is working the hostess stand, while I fill in as a waitress. It's crazy but I don't mind. Lucy even came back; she's been feeling so good lately that she wanted to make some extra money before the school year starts.

I've kept to my resolution and have started every morning with a sunrise run on the beach. It's actually helping me figure out what I want in life.

I thought that all the running I've been doing would make me hungry, but somehow, I've lost my appetite completely. I can barely force down a meatball a day, and you *know* how much I love meatballs.

Still, I must say that this new regimen of not eating and running has really improved my figure. I've lost the impossible five pounds from my gut, and now tote a flatter stomach than Lucy (Granted, she *is* pregnant, but not by that much). She laughs at me when I point this out to her in the waiters' station.

"I have a baby living inside of me!" she protests.

"Whatever Luce, that kid is barely a peanut. Just admit it, I'm skinnier than you for once in my life."

"Well enjoy these nine months, because I plan on bouncing right back after this kid."

We both laugh and I must say it feels good. I've been feeling so strange lately. I always get reflective as the summer winds down, but with all the changes that happened this summer, I'm even more so.

Tonight feels especially strange since tomorrow is my birthday. I honestly don't feel like celebrating at all, but Lucy keeps insisting that we go to the Beachcomber after work tomorrow night. I guess Lorenzo wants to go there. After all, it's his birthday too.

Besides Lucy and me, Dante and Ryan are working tonight too, and since it's only the four of us left on staff, we've been seeing a lot of each other lately.

The restaurant fills at 6:15, and since my mother can't say no to people, we all get double sat. We go from zero to one hundred, but that's how it is in the restaurant business, so I know we shouldn't complain.

At around 7:45 I'm the only one with free tables in my section. I can see Lucy is struggling a bit, so I go into the kitchen to help her run food, and when I come out, I see my mother seating Mr. and Mrs. Lancetti at my table.

My heart races.

Luckily they're alone.

I mean, obviously Roberto wouldn't have the nerve to come here. I haven't seen him since my brother's wedding, which is probably a good thing. I'm still totally embarrassed.

I approach the table and notice the extra menu and place setting sitting there.

Shit.

"Hello Mr. Lancetti. Hi Mrs. Lancetti," I say with a smile. He waves at me and opens the menu while she stands up to give me a hug.

I smile as she sits down. "Are you expecting someone else?" I say casually, reaching for the extra place setting.

"Robbie should be here in a minute." She winks at me. "Sorry about the whole flowers incident. Robbie was really mad when he found out. I never heard the end of it. Sheesh."

I force out another smile and ask them what kind of water they'd like, though I'd like to school her in the dangers of meddling in her son's love life.

"San Pellegrino," Mr. Lancetti says without looking up.

"I'll be right back with it," I say. I walk into the waiters' station to get it and thankfully Lucy is there at the credit card machine. "Roberto's coming in and sitting at my table."

She frowns. Lucy knows how much I hate waiting on friends of the family. There's something degrading about it. I'd much rather deal with strangers. At least strangers can be easily impressed with stories, and don't ask too many personal questions. And of course, I never threw myself at a stranger like I did with Roberto.

"Want me to take them instead?" she asks.

"I already greeted them, it would just look weird now," I reply. Why didn't I think of passing the table to Lucy? God, I'm *dumb* sometimes.

She looks out into the dining room. "He's sitting down with them now," she says. Then adds, "He looks good."

"He *always* looks good," I hear myself say. "Too bad he doesn't like me."

"It's just so weird," Lucy says while pouring coffee into a cup. "He asked Lorenzo if he could come to the wedding. He wanted to be your date."

"Probably so he could reject me. He used to torture me when we were little. I guess that's still his thing." I try to shrug it off as if I don't really care. In reality I've been replaying the scene in my head for two weeks now and I've come up with three possible reasons for his behavior. Number one: he's a player (though, then he would have taken me home and never called again), number two: he's gay (he does dress well), or the most likely scenario, number three: he's just not into me. Which of course, infuriates me. I mean, what's wrong with me?

Maybe I don't have a PhD or a corporate career, and maybe I'm not the best at holding down my alcohol, but dammit, I have good qualities. I can make people smile and feel welcome when they come in here; I can work an eight-hour shift in six-inch heels; I try my hardest to look on the bright side of things; I don't allow myself to be frumpy in public; older people tell me I'm sweet; and have you tasted my desserts? Most importantly, I'd bend over backwards for the people I love. If Roberto Lancetti thinks he's too good for that then he's no better than Drew. And they can both go to hell.

I grab the bottle of San Pellegrino and take a deep breath. I'll show him that rejecting me was a big mistake.

"Hi Roberto," I say as I reach the table.

"Hey Stella," he says not really looking at me.

I feel myself frowning as I pour the water into their glasses.

"You know, Stella's birthday is tomorrow. She's almost thirty," Mrs. Lancetti says, which makes me sound pathetic. For a minute, I feel like a fool. Why couldn't I be at the hostess stand wearing a cute dress, instead of standing here in a freaking tie looking like a twelve-year-old boy for God's sake? That's it. We're changing these damn uniforms. They're completely sexist. No woman should have to wear a tie. Ever. It's inhumane.

"Would you like to know tonight's specials?" I hear myself ask with confidence in my voice.

"Sure," Mr. Lancetti says looking at me. Mrs. Lancetti places her menu on the table then nudges Roberto to do the same. I feel my face getting hot as they all stare at me.

"We have osso-buco, served on a bed of saffron risotto…" I start. I can feel Roberto's eyes looking at me and I wonder what he's thinking. "Then halibut, wrapped in prosciutto and served on a bed of rosemary and fig polenta cubes…" They're all still looking at me.

"…And finally chocolate soufflé for dessert." I move to walk away from the table. "I'll give you a minute to decide."

"No need. I think we can all order now," Mr. Lancetti says.

Right.

I take a deep breath and smile.

"I'll start with an arugula salad and then I'll have the grilled salmon," Mrs. Lancetti says. "I'm on a diet you know." She winks at me then continues. "Speaking of diets, Stella honey you look *fabulous.* What have you been doing?"

"I run on the beach," I say without thinking.

God, why couldn't I just ignore her?

"Well it's working," she smiles.

I can feel my face flushing.

"You look beautiful. Doesn't she Robbie?"

God, please kill me now. Please just strike me dead.

"I'll take the Salumeria," Mr. Lancetti interrupts, thankfully. "And the filet with gorgonzola, medium rare."

I nod my head as I write down his order. Then I look at Roberto. Our eyes meet and I quickly look away.

"I'll start with a house salad," he says. "And then I'll take the sea bass."

I smile a little. That's my favorite dish on the menu.

"Stella makes the chocolate soufflés, don't you hon?" Mrs. Lancetti says. It seems like she's trying really hard to sell me and it's making me feel like a big loser.

"Yep," I reply. "I make all the desserts." Out of the corner of my eye, I see a man at table four waving his credit card in the air. Normally I'd want to ignore this public display of rudeness, but right about now, I could kiss that man.

"I'll take one," Roberto says, looking at me with a smile.

"Okay," I say scribbling down his order and walking away from the table.

Thankfully, the other customers in my section are equally as demanding as the man at table four, so I spend as little time at the Lancetti's table as possible. I barely check on them while they're eating their appetizers and once I place their entrées in front of them, I bounce to another table to take its order. I even forget to tell Roberto to watch out for pits in the olives of his dish, but I'm sure he'll figure it out. And if he cracks a tooth and has to leave before he gets his soufflé, well, I'm sure it'll be for the best.

But apparently, Roberto is a careful eater, because not only does he survive the olive pits, but he's also eaten his entire piece of fish without choking on a fish bone. Why does Lorenzo have to be so precise about removing *all* of the bones?

Thankfully, my soufflé puffs beautifully in the oven, and I admire it as I dust it with powdered sugar, a dollop of whipped cream, and two strawberry slices. Surprisingly, baking is the only thing that's going well in my life. So well in fact that I've gotten a few orders for whole cakes. I've also been toying with the idea of pastry school. I looked up a few programs for the fall and winter months, and have been emailing back and forth with an admissions officer for a program in Philly.

As I walk to the table I imagine myself cooking for Roberto in the Lancetti's enormous gourmet kitchen. I shake the thought out of my head and hurry to the table before the soufflé deflates.

"Here ya go," I say placing it in front of him. "Just be careful, the ramekin is hot."

He smiles. "It looks delicious."

Out of the corner of my eye, I see Mrs. Lancetti nodding with approval. Here we go again.

I meet Lucy at the coffee station as I move to make them espressos. I didn't even take an order, but I don't need to. They're Italian; they can't finish a meal without a nice stiff espresso.

"How's it going, Stell?" she asks.

"Fine," I say and tighten the hand piece.

"You seem a little… tense," she says looking at me.

"No, I'm fine."

"Okay," she says placing two cups of coffee on her tray and leaving me to make the espressos.

A few minutes later, I return to the table with the espressos and a sugar bowl. I place one in front of each person and Mrs. Lancetti smiles at me. Roberto is halfway through the soufflé. His face is twisted into a smile, the same way everyone looks when they take a bite. I've got him with this one.

"Stella this is amazing," Roberto says and looks at me with interest.

"Well, some people think I'm amazing too," I reply and turn to leave.

In the kitchen, Lorenzo and Mario are discussing football while they plate up food. I'm not really interested in what they're saying so I just sort of space out for a while, and take a breath. All of my tables are served, and I still have a few minutes before I need to drop off checks.

Suddenly, I see the kitchen door swing open. Roberto enters and walks over to my brothers. I want to leave the kitchen, but I'm pretty sure he saw me, so there's nothing I can do except look at the Bain Marie and pretend that I'm interested in salad ingredients.

They talk for a few minutes and then I hear Roberto say, "The dinner was awesome tonight. I had the sea bass."

"That's my sister's favorite dish," says Mario. God, why does everyone want to pawn me off on this guy?

"Really?" says Roberto looking at me. "I thought we had similar tastes."

Oh really? I thought we wanted different things. What a phony. I give him a half smile and look back at the fixings for the salad. I start counting black olives floating in their brine.

"The soufflé was excellent," he says, still trying to make conversation.

"Thanks," I mumble. Eight, nine, ten, eleven…

"And for the record, I think you're amazing too."

I want to disappear. My brothers both look at me for a minute. Then Roberto says goodbye to them and leaves the kitchen.

"What's wrong with you?" Mario asks.

"What do you mean?"

"He was trying to talk to you and you were just standing there." He points to the Bain Marie just as Lucy walks in the kitchen.

"Luce, your friend just blew it, big time," Lorenzo says.

"Whatever, he's a jerk."

"What happened?" Lucy asks.

"Roberto was trying to talk to her and she ignored him," Mario explains.

I leave the kitchen before they can say anything else. Thank God Labor Day is in five days. I'm so ready for summer to be over.

I walk back towards the table, and to my horror, my mother is talking to Anna Lancetti. I try to quietly drop off the check but they see me.

"Stella honey, are you excited for your birthday?" Mrs. Lancetti says looking at me.

I shrug my shoulders and drop the check on the table.

"Do you have any plans?" Roberto asks. I look at my mother, then at Mrs. Lancetti. This is getting ridiculous.

"I'm working."

"Teresa, you can't make your only daughter work on her birthday," Mrs. Lancetti says

"It's ok," I say quickly. "I like working."

"Stella, why don't you take the night off. You guys go out. Have fun," my mom says. I can't believe I'm being bombarded like this. As I see it, I have two choices: I can suck it up, say yes and go out with Roberto, or I can stand up for myself.

"I'd like that," Roberto says smiling at me.

For a split second, I consider going out with him, if only to appease our mothers. But then I remember his words of the other night. "Well," I say, looking right at him, "I guess we want different things." Before anyone can say a word, I turn and walk away.

Recipe: Sea Bass

Yields 2 servings

So what if we have similar tastes. Roberto Lancetti is a jerk and I'm glad I finally put him in his place.

2 sea bass filets
1/4 cup extra virgin olive oil
1 medium onion, diced
4 Roma tomatoes, diced
1/2 cup clam juice (or white wine)
1/4 cup dried black olives
salt and pepper to taste
fresh basil, chopped

1) Heat olive oil in a large sauté pan over medium heat. Add the onions cook until translucent.
2) Add the tomatoes and sauté together for a few minutes.
3) Push the tomatoes and onions to the side and place the sea bass in the center of the pan. Cook each side for about 2 minutes.
4) Add the clam juice and bring to a soft boil. Reduce heat and cover the pan.
5) Allow the sea bass to poach for 10-15 minutes, depending on the thickness of the fish.
6) Add salt, pepper, and black olives.
7) Top with fresh basil before serving.

Chapter 18

You can never go against Teresa DiLucio without facing her wrath.

Luckily, I am able to avoid her for the rest of the night because she leaves with the Lancettis. I'm just hoping that she's already asleep when I walk in the house.

Slowly, I unlock the door and try to creep in. But there they are, the DiLucio girls, waiting to judge me.

"Here she is, Ms. America," my mom exclaims when she sees me. She and Gina are sitting on the couch drinking tea. Lucy sits with her feet up in my Dad's La-Z-Boy. She smiles guiltily and I can tell right away they've all been talking about me.

"Stell, why don't you just go out with him?" Gina asks. "You looked so cute together at the wedding."

"You would think that, right?" I say, my head in the fridge. All of the sudden, my appetite is back, and, as usual, I missed dinner. The fridge is empty except for a gallon of milk and two cups of strawberry yogurt. I grab the milk and move to the pantry, where I find a box of Frosted Mini-Wheat's. Not exactly ideal Food Therapy, but at this point I'm pretty desperate. "But," I continue as I pour the cereal in my bowl, "he's not interested in me."

"Are you crazy?" my mom asks. "He asked you on a date."

"Because you and his mother forced him into it." I shovel cereal in my mouth.

"Why would you think that?" my mom asks.

"You sent me flowers and made me think they were from him!" I still can't believe I let that one slide so quickly.

"Oh please Stella," my mom waves her hand in the air.

"Come on Mom. You and Mrs. Lancetti have been planning our wedding for twenty years."

"Do you like him?" Gina asks.

"Of course," I reply automatically. I'm caught off guard by the question, but after I respond, I realize that I do like him. In fact, since the wedding I can't stop thinking of him. I just keep replaying the night in my head, analyzing every detail, right down to the minute I ruined everything.

"Then go out with him!" Gina squeals. "This is too cute. I mean, you guys have known each other *forever*. This could be *it,* Stella."

Suddenly I feel like I've stepped into a Match.com commercial.

"This is *not it*."

"You never know, Stella." My mom looks at me with a smile.

"Look, he's not into me."

"Yes he is," Lucy interjects. "I know it."

I shake my head. "He's not. And anyway, I want to be single for a while." This isn't exactly true, but I figure it will shut everyone up.

My mother scoffs at this. "You're not getting any younger."

"I'm only twenty-se…"

"Twenty-eight," Gina points to the clock. "You're twenty-eight as of one minute ago. Happy Birthday." The way she says it makes me feel like an old maid.

Happy birthday to me.

I don't really feel like running on the morning of my birthday, but like clockwork, I get up at 6:00 and, of course, I can't fall back asleep. I really want to just throw the covers over my head and camp out here until midnight. But I kick myself out of bed. I stumble around the bedroom, looking for running shorts and can't find any, so I pull on a pair of bright red boxers I've had since the nineties. I can't believe I actually used to wear these things as shorts. Why do I even still have them? I look at myself in the mirror. For the first time in my life, I'm down right *skinny*. If I lose any more weight, I'll look like one of those drug addicted Calvin Klein models. I debate just running in shorts and a sports bra but decide against it. I've never been a showy kind of girl and I'm not going to start now, *even if* I have the flattest abs of my life. I pull on a white cotton tank top, lace up my Nikes, and tip toe down the steps.

I start out with a brisk walk, and once I reach the dunes on 99th Street I lengthen my stride and begin to jog. It feels amazing to run on the beach in the mornings. The air is cool and tiny flecks of water from the ocean spray me.

By the time I loop back around to 99th Street, I've run four miles and my skin is glistening with a mixture of sweat and salt water. I'm panting and totally out of breath.

It feels like it's gotten so much hotter since I started running, and I can feel the sweat sliding down my back. I look down and see that my entire shirt is damp.

I'm officially gross.

And of course out of the corner of my eye, I see Roberto standing out by his porch.

What's he doing up so early?

For a second I think about turning around and running away, but it's obvious that he saw me.

Oh God, now he's walking towards me.

My heart is racing and the only thing I can think to do is sit down in the sand, my back facing his house.

I should have *known* I would see Roberto. Damn it. Why did I come running today of all days?

I can hear him approaching and without meaning to, I turn around.

There he is, standing a few feet away from me wearing gym shorts, a white t-shirt, and flip-flops. He's holding a bunch of flowers. Where did he get flowers at 7:00 a.m.?

"Quick Mart's finest bouquet," he says handing me the flowers. From up close, you can tell that they're old, but still, the thought was sweet. I sort of wish I'd seen him *before* my run, so I wasn't so sweaty. I stand up and reach for the flowers, trying to ignore the sand stuck to my legs like nylons. "These are one hundred percent from me."

"Thanks," I say smelling the flowers. "Your mom has better taste in flowers than you do."

"You got me there," he laughs. "Happy birthday, Stella."

I sigh and sit back down on the sand. "Thanks."

"Are you okay?" Roberto takes a seat next to me.

"Yeah," I reply. "It's just that I thought my life would be a little different by now. I'm twenty-eight."

"So what," he says and gives me a crooked smile. "I'm thirty-four. Now *that* is old."

"At least you've done something with your life."

"So have you."

His comment makes me laugh. Right. Like working in your family's restaurant is a big accomplishment. I'm about to say this when he interrupts.

"You're amazing at what you do. I've seen you in the restaurant and I don't think anyone else could do your job." He smiles. "And those pastries..." he kisses his fingers in the stereotypical Italian fashion.

"Yeah well, this is all just temporary." When I finally say the words I realize they are true. Now that La Cucina is closing, I'll need to get a real job, and depending on what I find, I doubt I'll have summers off. Roberto looks at me as if he understands.

"What do you want to do?" Roberto asks.

I take a deep breath and think about the question. The beach is starting to fill up with people staking their claim on a prime spot in the sand. I watch as a middle-aged man fumbles with an umbrella. His wife pulls a wheelbarrow full of beach toys, buckets, and a cooler.

I sigh. "Honestly, I have no idea. I just want things to fall into place. I want to be comfortable again. Is that such a bad thing?"

"Were you comfortable with your ex?"

His question stops me. I thought I was comfortable with Drew, but really I was just settling for a guy who treated me less than what I am worth. "I don't know. I guess not."

I expect him to roll his eyes, but instead, he smiles. "I was hoping you'd say that."

"So I wasn't comfortable with Drew, but I still want that life. I want a husband and kids and a nice house. I'm tired of waiting and wishing things would happen. I'm twenty-eight, for God's sake. When is my life going to start?"

Something in his eyes changes. "You really want all those things?"

"Yes," I say sincerely.

"You want those things now?" he asks as if he's calculating a plan.

"Yes. Yes I do."

"Will you have dinner with me?"

Oh God, here we go again. "Why do you want to have dinner with me so badly? Did your mom put you up to this?"

"Are you crazy?"

I snap. "Roberto, you said yourself that we want different things."

He softens. "I thought we did. I wanted to settle down and you wanted to run away."

"What are you talking about?"

"Rome."

At first, I have no idea what he's talking about. Then I vaguely remember telling him that I wanted to move there. But I was drunk. I mean, obviously I don't want to move to a foreign city. Though it would be nice.

"That was just drunk rambling."

"In vino veritas." He smiles. "Have dinner with me. How about Labor Day? We'll celebrate your unemployment."

This makes me laugh. "Fine."

He stands up and starts brushing sand off his legs. "Happy Birthday, Bella Stella. I'm going back to bed."

He turns to leave and I give him a little wave. I stand and brush the sand off my legs, then decide that I need a sticky bun.

Apparently, I'm not the only one who wants a pastry. The line for the bakery is wrapped around 96th Street, which gives me lots of time to think. By the time I'm facing the pastry case full of sticky buns I've worked out a life plan. I'll get a stable job and start dating Roberto. Eventually we'll have the big Italian wedding our mothers have been planning, we'll buy a big house, settle into it and have a few kids. It's the perfect plan. It's very comfortable. Very safe and comfortable.

Within three minutes, I'm out the door, sticky buns and cappuccino in hand, Roberto's flowers tucked nicely under my arm. I cross the street to the bookstore to grab a magazine, because, for the first time in weeks, I feel good.

No, I feel great.

Once I get all my goodies, I walk to the only place I can think of to have some peace and quiet on this Thursday morning. Lorenzo's.

I drop my stuff on the bench outside while I unlock the door. The cool air hits me in the face, and I realize I forgot to shut off the air conditioner last night. I walk across the restaurant and into the waiters' station to turn it off, then walk back to the front door and lock it. I unhook the phone and set up a little corner table all to myself.

Some people need spas, others fancy massages, but for me, the ultimate relaxation is a good cup of coffee and a few magazines. I place both sticky buns on a bread plate and grab myself a fork and knife to eat them with, that way I won't get the magazines dirty. I flip to the first page and take a big bite of the sticky bun. It's just as good as I imagined.

After a few minutes I come across an article on style tips for a first date. The page shows pictures of Drew Barrymore, Lindsay Lohan, and Penelope Cruz, all prepped for their big dates. Of the three, I lean towards Penelope's look, and start to imagine the exact dress I'll wear for my date with Roberto.

It's strange, planning a dress for a first date with a guy that I grew up with. I mean, he was there when I vomited all over myself at his dad's birthday party. Granted, I was only five and had a bad virus, but still, it was embarrassing, and I'm sure he remembers. Of course, I've seen him in his pudgy years, and I still agreed to the date. I smile. Maybe this isn't such a bad idea after all.

"What are you going to wear?" Gina asks the burning question once I tell her about the date.

"I'm not sure, probably a black dress…" I'm standing in the kitchen watching as she and my mother drink their morning coffee. It's eleven and they've only now gotten up.

"Black?" my mom interrupts. "You're going on a date, not to a funeral."

"Black is very classic," I say.

"Your mom is right. Black is a no go for a date," Gina adds. "Unless you're already an established couple."

I roll my eyes. Just because she works at Saks doesn't make her Rachel Zoë for God's sake. "I'm staying with black." I sit at the table next to them.

They both look at me horrified. "Stella, you should wear red. Red is a mysterious color," Gina suggests.

"How mysterious can I be? He probably remembers me in diapers."

My mom laughs.

"What about blue? You look *amazing* in blue," Gina says. I shake my head.

"White," my mom says. "You'll wear white." The way she says it, it seems like she's already planning our wedding.

"Mom for God's sake, it's a first date."

"White will look beautiful with your tan. I saw a gorgeous BCBG dress the other day. White satin strapless. We have it at Saks." Gina takes a sip of her coffee. Now even she's styling me in a wedding dress.

"I think white is too suggestive for a first date."

"Suggestive meaning what?" my mom asks, looking at me sternly.

"Meaning it looks too much like a wedding dress."

"Well is marriage the worst thing in the world?' my mom asks.

“Oh my God. It’s a first date,” I retort, although I *did* spend most of the morning envisioning myself walking down the aisle with Roberto. Still, no one needs to know that.

Recipe: Birthday Sticky Buns

Yields 1 serving

1) Decide that you are not cooking on your birthday.
2) Go to your favorite bakery.
3) Select sticky bun.
4) Devour, it's your birthday after all.

Chapter 19

Thankfully, we're fully staffed tonight. Both Brittany and Michelle came back from college for Labor Day weekend to make some extra cash, so I'm back to managing. I take extra time to get dressed for work because you never know if Roberto will stop in.

It *is* my birthday, after all.

I can imagine it already. Roberto will walk through the front doors holding a big bouquet of roses (from Dots and Bows, not Quick Mart). I'll be at the hostess stand, juggling a million things like I always do, but as soon as I see him the world will stop. Slowly, he'll walk towards me and hand me the bouquet. Before I can even say "thank you" he'll cup my face in his hands and give me a kiss. At this point, the entire restaurant will be watching; service will have stopped for a minute, as everybody awaits what's coming next. Then, without saying a word, Roberto will drop down to one knee and take my hand. He'll look up at me with those gorgeous brown eyes and say…

Ok, maybe I'm getting a little ahead of myself. But he *did* say he wants to settle down, and remember, he *does* think I'm amazing.

I decide on a red strapless A-line dress, with a full shirt. I pair it with brown open toe heels and wear my hair down. Gina has given me full permission of her Bobbi Brown case, so I'm all dolled up and ready for the night. I'm feeling so good that I wouldn't even mind going to the Beachcomber tonight.

"Wow, hot stuff," Gina says when I walk down the steps. I laugh, but inside I really do feel hot.

"You look beautiful Stella," my mom says. Then she looks me up and down and adds, "too elegant to go to work though."

Maybe she's right. Maybe I did overdo it a little, but hey, it's my birthday *and* Labor Day weekend. As far as I'm concerned, anything goes.

I change into flip-flops before heading out the door, carrying my heels in my hand. "I'll see you tonight," I say waving from behind the door.

I walk on the street hoping to see Roberto, but the only person I pass is Fr. Jim, walking his Golden Lab in front of the church. "Hello Stella," he says with a smile. "Off to work?"

"Yep," I reply picking up my pace. "Don't want to be late." The last thing I need is that dog drooling on my dress.

As I unlock the door my phone starts to ring. Of course, I'm carrying the biggest bag in the world and I can't find my phone. I sift through the various lip glosses, used tissues, and old receipts littering the bottom of my bag, until I finally grab my phone. I answer it without looking at the caller ID.

"Hi Stella. Happy Birthday."

The voice stops me dead in my tracks. I don't believe it.

"Hi Drew."

"How's it going?" he asks casually, as if he didn't completely crush me. As if he's not engaged to Trisha Motley.

"What do you want?" I snap.

"I just wanted to talk." He pauses. "I miss you. I made a mistake."

There they are, the words I waited months to hear. I've imagined this moment so many times. Replayed it over and over in my mind. Fantasized about it, believed in it. But now, it's all wrong. I don't care about Drew anymore. And I don't care what he has to say. In one swift motion I flip my phone shut. It's over. It's been over. There's no need to open that door ever again.

I turn off my phone and drop it in my bag.

"Stell, I need help on table four," Brittany says halfway through the night. It's 8:30 and we have reservations coming in until 11:00. I look over at the table and see six women laughing.

"What's going on?"

"They're not happy with me," she says looking down.

"They just sat," I say.

"I know, but they saw Dante and they want him."

"So just switch, what's the big deal?"

"I don't know, they said they wanted to talk to the manager about it."

I raise my eyebrow and walk towards the table.

They're still laughing when I arrive, and I can see that five of them look to be in their fifties. The younger girl looks about my age, though I'm always bad at judging these things. None of them look familiar, but like always, on holiday weekends the place gets full of strangers. The ladies have brought three bottles of red and two bottles of white. If they drink all that wine, I'm sure I'll be calling a taxi for them. "Hello, I'm the manager," I say loudly.

"Look at you, Ms. Thang," one woman squeals and they all laugh. I get the feeling they've been to happy hour before coming in for dinner.

"Can I help you with something?" I ask, trying to remain calm, though I'm slightly annoyed.

"I love your dress," a woman with long brown hair and a spectacular tan says to me. The dress would actually look great on her.

"Thanks, it's Marc Jacobs."

Did they need something? Or did they just want to talk fashion?

"You have lovely taste," she replies. She takes a sip of wine and continues. "This is my daughter, Caitlin," she says gesturing to the younger girl sitting at the table. Now that she mentioned it, I can certainly see the resemblance between them. Both of them have shiny hair and golden tans, though Caitlin looks fairer skinned than her mother. I smile.

"My daughter has impeccable taste as well," she continues. "And she knows what she wants."

Well good for her.

The other ladies laugh and I can see Caitlin's face get as red as my dress.

"That's great," I say. At this point, I'm finished with this table. They're just drunk and slightly obnoxious. "Can I help you with anything?"

"Well, as a matter of fact. We'd like *him* to be our waiter," the mother says pointing to Dante as he walks by.

"No problem, I already switched him to your table."

"What're his stats?" the lady asks me.

Stats? I have no idea what she's talking about, so I look at her blankly.

"Is he taken?"

I almost laugh. "No, no, he's not."

The lady looks me up and down and before she can say another word I continue. "He's my brother, Dante."

The ladies giggle a bit and the ringleader looks relaxed. Poor Caitlin is mortified and I can feel her pain.

"Do you think he'd like my daughter?" the mother asks me.

I glance at Caitlin, who as far as I can tell, is actually interested. "Of course he would, he's not *blind*."

The ladies giggle like teenagers. "Well send him over," the mother says. "And let's get this party started."

I smile tightly and turn away from the table. Thank God my mother is not *that* embarrassing.

"Good luck," I whisper to Dante as he approaches the table. Thankfully, he's a good sport about it, and as I watch him flirt with the table, I see that he's actually really good at it. Dante is by far the most quiet out of us, and I never would have thought he'd be able to play into them that much.

"What's up with that?" Lucy asks at the hostess stand.

"I have no idea," I say with a laugh. "People are so weird."

At about 9:30, my parents, Pietro, and Gina come in. My mom is carrying a huge cake decorated with "Auguri Lorenzo and Stella" piped on it. Gina is holding a signature bouquet from Dots and Bows. "Your table's right this way," I say very professionally. My dad hangs back as I walk, and while the others sit, he grabs my hand and squeezes it. "I heard about your date with Roberto," he whispers. "Good choice."

I smile and squeeze his hand again. I wonder if the Lancettis have called my parents to start arranging the wedding yet. If not, I'm sure they will while we're on our date.

My parents finish up their dinner at 11:45, and my mom disappears into the kitchen to get the cake. The last thing in the world I feel like doing is having birthday cake, but I don't want to make her feel bad for making it. The restaurant is almost empty except for a few campers who are sipping wine and lingering over chocolate soufflé, so my mom gathers all of the servers, bussers, and dishwashers around to sing to me.

I sit there watching my entire family and suddenly, the night doesn't seem so bad. I blow out my candles and wish for…

Well, I'm not telling you *that.* Everyone knows you have to keep your wishes secret if you want them to come true.

My mom moves to re-light the candles for Lorenzo but he stops her.

"I already have everything I could possibly wish for," he says grabbing Lucy's hand.

How lovely.

As soon as we finish the cake everyone gets up to leave. In the restaurant business the owners can never sit for too long. Before I can start clearing off the table, my dad pulls me aside.

"I have something for you," my dad says and reaches into his pocket. "I didn't have the chance to give it to you this morning." He holds out a mini manila envelope. My name is written on the front but I don't recognize the handwriting. I look at him.

"Open it," he urges.

I flip open the flap and peek into the envelope. I pull out a thin gold chain with a small cross dangling from it. It looks so familiar, but I can't figure out where I've seen it before.

"It's from Grandmom," he says and instantly. Her smiling face flashes before my eyes. I turn the envelope over and see that it's her handwriting on the front.

"I had it cleaned," my dad says. "She wanted you to have this when you turned thirty, but I figured you could use it now."

I reach up and clasp the necklace around my neck. It falls midway to my chest and looks so delicate against my skin.

"She got that necklace right before she came over to America and wore it every day of her life. It was precious to her, and I'm sure it will be to you too."

Tears start welling up in my eyes as I think of my grandmom. "Thanks," I say, more to her than to him.

"She'd be so proud of you Stella. You're exactly like her."

For the first time, I believe him. I am like my grandmother. Full of sass and ready to take on the world.

Less than an hour later, I collect everyone's checkouts and take the money into the office, where I can calculate the tips. As soon as I plop down in my chair, my foot hits my purse. I pick it up and shuffle through it, looking for my phone. When I turn it on there are seven full text messages from Drew. I delete all of them because that's exactly what my grandmom would do. She would never let a man treat her the way Drew treated me.

The next morning, I feel like a new woman. It's like as soon as I realized Drew was all wrong for me, the world sent me all kinds of possibilities. Namely, a new life with Roberto.

Instead of going for my usual run, I fix myself a steaming hot mug of coffee and enjoy the first rays of sunlight, creeping across the sky.

Recipe: Breakfast for a New Woman

Yields 1 serving

Sometimes Food Therapy really does work. Like today, for example, when I drank this steaming hot mug of espresso. It made me feel like a new woman, even though I drink it every morning.

But still, don't we become someone new every day?

1 shot of espresso
8 oz. of steaming hot whole milk

1) Combine the two together and drink.
2) Go outside and sit by the bay.
3) Contemplate your life and realize that, yes, it is wonderful.
4) Daydream about your wedding (obviously, Roberto and I will date first, but I have a feeling we're in for a whirlwind romance).

Chapter 20

I've never been so excited for anything in my entire life.

Ok, maybe that's an overstatement, but still you get the idea.

On Labor Day morning, I skip my run and sleep in, knowing that the extra hours of rest will show up on my face later. I haven't seen Roberto since he asked me out, and I want to look my best to impress him tonight. I didn't even partake in the end of the season party my brothers threw after work last night. Typically they drink in the restaurant until about 4:00 a.m., and I was in no mood to stay there that late, so Lucy and I left the party at around 1:00.

Now that summer is officially over, even the weather seems different. I feel the cool bay breeze as I get out of bed and the overcast sky tells me it's going to rain. This might change my outfit slightly, as I've never been able to sacrifice warmth for fashion.

Honestly, I don't know how those models do it. I've heard they shoot bathing suit catalogues on the beach in January.

I would die.

But when I open my closet and see the dress hanging there, I figure I'll have to just bear it. The dress is too gorgeous to change plans this late in the game.

As a birthday gift, Gina and my mom drove to Atlantic City and bought me an amazing cream-colored Betsy Johnson dress. Even though it's a little too white, when I tried it on, I knew this was the dress to wear on my date with Roberto. It's brushed silk with a sweetheart neckline and full tulip skirt. Paired with some nude heels and a gold clutch, this is the most amazing first date outfit ever. Plus my necklace really stands out.

Honestly, Gina should be a personal shopper; she nailed this one without even knowing how important it is.

By 6:15, my entire family is gone. I'm not sure why everyone is so concerned about beating the Labor Day traffic, but I guess it makes sense.

La Cucina reopens tomorrow at 11:00 a.m., and even Mario is excited to get back there. September is going to be a crazy month for the restaurant and he wants to get a head start. He and Lorenzo are going to use the last month to promote their new restaurant Fratelli's. If all goes as planned, they'll open in January, two months before the baby is born.

Dante and Lucy have a teachers' in-service meeting tomorrow at 6:00, and then the annual St. Iggy's faculty barbeque, and I know she's nervous about it. I would be too. Those Catholic School teachers are fierce. Plus, she's giving them a lot to gossip about considering she went from being a single girl at the end of the school year to becoming Mrs. DiLucio with a baby on the way. It's been a crazy summer. Honestly, I'm glad I never applied for the position there. Teaching is just not my thing.

Not that I know what my thing is. But who cares? Tonight we're celebrating my unemployment, remember?

By 7:00 my hair is in giant Velcro rollers and I'm putting the finishing touches on my smoky eyes. I'm in my robe, sitting in the den because the house was too quiet and I needed to turn the TV on to calm my nerves.

I reach for a Q-tip to rub the excess eye shadow off from under my eyes when I hear a knock at the door.

I get up to answer it thinking it's Mrs. Ryan from next door, but to my horror, I see Roberto standing in the doorway, wearing a charcoal grey suit, black t-shirt and his Ray Ban aviators. He's carrying a bottle of champagne.

Maybe he didn't see me. I can pretend like I didn't hear the door.

He knocks again. Crap.

"What are you doing here?" I say as I open the door. Who shows up thirty minutes early for a date?

"I couldn't wait," he says stepping into the doorway. "Plus I thought I'd give your parents a little gift to toast the season."

"No one's home," I say. He raises his eyebrow and follows me into the living room. "Have a seat."

He slowly sits on the couch and I survey the looks of the room. The coffee table is covered with make-up, a magnifying mirror sits in the middle of the table, and bobby pins are sprawled all over the carpet. I kneel down to collect everything, suddenly feeling a little self-conscious.

"I'll be right back," I say carrying all the makeup in my arms. "I just need like two minutes."

"You really don't need to change," he says with a mischievous smile. "I like what you've go on."

I laugh and turn to walk up the stairs as fast as I can.

Ok, that was *not* what I had planned.

I look at myself in the mirror and see that my make-up looks good. I step into the dress, then undo the Velcro rollers in my hair and flip my head upside down. I give my hair a little shake, then flip my head up and watch my hair magically fall into place. Works like a charm.

I grab my clutch and throw in the lip-gloss, my keys, and ID before heading downstairs. There's not enough room in the bag for my cell phone, but really, who needs it?

"Stella, you look amazing," Roberto says when he sees me.

I feel my face flushing. Without saying a word, he gets up and wraps his arms around me. My heart races and my stomach does a flip. Is he going to kiss me?

He looks me in the eyes.

This is it! My first kiss with Roberto. I close my eyes.

Only, he doesn't lean in.

I wait another second. Nothing.

I open my eyes and we look at each other for a few seconds before he starts laughing.

Ok, this is a little weird.

I giggle, just to keep him company, but his laughter grows.

What the hell? Am I some kind of *joke*?

I'm not the one who goes around saying *he's amazing.* I don't even think of him like that. As far as I'm concerned, he can just leave right now...

I'm sorry," he says composing himself. "It's just a little weird to be on a date with you."

"Why is that?" I ask, suddenly cross.

Oh God, what if his mom really *did* put him up to this?

"I just…" he looks at me for a second. "I never thought it would happen."

My heart leaps up to my throat. We *are* perfect for each other. I knew it! I always knew it!

"We're not really on a date yet," I say casually looking at the clock. It's 7:20. "You showed up early, so we still have ten minutes before our date officially starts."

He laughs. "Should I go outside?"

"Why don't we both go outside?" I say motioning to the sliding glass doors. "Let's sit on the dock for a while."

"I have a better idea," he says. "Let's get a head start on our date."

I smile. "Ok. Where are we going?"

"It's a surprise." He starts walking towards the door and I follow. He opens the passenger door for me and holds his stare as I get in. I'll have to hug Gina the next time I see her. This dress is magic.

As we pull out of the driveway I wonder where we're going. I'm sure it'll be somewhere off the Island. Maybe Atlantic City. Or Cape May.

After a minute, we pull up to the Lancetti's house. Are we making a pit stop?

"Here we are," he says shutting off the engine. He looks at me. "Ready?"

I'm not sure how to take this. This is our first date and I wish he'd at least planned something special. "Ok."

We walk into the foyer and I breathe in the familiar scent of this mansion. It's a mixture of white musk and eucalyptus, and just smells, well, rich. "Wait here one sec," Roberto says and darts off towards the kitchen. I can only assume he's getting some wine.

He returns a few seconds later holding a red and white gingham apron. He hands it to me and I give him a blank stare. "What am I supposed to do with this?"

"Put it on. Your dress is too nice to risk getting dirty." He starts walking towards the kitchen again. I slip the apron over my head and follow him.

The marble countertops are full of fresh fruit and vegetables from the farmers' stand right off shore. "Are we cooking?" I ask. Come to think of it, this is a pretty cute first date. I can roll with this.

"Yup" he says but doesn't move.

"What do you want to eat?"

He smiles. "Tell me about your summer. Use whatever you want, I stocked the fridge too." He leans back in his chair as I survey the veggies.

"Ok, we're gonna need some wine."

"Red or white?"

I open the fridge to see what we've got. "White."

By the time Roberto returns with a bottle of Riesling and two glasses I know what I'm going to cook. This summer was tough; it started out bitter and ended up sweet, and my menu will do the same.

Roberto hands me a glass. "Cheers to your unemployment." He clinks my glass. "So, what are we having?"

"The story has three acts," I say and take a sip. The crispness of the wine hits my palate and makes me smile. "We're going from bitter to sweet."

"Agro dolce," he says. "I like it." He starts to sit back down.

"I'm not cooking alone though," I say. "Grab an apron."

He laughs and walks toward the pantry. He finds himself an apron that says "Kiss the cook." He walks over to me, pointing to the words.

"That's cute," I say coyly. "But I'm the cook."

He leans closer to me. "I know." He leans down and kisses the top of my head.

About two hours later we're done cooking the first two courses and I still haven't gotten a proper kiss. I mean honestly, if I have to do all of the cooking I should get some rewards. Regardless, the meal looks great. We've made bruschetta topped with radicchio and Grana Padano cheese and halibut wrapped in prosciutto and served with fig and goat cheese polenta cubes. We've finished the bottle of wine, and as Roberto goes to fetch another one, I have a brilliant idea.

"Let's eat outside," I say when he returns. "Go set up the table while I make dessert."

He gives me a sneaky smile. "Ok," he says. "Whatever you want."

Truth be told, I don't want him in the kitchen while I'm making dessert. I need full concentration to make these damn profiteroles and analyze the situation. Why hasn't he kissed me yet? Does my breath stink? Do I have something in my teeth? Or worse, did his mother really put him up to this? As I spoon the dough onto a sheet pan I'm half expecting Anna Lancetti to jump out of the closet.

By the time I'm finished baking it is totally dark outside. Roberto has lit all the votive lanterns on the back porch; there must be at least fifty of them in different heights and positions, all twinkling like stars. "Surprise," he says when he sees me holding the tray of bruschetta. And just like that, all my worries melt away.

We eat and drink and laugh for the next few hours, totally entranced by the moment. We're so into each other that we don't even notice the lightening dancing in the sky over the ocean. It's only when I go inside to assemble the dessert that I hear the thunder rumbling. I work fast so we can finish our meal outside.

For the first time all summer, my profiteroles are perfect. The pate a choux has puffed perfectly and looks spectacular stuffed with vanilla ice cream. The hot chocolate sauce on top is just the right compliment, really symbolizing the sweet turn my summer took in the end.

A lightning bolt flashes in the sky just as I am carrying the profiteroles to the table. "This is the grand finale. I've been working on these all summer." I place the dish on the table with a big smile. "Dig in."

Roberto's eyes light up. Without saying a word he reaches for a spoon and plunges it into the pastry. Just as he's putting the spoon into his mouth, the sky opens and pours down on us.

I squeal and head for the door, but before I reach it Roberto grabs my hand and swings me toward him. He wraps his arms around me and pulls me close to his chest, which feels warm and familiar, despite the pouring rain. We look at each other for a minute and then he cups my face and kisses me.

Even though it's our first kiss, it feels as though we've been kissing each other our whole lives; it is comfortable, sweet, and confident. Just what I imagine our relationship will be like.

I don't know how long we stand there kissing, but I do know that I would have stood there forever if it weren't for the crack of thunder which sounded like it was way too close.

Roberto pulls me inside a little too forcefully and that's when it happens. My shoe catches on the doorframe and I tumble forwards flailing my arms out in front of me. As if in slow motion, I try to break my fall by catching the sleeve of Roberto's jacket. I guess my weight is too much for the fabric, because it gives with a loud tear. I fall backwards on my butt and Roberto falls face down on top of me.

We look at each other for a second. My tailbone hurts so bad that I don't know whether to laugh or cry but Roberto starts laughing and before I can stop myself, I join him.

"I think my butt is broken," I say.

Roberto gets up then reaches his hand out to help me off the ground. I stand in the puddle of water we trailed in. He peeks behind me and looks at my butt. "Nope. It's still perfect."

I laugh, but now it really hurts. For real. "I'm serious."

"Ok, hold on. I'll fix everything." He runs upstairs and comes down two minutes later wearing sweat pants and a t-shirt. He holds out mesh gym shorts and an oversized sweatshirt. "Put these on," he says, and even though I love my dress, it's now a soaking wet mess. At least these are dry.

I shuffle into the bathroom and peel my clothes off. I get dressed as quickly as I can. On the way out of the bathroom I spot myself in the mirror. My hair is hanging down like a wet cat, and my smoky eyes are more crack-head than heroin-chic. I grab a towel off the hanger and rub my face off. Even though my face is bare, it looks much better.

In the kitchen, Roberto stands holding one of those inflatable butt pillows for people with severe hemorrhoids. "I got you this," he laughs.

"Eww. I am *not* sitting on that thing." I move towards the counter to prep some new profiteroles.

"Come on Stell, it's me. I've seen you at your worst. Remember when you threw up all over yourself at that party?"

"I was five!"

"That makes it even worse. We made fun of you for months." He puts the pillow down on a chair and gives it a pat. "Now come sit."

I plate up the profiteroles and bring them to the table. Slowly, I sit on the pillow and I have to admit, it is quite comfortable.

"So did you like playing house here?" he asks between bites. "Was it comfortable?"

I look at him like I have no idea what he's talking about.

"All this, would it satisfy you?" he waves his hand around, emphasizing his point.

He looks at me with sincere interest. I actually need to think on this one. Would this satisfy me? Sure, I like Roberto and can even envision a future with him, but satisfaction? I take a bite of my profiterole, hoping it will give me the answer.

As I'm chewing, he reaches into the pocket of his sweatpants and pulls out a small box. My eyes widen. "I want to make you an offer," he says with a smile.

My heart jumps into my throat. I mean, I figured we'd eventually get married, I just didn't think he'd propose on the first date. Not that this is really a first date, but still. He moves fast.

Before I have a chance to say anything, he opens the box.

A rusty skeleton key sits on a bed of red velvet.

I'm not sure what to say. Is this some kind of weird necklace? I mean, he did study Latin for God's sake. Maybe this is some sort of artifact.

"It's beautiful," I say finally. Roberto gives me a strange look.

"It's the key to my place in Rome. It's yours for as long as you want it."

His *place* in Rome?

"You have a place in Rome?" I ask, shocked.

"Stella I did *live* there for eight years. What was I supposed to do? Rent the whole time?"

Right. Why would he rent? Why not just buy a place?

"Where is it?"

"In Trastevere. That's near St. Peters."

"You own a place in *Trastevere*?" This is too much for me to handle. Trastevere is, by far, my favorite neighborhood in Rome. It's such a totally Roman mix of ancient and modern and it bustles with life 24/7. "How did you afford an apartment in Trastevere?"

"My dad bought it before I went to grad school, and little by little I paid him back. Now it's mine."

"Why don't you sell it? You could make a fortune." After the words come out of my mouth, I realize how stupid I sound.

He raises his eyebrow. "Would you sell a place in Rome?"

I shake my head and reach for the key as if it is the Holy Grail. "Is it empty now?"

"I'm not sure. But it will be in October."

"How do you not know if your place is empty or not?" I raise an eyebrow. Does he have a woman living there? Suddenly I imagine Roberto as some international playboy with women all over the globe. Does he have apartments in any other countries? When we're engaged I'll have to nix all of that.

"I gave the keys to an agency before I left. They said they were renting it out on a week-to-week basis for the summer. I'd make more money that way."

"Still, don't they let you know if it's rented?"

"I just told them to send me a check each month."

"So you don't even *care*?" I'm shocked. I look at Roberto and see him in a different light. For the past eight years I had him pegged as a nerdy grad student, now I'm beginning to see him as an international businessman.

He shrugs his shoulders and finishes off the profiteroles. "Anyway, it's yours if you want it."

"Why are you offering me this?" I ask.

"Because I care about you."

For a minute I don't know what to say. No one had ever been so nice to me.

"Stella, I never want you to settle. On the beach the other day, you sounded a little desperate. The Stella DiLucio that I know is not desperate. Go to Rome. Get out of your funk."

This offer changes everything. Of course I'd love to live in Rome and this is the one time in my life I'd actually be able to do it. I have no obligations here, no job, no boyfriend…

I look at Roberto. If I did take his offer, it would mean letting go of this new relationship, and possibly a future together. Am I willing to give up this stability for the unknown?

"Don't worry," he says as if reading my thoughts. "I'll still be here when you get back."

This makes me smile. I clutch the key in my hand. "And what if I don't come back?"

"Then I'll come find you." He leans over and kisses me.

And just like that, everything falls into place.

Recipe: Profiteroles

It took all summer, but I finally got it right.
Yields 20 medium creampuffs

The Puffs-
1 stick of butter
1 cup of water
1 cup of flour
4 eggs at room temp.

1) In a medium saucepan on low heat, melt the butter.
2) Add the water and bring it up to a boil.
3) Once the butter/water is boiling, add the flour and stir, making sure to "cook" all of the flour so that no white is showing. (You'll be able to hear the sizzling of butter on the sides of the pan—this is a good thing!)
4) Remove the dough from the stovetop and spread it on a flat plate to cool.
5) Once the dough is cool, transfer the dough to a mixing bowl. Beat in eggs one at a time on a low speed. The dough will appear sticky. This is good! Preheat oven to 400 degrees F.
6) Lightly grease a baking sheet. Drop teaspoons of dough on the sheet, about 1 inch apart.
7) Bake on the middle rack at 400 degrees for 15 minutes. DO NOT OPEN THE OVEN!
8) Lower the oven to 350 degrees F and bake for an additional 20-30 minutes, until golden. (If you have to peek you may at this point.)
9) Cool on a wire rack.
10) Once cooled, slice in half and stuff with vanilla ice cream. Serve with warm chocolate sauce.

Chocolate sauce:
1 can sweetened condensed milk
3 oz bittersweet chocolate

1) Melt chocolate and condensed milk together over a double boiler, stirring until smooth.
2) Pour over profiteroles.
3) Revel in the new possibilities of your life.

Acknowledgments

I am so grateful to have amazing family and friends who have supported me through every step of this book. Many thanks go out to my husband, Gian Luca and son, Francesco. My parents, Joe and Graziella, who taught me everything I know. My brothers, Donato, Gianni, Joey, and Luciano, and my friends Mary, Shelby, Ashilee and Andrea. You are all a part of this book.

I'd also like to thank Elizabeth and Robin for their comments and suggestions, and Tom for his amazing artwork.

About the Author

Antonietta Mariottini has an MA in Creative Writing from Rutgers University and has taught writing at the high school and college levels. Before writing this book, she managed her brother's restaurant for seven summers. She is now a proud stay- at- home mom who writes when her baby is sleeping. This is her first novel.

For more info, please visit antoniettamariottini.blogspot.com

Stella is moving to Rome to start a new life… but will her past follow her?

Look for

The Queen of Roman Disasters

Coming early 2014

Made in the USA
Charleston, SC
28 June 2013